The Prince of Warwood
and
The Fall of the King

J. Noel Clinton

Cover Design by C^2 Publishing
Cover Photos from thinkstockphotos.com
Book Design by Angel Editing

C^2 Publishing
P.O. Box 5269
Vienna, WV 26105

Library of Congress Control Number: 2013902926

ISBN: 0-9773115-3-8

The Prince of Warwood
and
The Fall of the King

J. Noel Clinton

Chapter 1

Responsibilities

Xavier's eye throbbed and burned, and he could taste blood in his mouth. The rugby scrimmage had turned out to be quite violent; he should have insisted on referees. He tucked the rugby ball in the crook of his arm and lunged forward. Ken Calhoun intercepted him and tackled him to the icy turf, stabbing an elbow into his ribs. A struggle for possession of the ball and to continue the game ensued. Xavier's teammate, Beck Wilcox, snatched up the ball and tossed it to Erica Jefferson. She raced along the sideline and crossed the goal line, planting the ball to score a try to win the game.

"In your face, Calhoun! You couldn't beat us even with all your fouls!" Court Hardcastle, one of Xavier's best friends, chastised as he stormed over to the other boy.

"Are you calling me a cheat?" Ken challenged, bumping into Court.

"You're bloody right, I am! You and Mac deliberately blocked us when your team had the ball, and you know it!" he growled.

"Court, just let it go. We won," a small dark-haired girl murmured, pulling at him.

"Letting a girl fight your battles, mama's boy?" Ken jeered.

Court's face turned bright red, and he charged toward the other boy. Xavier was at his side in an instant, grabbing him. The other boys turned and walked off the rugby pitch, laughing. As if to emphasize Courtney's bad mood, the wind intensified and snow began swirling to the ground.

"You know what, Robbie?" he spat, turning toward the petite girl. "I'd appreciate it if you'd butt out of my business in the future."

"What are you talking about? I only said that we'd won. It wasn't worth fighting a bunch of sore losers!" she implored, her dark eyes large.

"Yeah, well, you made me look like a complete git! Just keep your mouth shut next time!" he spat out before storming out of the stadium.

"Jeez, what's with him?" she sulked.

"Well, you kinda put him in a bad spot!" Xavier told her. "You made it look like he couldn't handle those guys on his own."

"Fine, take his side! You always do!" she complained, stomping away.

"What? Robbie!" Xavier called with a nervous laugh. "Don't be ridiculous! I'm not taking sides; I'm just saying..."

She whipped around and glared at him, tears welling in her eyes. "Yes you are! You are taking his side! Otherwise, you would have said that you agreed with me! Otherwise, you would have said... Oh, just forget it!"

Xavier stared after her as she stormed away. He didn't think he was taking sides. What was wrong with her? Robbie had always been levelheaded, with the ability to see all sides of an argument. This was completely out of character for her. He looked at Erica, silently pleading for help, but Erica simply shrugged, looking just as puzzled as he and ran to catch up with Robbie's fleeing figure.

"Women!" Garrett hissed, shaking his head in disgust. "Who can ever figure them out?" At this, the other boys chortled, and Xavier couldn't help but smile. "Well, Your Highness, it was a good game," Garrett announced, clapping him on the back.

"Yeah! They wouldn't have stood a chance against us even if the Chosen himself had played for them!" Beck boasted loudly, which was followed by a cheer of support.

When the boys exited the huge gothic coliseum, Xavier separated from the group and sauntered across the field toward the soaring fifteen-foot wall surrounding the palace.

"See ya, Your Highness!" Garrett called, waving.

"How many times do I have to tell you guys? Call me Xavier!" he bellowed back.

The boys stopped abruptly and stared at one another as if hearing this for the first time. Then grinning broadly, the group chorused, "Yes, SIRE!" and bowed for added emphasis.

"You're all hopeless!" Xavier yelled with a snicker.

Xavier Wells was indeed a prince. Up until six months ago, he had believed that he was a normal, typical boy, aside from his unusually white, curly hair. But, this couldn't be further from the truth. Not only was he the future leader of a kingdom, he was an empowered human. He possessed abilities a normal person could only dream of. His entire kingdom was full of supernatural humans who had abilities ranging from telepathy to teleportation to telekinesis.

Xavier chuckled at his friends' teasing as he continued across the barren field, huddling deeper into his coat as a vicious wind howled around him. He couldn't believe how quickly the weather turned in Warwood. When they had started their rugby match, it was sunny and nearly fifty degrees, chilly but bearable. Now the temperature was a good twenty degrees colder, and snow swirled down in angry spirals. It didn't take long for the ground to be dusted in white. He had been told once that the weather in the Newfoundland territories was as moody as an old hag. It had a way of changing from beautiful sunshine to blizzard-like conditions in a matter of minutes or even seconds, and it could be harsh and unforgiving. He looked up annoyingly at the darkening clouds as he fought against the icy wind lashing at his face and body. Harsh he could understand, but this weather was ridiculous!

He squeezed behind the large, blue spruce growing against the palace wall. The tree hid a secret passage in the wall that provided a short cut to the palace, if you knew where to look. Carefully, Xavier ran his hand along the wall, feeling for the smoother, polished surface of the fabricated stone. He found it easily, revealed the hidden lever, and opened the secret door. He stepped through and found himself between the rows of pines in the back garden of the palace. He quickly closed the passage and maneuvered out of the trees. When he walked around to the front of the palace, Court was leaning against the building waiting for him.

"You okay?" Xavier asked.

"Yeah. It's just that Robbie can be so nosey sometimes. It's infuriating!"

"I know. I've been there, but she means well. And you have to admit, she did have a point," he commented.

"Yeah, but don't tell her that! It'll only encourage her," he replied, falling into step with Xavier as they walked to the palace's entrance.

"You still on for the camping trip tomorrow?" Court asked, changing the topic.

"You bet! It should be a blast!" he grinned as they entered the palace, shaking the snow from their clothing and hair. They continued down the long hall and into a large antechamber where a grand stairway led up to the royal chambers.

"Well, see ya later," Court announced, moving toward a door to the left that led to the Hardcastle residence.

"Hey, Court?" Xavier began, and Court turned and faced him. "Who's the 'Chosen'?"

"The Chosen?" he asked with a snort.

"Yeah, the guys were talking about it, and when I was held at the Institute this summer, I heard the guards talking about it too."

"You're off your head! You really don't know?"

"Well, no. I didn't grow up here, remember?" Xavier pointed out defensively.

"Yeah. I'm sorry, Xavier. I forget that sometimes," he replied, shifting awkwardly. "The Chosen is folklore, a message of hope really. It's described in the Dead Sea Scrolls."

"The what?"

"You've never heard of the Dead Sea Scrolls?" Court gaped at Xavier. "Jeez, X! They're only the biggest biblical find since... well, since the Ten Commandments!" Xavier's dumbfounded look didn't alter, so Court gave a great sigh as he went on to explain. "Folklore tells us that, supposedly, there will come a time in history when the sons of the dark lord will try to overtake the sons of the light."

"Who's the dark lord?" he asked.

"No one knows. Though legend says he and his army will succeed in the first wave and beat the army of the light, but then the Chosen will lead his army into the greatest battle mankind has ever seen. This battle will not be just for the freedom of one kingdom or the empowered world; it will be a battle for everything and everyone—common and empowered! It's like the pre-apocalypse test. If the Chosen doesn't accept his destiny, if he fails, mankind will experience despair and darkness for hundreds of years. The events can only be described as doomsday, the end of the world!" Court looked at Xavier's shocked, disbelieving face.

"What happens if the Chosen succeeds?" he asked.

"Well, then we'll all live happily ever after on Earth for another millennium, or something like that." he shrugged nonchalantly. "I don't know if it's all true, but that's what the secret scroll foretells. But, for all we know, this may not happen for millions of years."

"Wow," Xavier muttered.

"Yeah! Kinda blows your mind, huh? Could you imagine being the poor bloke who suddenly finds out that he's responsible for the future of the entire world?" Court said, shaking his head.

"Yeah," he mumbled.

"Well, I better go. Mum will be ticked if I don't help set the table. See ya at the camp out. After all, according to Beck, there's nothing like camping outdoors when there's a major threat of frostbite and hypothermia." He laughed as he entered his residence.

Xavier climbed the staircase, entered the royal residence, and slammed the door shut behind him, still preoccupied with the Chosen Prophecy. Imagine! Some poor unsuspecting dude would be responsible for preventing Armageddon. And he thought he had it bad as future ruler of a kingdom. Slowly, he began climbing the stairs to his room. Suddenly, he froze.

"Oh, no! Oh, darn it!" he muttered as he sprinted up the last of the stairs and into his bedroom. He looked frantically around at the disheveled room as dread seized him. He hadn't cleaned his room. Father was going to kill him! His room was so cluttered and messy that the maids hadn't been able to vacuum or dust for nearly three weeks. So, Jeremiah had given him the ultimatum to have the room in order by the time he got home from work or there would be no camping trip. Xavier had joked, what good was it to have maids if they didn't clean up after him, but his father hadn't been amused.

He looked at the clock—a quarter to five! Oh, great! Father was due home any minute, and his room was in such disarray that he would have to use a bulldozer to get it cleaned up in time. Frantically, he began throwing toys onto shelves and into a large wooden chest. He had managed to clear a path to his bed when he heard the door downstairs shut and his father announce, "I'm home!"

Great! Goodbye camping trip. Xavier sighed dejectedly. If only the mess would pick itself up! Wait! It could if he'd use telekinesis! With a grin, Xavier closed his eyes and eagerly reached into his consciousness where his abilities laid quiescent. Almost instantly, his body grew warm as the power stirred within him. It began very gently with a book here, a toy there, floating across the room toward the bookcase or chest. Then, like a growing typhoon, the mess that once lay on his floor flew into the air, swirling and smashing violently around the room. A remote control car zipped past his head, grazing his left temple.

"Stop! Stop!" he screeched, raising his hands and trying to muster up the power that had started the storm of toys, books, and clothes. But the whirlwind didn't stop; it intensified. After another near miss, this time from a baseball, Xavier abandoned his attempts and dove under his bed for cover.

Moments later, his bedroom door swung open and his father stood in the doorway. A book, *Treasure Island*, propelled past his head.

"What the...?" the king spat, ducking and dropping to the floor. He scanned the room and found Xavier. "Son? What's going on?" he shouted over the clattering and crashing.

"I don't know! It just... happened! I can't stop it!" he exclaimed.

The king studied the boy a moment before jumping to his feet and thrusting his hands toward the storm of belongings. Instantaneously, a resounding golden force erupted from his hands, vibrating through Xavier's body. Toys and books dropped to the floor and the force evaporated. Slowly, Xavier wiggled out from under his bed and stood. With his heart lodged in his throat, he surveyed the damage. If his room had been messy before, it was a disaster area now. The force had shredded books, demolished toys, and, he noted with apprehension, shattered his computer monitor.

His shoulders slumped as he gave his father a sidelong glance.

For several long seconds, Jeremiah regarded him in silence. Then, he pulled a handkerchief from his suit jacket and gently dabbed at the oozing scratch on the boy's head.

Finally, he spoke quietly, "Let me guess, you didn't clean your room today and attempted to do it at the last minute using telekinesis. Right?"

Xavier nodded dejectedly. "I didn't mean to do this. It just... happened."

"Mm hm. But, didn't I ask you last night to have this room picked up by the time I got home from work? You had all day to get it done. Why didn't it get done, son?" he asked.

"I...I guess I just forgot about it. And, I had a rugby scrimmage with the guys this afternoon," he muttered.

Jeremiah sighed, giving him a stern glance. "I see. So, you chose games and friends over your responsibilities. Well then, as a result, there will be no camping trip."

"Oh, come on, Dad! I can have this room picked up before tomorrow afternoon," he begged.

"I'm sure you could, but when did I ask you to have it picked up?" the king rebuked.

"Today, sir," he mumbled, fully aware that his father wouldn't recant on his decision.

"That's right, and if you cannot take care of your responsibilities, then your special privileges will suffer," he replied matter-of-factly as he crossed the room, picked up a broken toy, examined it, and then placed it on the shelf. "And speaking of responsibilities, I received your first term report from the academy today." He turned and pinned Xavier to the spot with steely eyes.

Xavier's heart sank. If he had any hope that his father would change his mind about the camping trip, it evaporated the moment he uttered the words, "first term report."

"A 'D' in Latin?" Jeremiah questioned. "Why didn't you tell me you were having difficulty? This could have been prevented."

"I guess I didn't realize I was having that much trouble, sir," he lied. The truth was that he had been so preoccupied with setting up a rugby team and hanging out with his friends that he had given little time to practicing or studying his Latin.

His father knew this as well and interjected, "Or maybe rugby and time with friends have taken your mind off the most important part of school: to learn!"

He looked up at his father's displeased face. "It's not that...I..."

Jeremiah raised his hand, silencing the boy. "Don't," he warned quietly. He took three long strides toward him and continued sternly. "You've allowed friends and rugby to occupy too much of your time. Consequently, you're not doing as you're told and your grades have suffered. I dare to say the marks from your other classes could have been higher as well. So, you won't be going on the camping trip with your friends this weekend, and there will be no rugby for three weeks!"

"Three weeks! But..." he blurted.

"Yes, three weeks," his father interrupted loudly. "And if your Latin grade doesn't improve, there will be no rugby at all in the spring. Do you understand me?"

Xavier bit his lip and grimaced. "Yes, sir," he muttered.

"Now, you're grounded to this room for the remainder of the evening. I want this room cleaned and straightened. In the future, do not use your abilities without adult supervision. I'm sure they've told you that at the academy. I'll speak to Spencer this week about adding a telekinesis course to your schedule for the new term."

"Yes, sir," he agreed without meeting his father's hard stare.

"All right then, get started. I'll be up after dinner," Jeremiah concluded, leaving the room.

Xavier released a long slow breath and began picking up his broken things, muttering grievances under his breath.

Much later, he had most of his toys put away when Mrs. Sommers came swaying into the room carrying a silver serving tray. "Master Wells, here's your dinner. Why don't you take a breather and eat? It's pot roast," she sang out as she set the tray on his desk.

He dropped an armful of toys into the chest and crossed the room toward her. "Thanks, Mrs. Sommers," he muttered, throwing himself into the chair.

"I'm sorry you're not permitted to go on your camping trip. I'm sure there'll be others. Besides, who would want to go camping this time of year? It gets bitterly cold in the fall."

"I would," he grumbled. "We were going to have a huge bonfire. It wouldn't have been so bad."

She smiled down him. "You know, you remind me so much of your father when he was your age."

"Yeah?" he mumbled. "I bet he didn't screw up as much as I do," he pouted, toying with his food.

"Well, I don't know about that!" she chuckled. "Your father got into plenty of mischief in his day."

"Really? Like what?"

Grinning, Mrs. Sommers pulled up a chair beside him. "Let's see. Oh, he was suspended from school when he was about your age. You see, back then, the church had more of a hand in running the academy, and the church isn't known for sparing the rod. Children were often struck for simple misdemeanors such as daydreaming, forgetting homework, or passing notes. Your father had a huge crush on Lucy Michaels at the time."

"Lucy Michaels?" he asked, taking a bite of roast.

"Well, you know her as Lucy Jefferson," she said, winking at him.

"Loren's wife?" he gasped and Mrs. Sommers nodded.

Loren was a general in the Premier Royal Guard, and the king's childhood friend. A few months ago, Loren had helped rescue him from the clutches of his father's arch-nemesis, William LeMasters. For reasons unknown to him, LeMasters had a sick fascination, an obsession really, with inflicting pain and suffering on his father through any means necessary. William had kidnapped him from the woods behind his grandparents' home. Then, when he discovered Xavier true identity, he found great joy in torturing him. He was held captive and tortured for nearly three months, and he began longing for death. He was certain LeMasters would have accomplished that if his father and Loren hadn't rescued him. This failure had infuriated LeMasters, and he set his sights on his next vulnerable target: Xavier's mother. Unfortunately, Julia Wells hadn't survived her encounter with William LeMasters. The raw grief of his mother's death still tugged at him, and now, with his thoughts back in his room, he sighed.

"Are you all right, young sire?" Mrs. Sommers asked.

"Yes, ma'am," he replied, trying to smile. Feeling her eyes burrow into him, Xavier quickly resumed the subject of his father's mischief. "So, Dad had a thing for Lucy when they were kids?"

"Ah, yes, Lucy. Anyway, he was caught passing her a note in history and was sent to Headmaster O'Brien, who took a switch to his hands and then called your grandfather. Poor boy had marks on his hands for weeks. Anyways, your father, being the perpetual hot head, vowed to get even with Headmaster O'Brien." Mrs. Sommers chuckled. "And, boy, did he ever! Your father..."

"Is quite certain that he doesn't want his son to hear any more of that story," Jeremiah's voice interrupted from the door.

"Now, Jeremiah," she chastised, "are you going to try and tell this boy that you've never stepped out of line?"

"No, but I don't want to encourage his knack for trouble either," he noted ruefully.

"What did Father do?" Xavier asked, hoping Mrs. Sommers would continue despite his father's protests.

"He filled the headmaster's desk with manure," she whispered melodramatically.

"Ewww! He didn't!" Xavier exclaimed, his eyes darting to his father, who seemed to be squirming uncomfortably in the doorway.

"Emma..." Jeremiah began but she cut him off.

"Yes, he did. Your grandfather was furious beyond words, and I must say I truly felt sorry for him. You may think your father is tough with you, but believe me, King Wells Senior was an even more severe disciplinarian. I always thought he was way too harsh," Emma concluded, looking at Jeremiah with empathy. "I'm not sure how many times he struck him, but I do know I had to run him an oatmeal bath to ease the pain afterwards."

"All right, Emma. That's enough. No more stories for tonight. Thank you," Jeremiah sighed, stepping into the room.

"Yes, sire." She smiled at Xavier and kissed him on the forehead. "Goodnight, sweetie."

"Goodnight, Mrs. Sommers. And, thanks for the story."

She smiled conspiratorially. "Oh, I have plenty more, but they'll have to wait for another day." Then she stood and left the room.

Silence hung heavily in the air as Jeremiah surveyed the room and Xavier continued to pick at his meal.

"Well, it's looking much better," his father finally noted. "If you hang up your clean clothes and put the dirty ones in the hamper, the rest can wait until the morning. I'll have Milton install a new monitor tomorrow," he added, inspecting the computer.

"Yes, sir," Xavier muttered. He pushed the mostly full plate away from him and looked up at his father's studying eyes. Without a word, Jeremiah pulled out the chair next to him and sat.

"Okay, here's the deal," he began. "For the next three weeks, you and I will work for one hour every night after dinner to get you caught up in Latin. Then it will be up to you to keep practicing and studying."

"Yes, sir," Xavier replied.

"But, next time you start falling behind in your studies ask for help. I don't ever want to find out that you're struggling with a class like this again. Got it?"

Xavier nodded. "Yes, sir."

Chapter 2

Dreams

Following the brutal murder of Julia Wells, William LeMasters began working on another plan to bring King Wells to his knees and ultimately gain control over Warwood. This time LeMasters' goal was to use the King's Key, a small, magical staff, to obtain additional powers so that he and his army could sweep through Warwood invincible. However, only the king or his heir could wield the key. So, he kidnapped the prince and held him captive in the ruins, an underground system of passages and chambers, where he attempted to coerce the boy into using the key and endowing him with every power known to empowered-kind.

But, LeMasters had miscalculated the power of the key in the hands of the boy. If it hadn't been for the key, Xavier wouldn't have obtained the ability to expose Dr. Angelo who had transfigured into his mother's image in attempt to manipulate him. If it hadn't been for the key, the king wouldn't have materialized in the ruins and rescued him. If it hadn't been for the key, they would have all been blown to smithereens. The key had saved his life.

The night following the telekinetic tornado in his room, Xavier dreamt of his mother for the first time since after his father had rescued him from the ruins. The dreams he had back then had been nightmares that depicted his mother's torturous death at the hands of William LeMasters. But, on this night, the dream was different, peaceful, and a longing for happier times.

In the dream, he found himself on a familiar beach with a small bungalow behind him. The surf rumbled onto the shore, and the sun began to slip behind the trees, casting a warm golden hue over the area. Xavier heard a chuckle to his right and turned to see a couple strolling up the shore. The woman was carrying a blanketed bundle and the man, peering at it, chuckled again, louder this time.

"Look! Look! He smiled. He smiled, Julia. Do you think he knows that I'm his Daddy?"

He instantly recognized his father's voice and timidly moved toward the pair for a closer look. His parents stopped and sank onto a blanket spread over the sand. His mother looked beautiful and young, not beaten and tired like she had been in the last memory he had of her. His father's face was clean-shaven, and he too looked young and handsome.

"He's perfect," his mother choked, fighting back tears as she looked down at the gurgling baby.

Jeremiah stroked her cheek, whisking away her tears. "Yes," he murmured. "He's perfect, just like his mama." He kissed her tenderly and pulled her to him.

They snuggled against one another, reclining on the blanket. Julia lifted the infant and nestled him against her, kissing the crown of wispy white curls. Jeremiah lay next to them, stroking the baby's back, and soon both mother and child were fast asleep. As he watched his sleeping family, his father's face contorted with an emotion Xavier didn't understand. He looked...grief-stricken.

When he woke, Xavier opened his eyes to moonlight spilling across his bed in a pale, mournful glow. The sounds, smells, and sights of the dream quickly slipped away, but the loneliness it stirred in him did not. He thought of his mother and what his life would have been like if she had lived. She would've been asleep beside his father in the next room. He could have gotten up and gone to her after a bad dream. He would have been able to feel her warm arms around him and heard her soft, soothing voice again. He would even welcome the impatient sigh and sharp tone she'd use whenever she was cross with him. Oh, and her laughter. What he wouldn't give to hear her laugh again. Whenever she was really tickled, her laughter would hiccup with the occasional snort. He smiled wistfully at the memory. Lord, he missed her! He would do anything to be in her arms at that very moment, inhaling her perfumed skin. Suddenly, the room felt too big and empty, and he longed to be near his father. Without any effort at all, he telepathically reached out to his father and was surprised to find him awake.

"I need to remember to meet with Yaman and Bracus come Monday. We've got to stop that legislation before it gets organized. And, I should call Michael too. I can't believe Xavier has...what is it now? Four or five abilities? I'm sure using the key last month is what gave him the telekinesis and summoning abilities." Jeremiah chuckled. *"The boy sure surprised the hell out of me by teleporting me into the ruins. I'm still not sure how he did it. Every chambers and passage in that place is lined with lead... Xavier? Why are you in my thoughts?"*

"Uh...I... had a dream about Mom, and now I can't get back to sleep. I just...I was wondering... do you think... can I sleep with you?" he stammered.

After a moment of silence, Xavier heard his father's

voice answering in his mind, *"Sure. Come on."*

With a grin, Xavier jumped from his bed and tumbled to the floor with a thud, his legs tangled in his sheets. After a brief wrestling match with the covers, he scrambled to his feet and hurried to his father's room. He entered the room quietly as though he were entering a sacred temple and found Jeremiah sitting on the edge of the bed, wearing a pair of flannel pajama bottoms and a t-shirt. He was rubbing his hand through his hair and looked up as Xavier approached.

"Well?" Jeremiah stated with a brief smile, patting the mattress next to him. "Hop in."

Grinning, Xavier sprinted to him and bounded to the other side of the bed. Jeremiah tucked him in, turned out the light, and settled into bed, pulling the boy close. Xavier burrowed under the covers and snuggled against his father's warmth. He sighed heavily, feeling utterly content.

After a moment, Jeremiah spoke. "Son? What was the dream about? Was it another nightmare?"

Xavier yawned. "No, sir. I dreamt of Mom and you on the beach with me when I was a baby." He felt his father's body grow tense beside him.

"Go on," Jeremiah muttered.

"It was nothing really. We were having a picnic or something on the beach. We were at that little beach house where we stayed after you busted me out of the Institute. It was kind of a nice dream actually. It just made me miss her. Why? Did that really happen? Did you and Mom go to the beach house after I was born?"

"Yeah, we did," he replied.

They lay in silence for several moments until Xavier asked, "Dad?"

"Hmm?" he mumbled lazily.

"Why didn't Mom and I stay with you? I mean, why were we sent away to live with Grandma and Grandpa?" he questioned.

Jeremiah didn't answer straight away, but when he did, he spoke so softly that Xavier had to hold his breath to hear him. "It was because of LeMasters."

"William LeMasters?"

"Yes. He was a citizen of our kingdom at one time. In fact, his mother raised him here. My father had always believed that any empowered person who sought citizenship should be granted it. William was a bad seed; everyone saw it except his mother, of course. She was a sweet lady, Daphne LeMasters. Growing up, I often butted heads with William. I'd bet that most of the trouble I got into as a kid was in some way connected to him. After we grew up, our childhood petty differences grew into something more sinister. Then, on the day of your christening, the prophet came to perform his part in the ceremony..."

"The prophet?" Xavier interrupted.

"The prophet is an old hermit who lives...well, no one is quite sure where he lives, but he always manages to show up whenever he's needed or has a duty to perform. The prophet is the most powerful oracle in the world. His visions are extremely accurate and nothing to trifle with. Whatever he says is going to happen *will* happen unless something is done to actively interfere with it." He sighed before continuing. "Anyway, the prophet came and performed the divination during your christening. The reading was going along normally until suddenly the prophet went rigid and began speaking in a monotonous, bizarre voice."

Xavier wasn't sure what a divination was, but he held his breath and waited for his father to continue. When he didn't immediately, his impatience got the better of him, and he whispered, "What did he say, Father?"

"He repeated one phrase over and over. He said that you would be killed before the end of your first year."

"He said that...I would...die. Someone would kill me?" he asked, feeling cold and uneasy.

His father, sensing his fear, pulled him closer. "William wanted the throne so badly that he would have killed anybody to get to it. So, after a close call with your lives, I took you and your mother out of Warwood. Your dream was a post-monition, a vision of a true event that has already occurred. It was a vision of that day. The day I took you both to the beach house to protect you. The day I had to tell your mother to leave Warwood with you."

There was another long pause, and Xavier snuggled closer to his father, feeling his regret and despair. Now, he understood the expression on his father's face during the dream. He had been preparing to send his family away, and for the first time, he realized how hard that must have been for him.

"Dad?" he muttered.

"Hmm?"

"I'm sorry I yelled at you when you tried to tell me this at the beach house. I'm sorry I ever blamed you for any of it."

"Oh, son. It's not your fault. You had every right to be angry. You weren't brought up in the most loving of homes. It ate away at me to read your thoughts when your grandparents were mistreating you. I begged your mother to come home to me after William and his followers were disbanded, but she refused. She was still fearful something would happen to you. I wish now that I had insisted." He patted the boy affectionately and sighed. "It's getting late, son. You better get some sleep."

"Yes, sir. Goodnight, Father," he muttered, though it was some time before sleep would come.

Xavier stood next to his father in Center Square, facing a pudgy man who was in a heated discussion with a panel of four high-ranking officials. He recognized two men from the group at once as Governor Bracus, of the Merchant District, and Governor Yaman, of the Wellington Area. The Square had been cleared of all its shops and booths, and all that remained was a small, marble altar. A large crowd gathered behind them, and a thick air of apprehension lingered like a fog. The man turned his gaze to Jeremiah, and nothing short of contempt contorted his round, ruddy face. After the long glare, he turned and nodded briskly at Loren and Ephraim. Without a word, Loren drew Jeremiah toward the altar in the center of the Square. The crowd around them began to chant and shout viciously. Xavier spun around staring bewilderedly at the mob's sudden change in demeanor.

Loren spoke to Jeremiah, but Xavier couldn't hear what he said over the ranting crowd. As he watched, Loren grasped the king by the shoulders and drove him to his knees. He knelt without resistance, and Loren peeled back the white cloak draped over his shoulders. The king rose and grasped the edges of the altar, his face unreadable and rock hard. The hair on Xavier's body stood on end, and he suddenly felt very afraid. Then, begrudgingly, Loren stepped forward, pulled a whip back and over his head, swung it, and struck him across the back. With the briefest of hesitations, Ephraim stepped forward and followed with a blow of his own. Repeatedly, Loren and Ephraim pelted the king with lash after lash.

Xavier was stunned. Why? Why were his father's

closest companions beating him to a pulp?

"NO! Stop! Loren, Ephraim, stop! You're hurting him! Please, stop! Dad! Daddy! No!"

Xavier bolted upright in bed, sweating and gulping for air.

Jeremiah barged out of the bathroom, hastily wrapping a towel around his waist. "Xavier?" he called. He crossed the space between them in four long strides. "Are you okay?"

Xavier surveyed his father's dripping wet face and hair and nodded. "Yeah, I had ...a nightmare," he answered meekly.

"About me?" Jeremiah asked.

"Yeah. We were in Center Square, but all the little shops were gone. There was only a white table-like thing. Loren made you kneel and then...he and Ephraim started beating you with whips in front of everybody," he explained miserably.

"What?" Jeremiah guffawed.

"It's not funny, Dad!" he blurted indignantly. "I'm telling you it..."

"Was just a dream. It was only a dream, Xavier," he soothed, stroking the boy's cheek.

He blinked heavily, staring up at his father's gentle face.

"Loren and Ephraim would never betray me. There's nothing to worry about. It was only a dream," he insisted, giving him a reassuring smile.

Xavier nodded and tried to smile back. It hadn't felt like a dream. It had felt real, concrete, and inevitable, but he didn't say a word as his father patted and kissed his head, before returning to his shower.

Chapter 3

Rivals

After spending the entire day Saturday cleaning his room, Xavier had plans to sleep in on Sunday morning, but his father had other plans.

"Church? You go to church?" Xavier asked, astounded, at the breakfast table.

The king nodded without looking up from his newspaper, *The Empowered Press.*

"How come we've never gone since I've been here?" he asked.

"I wanted to give you time to adjust to your new life before I exposed you to the entire kingdom's population every Sunday," Jeremiah answered.

"Do I have to go? I mean, why do I have to go?" he beseeched.

His father peered up at him then. "Stop whining, son. Attending mass is your duty not only as the Prince of Warwood, but as a child of God."

"But, I've never been to mass, Father. I haven't got a clue of what my duties are! It's a Catholic Church, right? Well, when do I kneel, when do I chant prayers, what *are* the prayers, and when do I use holy water?" he blurted anxiously.

"Your mother never took you to mass?" Jeremiah

frowned.

"No, sir. Never!" he answered, his voice squeaking.

"It'll be all right, son. I'll help you through it; just follow my lead, and you'll be just fine."

When father and son exited the royal residence an hour later, they found the Jeffersons and the Hardcastles standing in the lower foyer waiting for them. The Hardcastle boys stood behind their parents, fidgeting with their suits and ties, looking meek and miserable. Then, one by one, the group stilled and grew quiet as their eyes drifted up the grand staircase to King Wells and Xavier.

"The cars are ready, sire," Ephraim announced, as Jeremiah and Xavier descended the stairs to join them.

Xavier walked over to Courtney, who was pulling at his tie with a grimace. "It's choking me, Mum! Why do I have to wear the sodding thing, anyway? Can't I wear the suit without a tie?"

"Courtney Aaron Hardcastle, watch your language! Now leave the tie alone and stop complaining," Rebecca scolded.

"Mum!"

"Courtney!" Ephraim snapped, turning a harsh glare on the boy. "That's enough! Mind your mother."

Court tucked his head and sulked. "Great! Not only do I have to sit and listen to that fire and brimstone screaming priest, I get to do it while wearing a miserable, sodding tie," he muttered softly so his parents couldn't hear.

"I think you look absolutely handsome, Courtney," Loren's oldest daughter, Sarah, said with a coy smile. "And you as well, Your Highness," she added, directing her attention to Xavier and brushing a curl away from his eyes. Xavier's body blushed as her gaze traveled up and down his immaculately pressed double-breasted suit. Her smile widened as she smoothed out the blue royalty sash draped across his chest.

The boys smiled back and fidgeted under her approving stare. Erica rolled her eyes in disgust behind her sister. "Oh, please!" she spat, shoving Sarah aside and wedging herself between her sister and the goggling boys.

Sarah flashed them another smile and a small wave as she crossed the foyer to her mother. Still entranced, the boys waved back, grinning like fools.

"Hey, snap out of it!" Erica yelled, snapping her fingers in front of their faces. The boys jerked to attention and smiled feebly under Erica's glare.

"Let's go, kids," Rebecca Hardcastle called and the children followed the adults down the hallway.

"Did you hear? Madam Crabtree retired!" Erica whispered to the boys.

"Crabby Tree retired? Now I *truly* have a reason to go to church and praise God!" Court exclaimed. "Did you know that old bat gave me a 'C minus'? A 'C minus'! Mum wasn't happy." Court complained. He screwed up his face and impersonated his mother, "Courtney Aaron, doing your best and earning a 'C minus' is one thing, but I know you can do better than that! If you don't start applying yourself and bringing up those grades, I will lock you in your room with nothing but your books, paper, and pencils!"

"Courtney! I don't appreciate being mocked!" his mother called from the crowd of adults, and his father turned and pinned him with an ominous stare.

Courtney's head and shoulders cowered under his father's silent reprimand, and Erica snickered at him.

"You did better than me. I got a 'D'. Daddy grounded me for two weeks. How did you do, Xavier?" she chirped, not at all concerned.

"D," he grumbled. "Father's tutoring me, and he says I can't play rugby for three weeks. And if my grades don't improve, he says I can't play in the spring league."

Erica and Court both gave him a horrified look. "You don't think he meant it, do you?" Court questioned, glancing at Jeremiah as if the man's smiling face would rebuke the statement.

He nodded in response. "He definitely meant it! Have you ever known him to say something he didn't mean?"

The church was a short drive from the palace and as the limo pulled up to the entrance of the gothic-influenced cathedral, Xavier's stomach rolled with anxiety, and he looked up at the enormous building that dwarfed everything around it. The cathedral's turrets jabbed up into the sky like holy swords, and weather-stained angels peered all-knowingly down at him from the flying buttresses. The stone walls had darkened from age and weather, giving it an ominous feeling, and the dreary morning did little to improve its initial impression. The church was quite simply spooky. Xavier's eyes dropped from the building to the stream of well-dressed citizens migrating toward the grand vestibule where a priest stood greeting his parishioners with zealous.

"Ready?" his father whispered, squeezing his hand.

No. He wasn't ready. He didn't want people staring and ogling at him. But, he was the Prince of Warwood, and he had better get used to the stares and whispers. Sighing, he nodded at his father, and they climbed from the vehicle.

Then, Jeremiah turned, stooped in front of him, and smoothed out his tie and jacket. "Nervous?" he asked softly.

Xavier shrugged, painfully aware that the crowd filing past was staring at them. "Yeah, a little." No, he was a lot nervous.

"Don't worry. Just watch me and do what I do. You'll be fine." His father gave him a reassuring smile, took him by the hand, and led him up the walkway to the church. Xavier looked around at the staring crowd who were now whispering excitedly and pointing at them, and he tucked his head bashfully.

"Sire Wells!" a voice boomed from the doorway. "It's so good to finally see you back at church, and I see that you brought young Xavier as well."

Xavier looked up at the priest standing in the entrance, and his heart stuttered in his chest. The man from his dream, the fat man who had directed Loren and Ephraim to beat his father, was standing right in front of him. He was a priest! His gray hair was combed neatly to one side on his forehead, and although his voice was friendly and he smiled at them, his pale blue eyes were cold and disapproving.

"Yes, it's good to be back, Father O'Brien," Jeremiah replied, shaking the older man's hand heartily.

"Father *O'Brien*?" Xavier blurted in disbelief. "Headmaster O'Brien?"

"Why, yes. I was the headmaster of the academy when your father was about your age," the priest noted.

Jeremiah shifted uncomfortably and quickly changed the subject, "Although, I imagine being Bishop of the North American Empowered Societies is a more fulfilling job for a priest of your standing."

Father O'Brien smiled and lifted his head and shoulders importantly. "Yes. Yes, it is, and it keeps me quite busy."

The king nodded in agreement. "I image it does. Well if you'll excuse us, we won't keep you any longer. It's good to see you again, Father O'Brien."

He shook the priest's pudgy hand and nudged a smirking prince into the church.

"Emma and her big mouth. No more stories for you, blabbermouth," he hissed teasingly. Xavier giggled, finally feeling relaxed.

When they entered the sanctuary, his father immediately dipped his fingers in a basin of water and looked at his son to follow his actions. Then, he prayed while slowly producing the sign of the cross.

"In the name of the Father, and of the Son, and of the Holy Spirit. Amen."

He copied his father's actions and words before following him slowly up the aisle toward the pulpit. They paused next to the first row pew, knelt, and again crossed themselves before moving to sit next to Dublin and Tamarah Minnows and their two daughters. Xavier eyed Robbie anxiously before nudging her.

"Robbie? Are we okay?" he whispered.

The king elbowed him, shook his head, and slowly raised his index finger to his lips. Sighing, Xavier slouched, and after another prod from his father, he straightened and muttered, "Jeez!"

Robbie snickered and bumped into him with her shoulder, smiling broadly. With that simple gesture and smile, his bad mood lifted, and he grinned back.

Since Xavier had never been to church before, he hadn't quite understood what Court had meant when he described Father O'Brien as a fire and brimstone priest, but the moment he began his sermon, Xavier was left with little doubt of its meaning. The sermon focused on the burdens of a Christian with an emphasis on church attendance. Although the priest never said it outright, the undertones of the sermon made it clear that King Wells had been its inspiration. The rustling and uncomfortable coughs scattered among the congregation made it painfully clear that Xavier wasn't the only person who realized this. He peered up at his father expecting to see anger kindling in his eyes, but he saw nothing. If Jeremiah had any inkling that Father O'Brien was desecrating him in front of most of the population of Warwood, it wasn't apparent in his proud, unreadable face.

After church services, Jeremiah and Xavier were permitted to leave before the rest of the congregation, and they followed Father O'Brien outside the church.

"Have you contacted Abraham about the boy's return?" Father O'Brien asked.

"No, Father, I haven't," Jeremiah answered with a slight edge to his voice.

His father's response resembled the answer he had given just two days ago when asked why his room hadn't been cleaned like he had promised. Xavier would have smiled at the irony, but the air between the men was extremely hostile and tense. It was obvious that neither man liked the other.

"You really should, Jeremiah. The boy's divination may have altered or he could still be..."

"I appreciate your concern, Father, but I really don't find this to be the best of places to discuss it," he ordered firmly.

The priest wasn't used to taking orders and contempt flickered briefly in his eyes. "Yes, sire," he forced out, his face strained and red. "You're right. We'll discuss this at another time. Just keep in mind that the High Counsel of Warwood is extremely interested in the future divinations performed on the boy, and we demand that the counsel be present when you call on the prophet."

The conversation ended as the congregation emerged from the chapel and stood eagerly in line to shake hands with Father O'Brien, King Wells, and their prince. Governor Yaman was one of the first to emerge from the building. He approached the trio with an enormous fake smile plastered on his face. A pretty young woman followed him, looking anxiously at the king.

"Governor! It's so good to see you. How's the family? Grandchildren still growing like weeds?" Jeremiah asked and shook the man's hand, eager to have a distraction from his uncomfortable conversation with the priest.

"Yes, sire. Thank you for asking," Governor Yaman replied, turning to the young woman behind him. "I'd like to introduce you to my niece."

The young woman stepped forward. "How do you do, sire? We've met once before in Nottingham's," she announced sweetly, as she curtsied and extended her hand.

For a moment, the king simply stared at the voluptuous, golden-haired woman. "Ah, yes," he replied finally as he took her hand and brought it to his lips. "I remember. Catherine Stokes, right?"

She beamed up at him. "Yes, that's right." A long awkward silence filled the air between them as they stared at one another, still holding hands. Xavier looked from his father's goofy smile to Miss Stokes' blushing cheeks, and suddenly, he felt uncomfortable and annoyed. He didn't want this woman making moves on his dad!

Frustrated and angry, he stomped on his father's toes.

"Ouch! Xavier, what are you doing?" he hissed, pushing the boy at arm's length.

"Ah...I...I'm sorry. I didn't mean to! C...can we go now? I'm hungry." Xavier was very aware that he sounded whiny, but he didn't care. He wanted to leave and get his father as far away from this woman as possible.

Jeremiah looked down at the boy, looking a bit

annoyed himself, but after a moment, he nodded. "All right." He turned back to Miss Stokes and shrugged. "Kids! Everything is a dire emergency especially when it involves their stomachs. It was nice to see you again, Miss Stokes. Please excuse me?"

"Oh, yes, I understand. It was nice to see you, King Wells." She bowed.

Taking Xavier by the hand, King Wells turned to leave but then stopped and addressed the woman once again. "Miss Stokes? Would you and your uncle like to have dinner with my son and me at the palace this evening?"

Catherine seemed flustered by the question and didn't answer immediately. It was her uncle who finally spoke, "We would love to, my king."

"Wonderful! I'll have Milton contact you later this afternoon with the details. Have a good day."

During the ride home, Xavier sat with his arms folded across his chest scowling out the window. As soon as the car came to a stop in front of the palace, he bolted from the car and into the building without waiting for an escort. He heard his father's voice calling after him, but he didn't stop. He raced into the royal residence, up the stairs, and into his room, slamming the door shut behind him. Then, he jumped onto the bed with a bitter groan and punched at his pillows until his arms ached. Finally, he collapsed on to the bed, burying his face in his pillows and trying to calm his raging emotions.

"Feeling better?" his father asked softly from the doorway.

Xavier hadn't heard him enter. He jolted upright, sitting on the edge of the bed, but didn't look at his father nor did he answer the question.

"What's going on, Xavier?" he asked simply.

"Nothing. Just tired I guess," he grumbled.

"Why the anger?"

"I don't know. I guess I'm mad that I can't play rugby with the guys today," he lied.

If his father knew he was lying, he didn't call him on it. Instead, Jeremiah nodded as he spoke. "Well, take a nap and see if that doesn't cure your moodiness. Lunch is in an hour, and then we'll work on some Latin before our dinner guests arrive."

"Yes, sir," he mumbled.

Chapter 4

Dinner

The Latin lesson went as well as could be expected considering he was weeks behind. Jeremiah was fluent in Latin and was a very patient teacher, which helped considerably. Madam Crabtree got her nickname of Crabby Tree honestly. Aside from Dr. Angelo, she was possibly the most impatient, ill-tempered woman Xavier ever had the displeasure of meeting. She often snapped at the students whenever they tried new words and mispronounced them, unlike his father.

"Courage, v...eye...ert...us," Xavier stammered.

Jeremiah smiled. "No, son. Vir-toos," he pronounced slowly.

When he mimicked the word successfully, his father beamed. "Excellent!"

Father and son had been struggling through the first year Latin book for nearly an hour in the king's study. He had never been in this room before and had been surprised to find it a bit chaotic. Numerous books on law, economics, and government were strewn over two large bookcases, and papers, folders, and mail littered his desk and conference table. It had taken Jeremiah a couple of minutes to clear an area at the table for their tutoring session.

"Good, son. Now translate the next words."

"Dad? Who's Abraham that Father O'Brien was talking about at church?" he asked.

The king looked down at him, uncertain. "Abraham Vincent is the prophet."

"Oh." He frowned. "So, he thinks you should contact him and tell him I'm back?"

"Yes," he stated simply.

"Why? And, why does he want to counsel me?"

"Counsel you?" he asked, bemused.

"Yeah, he said he wanted the High Council of Warwood to be there."

"Oh," Jeremiah snickered. "He doesn't want to counsel you; he wants the high council to be in attendance for the divination ceremonies. The High Council of Warwood is an elected panel of citizens who gives the king advice when he needs it, and they oversee that the king doesn't infringe on any of the codes."

"Codes?" Xavier asked.

"Yes, son. The codes are laws found in *The Chronicles* that everyone must abide by and follow. You'll study them at the academy in your citizenship class when you get a little older."

"A king has laws he has to follow? I thought you could do whatever you wanted," he questioned.

"No, son. No one is above the law, especially the king. Otherwise, how would the people stand a chance against a king who's a tyrant?" his father inquired.

"What happens to a king if he breaks the codes? Does he go to jail or something?" he asked.

"Well, he can. It depends on the level of the infraction. A king could face a suspension of his duties, a prison sentence, a royal caning, banishment, removal of his royal title, or even death for a serious crime," he told him before looking back at the Latin book. "Well, I think we've had enough Latin for one afternoon; let's pick up here tomorrow, shall we? I have a lot of paper work I need to do before dinner."

Xavier bit back the swarm of questions buzzing inside him and nodded. He scooped up his belongings and walked toward the door, but his father's voice stopped him.

"Mrs. Sommers will be up in an hour or so to help you find something appropriate to wear to dinner this evening."

Xavier made a face but didn't argue.

When Xavier begrudgingly trudged down the steps for dinner a couple of hours later, he felt the sudden urge to lock himself in his room and hide. He didn't want to have dinner with Governor Yaman and his flirtatious niece. Robert Yaman made him extremely uneasy and suspicious. He didn't like the way the governor looked at his father. Whenever the king had his back turned, the older man would glower at him, but as soon as Jeremiah would turn, his expression would lighten, and he presented a fake, cheesy smile. As for Miss Stokes, she ogled and gawked at the king. It was obvious that she liked him and would stop at nothing to get what she wanted. No, Xavier didn't like Governor Yaman or his niece one iota.

With his stomach twisting itself into knots, Xavier descended the stairway to the reception room where his father, Governor Yaman, and Catherine Stokes stood talking. Jeremiah looked exquisitely imposing dressed in a navy pinstripe suit while leaning casually against the fireplace mantel. The moment Xavier stepped from the stairwell his father looked at him and smiled broadly.

"Ah, here he is!" he announced jovially, waving him over to the group. "Xavier, Miss Stokes was just telling me that Madam Crabtree retired. She..."

"Yeah, I've known about that for ages," Xavier interrupted haughtily but stopped short from rolling his eyes when the king arched his brow. Clearing his throat, he added quickly, "I mean, yes, sir. I heard about it this morning."

With a small nod of approval with the change in the boy's attitude, his father continued, "Well, she also told me that she applied for the position. The headmaster called her today and told her that she was the best candidate for the job. She starts teaching at Wells Academy tomorrow! Isn't that terrific?"

Catherine tucked her head in contrived modesty and giggled. "Please, sire. You're making me blush."

"Congratulations, ma'am," Xavier responded with a grimace.

"Thank you, Master Wells," she replied in a sticky, sweet voice.

At that moment, Milton announced that dinner was ready to be served, and the group moved into the dining hall. Jeremiah sat in his customary chair at the head of the table with Xavier to his right. Catherine found a seat to the king's left, and her uncle sat next to her. Dinner was extravagant to say the least, and the kitchen staff left no luxury out.

As Milton served the third course to the meal, Xavier grew disgruntled. He just wanted this torturous dinner over. "Milton? Why are we eating...like this? Can't you just bring out the food so we can eat and be done with it?"

Milton chuckled. "King Wells requested that a seven-course meal be served this evening, young sire," he answered, continuing to serve the meal.

Xavier looked at his father, who was smiling at a story Governor Yaman was telling, and he couldn't help but notice how often his father's eyes trailed toward Yaman's niece. A dark, deep-seeded emotion began to swell inside him, and each time Catherine laughed, coyly batted her eyes, or caressed his father's arm, the feeling grew.

The king relished in this beautiful young woman's attention, and his conversations and corny jokes grew bolder and more animated as dinner progressed. Xavier rolled his eyes. It was nauseating to witness, and he tried not to watch the couple. But, when Jeremiah caught Catherine's eye and held it for an uncomfortable length of time, the darkness inside him began pulsating through his body. Lord! He hated this woman! He hated the way she looked at his father. He hated the way she kept touching him. He hated the way she laughed and the way she smiled. Her voice even grated on his nerves. He hated everything about this woman. His hatred and anger became so ferocious that if Governor Yaman hadn't stood and announced his departure Xavier wasn't sure what he would have done.

"Well, I'm afraid that I must say goodnight, Your Highness. I appreciate your hospitality, but I have an early day tomorrow. There are several issues coming up for discussion on public relations and building camaraderie between the Wellington and Merchant Areas," Yaman told his host.

"Thank you for coming, Governor." Jeremiah stood and shook the older man's hand.

Catherine got to her feet and dejectedly looked for her belongings.

"Oh, no, my dear," her uncle told her, patting her shoulder. "Just because your old, tired uncle must go doesn't mean you should. Stay. I'm sure King Wells will see to it that you get home safely."

"Of course," Jeremiah reassured him.

"I don't want to outstay my welcome," she protested.

"Too late," Xavier thought bitterly.

Jeremiah's head whipped in his direction. Though Xavier was fairly certain he hadn't said the words aloud, his father's frosty glare made him question it. Aloud or not, it didn't prevent the telepathic reprimands bombarding his mind, and Xavier tucked his head submissively.

"Are you sure, Your Highness? I would like to stay for tea and dessert. I'd really like to try the Crème Brûlee your chef has prepared," she noted softly.

"Yes, by all means, stay. I'd like for you to stay, Miss Stokes," Jeremiah insisted, turning his attention back to Catherine.

She smiled. "Well, okay, if you insist, Your Highness."

"I do," he replied, flashing a devilish grin to her before turning to the governor. "Your niece is in good hands. I'll see to it that she gets home safely."

"There's no doubt that she's in good hands, my king. Well, good night sweetheart," he said, kissing her cheek.

"Goodnight, uncle."

Sometime later, the three of them sat around the hearth in the reception room sipping tea, their deserts long gone. Catherine was giggling like a child over a stupid joke Jeremiah was telling her. Xavier eyes shot heavenward, and he groaned flippantly. The king was eating up the attention. At the punch line of the joke, Catherine burst into wild laughter, grasped his father's arm, and buried her face against his shoulder, causing Xavier's irritation to escalate into full-blown fury. So when Catherine turned to him, he had little control over what came out of his mouth.

"So, Xavier, your father tells me that you're having trouble with your Latin. If you'd like, I can tutor you after school for the next few weeks until you catch up. He thinks it's a good idea. What do you say?"

He glared incredulously at his father and growled, "I think it's a terrible idea! Father is tutoring me. I don't need *your* help."

"Xavier! Don't be rude!" Jeremiah told him severely. "Apologize to her at once."

His weak grip on his temper shattered. "No! She's known me for barely two hours, and now she thinks she can tell me what to do! She should apologize to me!" he roared. "She shouldn't be here! I don't want her here!"

"Maybe I should go," Catherine interjected timidly.

"Yes!" Xavier blurted just as his father gave a firm no.

"No," Jeremiah repeated. "Please stay, and forgive my son's insolence. Please stay, I want you to stay." When Catherine finally nodded and agreed, Jeremiah turned on Xavier. "I think it's your bedtime, son," he announced harshly, standing and waiting for him to do the same. Then, grasping him by the arm, he led him up the stairs and into his room, shutting the door behind them.

"That was intolerable!" the king hissed, spinning the boy to face him.

"What? That I spoke the truth? That I spoke what was on my mind?" he spat out.

"She is our guest! You should..."

"No, she's not! She's not our guest! She's YOUR guest!" Seeing his father's bewildered look, he pressed on. "Don't you think I have eyes? I see how she looks at you and how you look at her!"

"What are you talking about?" his father spat.

"Oh come on, Father! Did you really think I wouldn't notice? I may be only twelve years old, but I'm not a complete idiot!"

"Obviously, you've planned for this to be a long, drawn-out discussion; unfortunately, you will not be getting it. There is a guest in our home, and I will not keep her waiting any longer. Now, change into your pajamas and go to bed. We'll finish this discussion in the morning." Jeremiah turned and left the room.

Xavier paced around the room, fuming. He punched at a model airplane he had been meticulously working on for nearly a month, propelling it across the room and shattering it against the wall. He spat a string of curses, threw himself onto his bed, and worked to suppress his raging anger.

He lay on his bed for some time until his father's bellowing laughter drifted up the stairs, drawing him out the door and onto the landing. When he peered over the banister, he found his father standing in front of Catherine with his hands stuffed into his front pockets, his jacket long gone. He chuckled softly at a comment from Catherine as he pulled and loosened the tie at his neck. Xavier could see why Loren had called his father a lady's man. His movements were smooth and suave. His voice was steady and silky. He had the woman utterly enchanted. Finally, he extended his hand and helped her to her feet, but she stumbled and fell against him. As she clutched his biceps to keep from crumpling to his feet, the king's hands swiftly grasped her hips, steadying her.

"Excuse, me, Your Highness," she whispered, her eyes fluttering up at him.

"It's quite all right, Catherine. Come. Let me walk you to the door. Milton has the limo out front. He'll drive you home."

Hand in hand, Jeremiah led Catherine to the door and turned to face her. "Good night, Catherine. Your company this evening has been very refreshing."

"Thank you, sire," she said shyly, looking at her feet.

A long pregnant pause extended between them, and Catherine stood fidgeting before the king. She was waiting for something. Then, it happened. His father pulled her closer, gently lifted her chin so that her eyes met his, and kissed her. It was exactly what Xavier had been dreading would happen since he first saw Catherine Stokes, and his stomach dropped like a cold lead weight.

Xavier had never felt so enraged in his life. Seeing this woman in his father's arms, kissing him, was more than he could bear. Xavier's control snapped and he shouted, jutting his hands out toward the couple. Instantly, the front door swung open, smacking the king and his harlot to the floor. Then, with a flick of his hands, he began pelting the couple with books, paintings, vases, pottery, and anything else in the room that wasn't securely fastened down. Jeremiah quickly grabbed Catherine and drew her toward him, shielding her from the missiles of household items. Catherine's blood-curling squeal and his father's angry shout sent Xavier racing into his room. He dove into bed, switched off the light, and pulled the covers over his head.

It was several minutes before Xavier heard the door to his room open. His entire body went rigid with dread as he listened to his father stomp across the room and flick on his bedside lamp. Abruptly, his covers were torn away from his body and tossed to the floor. He stared into his father's unbridled, stormy eyes.

"Get up," he growled.

"Father, I...I didn't mean for that to happen. I just thought...I..."

"Get up."

"Father..."

"Xavier, if I have to say it again, so help me, I'll haul you out of that bed myself and give you a spanking you won't soon forget."

The young prince climbed from the bed and found Catherine standing apprehensively by the door looking disheveled. His father yanked him toward the woman.

"That was a dangerous stunt you pulled. What if you had hurt her? How would you have felt if we had to rush Miss Stokes to the hospital?" he spat.

Xavier shrugged, avoiding his father's cold eyes, choosing instead to stare at his highly polished wing-tipped shoes.

"A shrug? That's all you can come up with? You have nothing to say about your behavior?" Jeremiah drilled gruffly. When the boy continued to silently stare at his feet, the king added sharply, "You owe Miss Stokes an apology, boy!"

Xavier grimaced and looked up at the woman with dread. His gaze dropped, and he sang condescendingly, "Sorry."

No sooner had he uttered the word than his father grabbed his arm, jerked him around, and swatted his backside with three sharp smacks. Xavier flinched, tears springing to his eyes. Then, spinning him to face the woman again, the king growled, "You'll apologize properly, and if I hear even a hint of disrespect in your tone again, boy, you won't be able to sit for a week."

When Xavier glanced up at Catherine's face, he saw a glimmer of triumph flash across her features, and she smiled at him. He narrowed his eyes at the woman trying to read her thoughts, but for some reason, he couldn't. He was blocked from her mind.

"Xavier Wells!" Jeremiah barked.

Xavier dropped his gaze and stared at the floor as he

muttered, “I’m sorry, Miss Stokes. I lost control of myself, and... I’m sorry.”

Catherine stepped forward with an air of superiority and knelt to eye level with him. “I appreciate the apology, young sire. I don’t think it’s a good idea to begin our academic relationship on the wrong foot, do you?” she said evenly. “After all, we’re going to be seeing quite a lot of each other,” she finished with a note of disdain so subtle that Xavier wasn’t sure he even heard it. He glanced up at his father’s agreeing stare and knew that he was alone in his distrust of this woman.

Chapter 5

Madam Stokes

The next morning, Xavier, Courtney, and Erica slipped through the secret passage in the palace's wall and trudged across the field toward the enormous school. Like most old buildings in the kingdom, its limestone walls had blackened over the years, giving it an archaic look. Xavier followed Courtney and Erica as they approached the school, chattering excitedly about the prospects of a new Latin teacher.

"I heard the new Latin professor is a woman," Court noted gleefully, "a fairly young and pretty woman. Boy, it'll be nice to learn Latin from something other than a raisin-faced, crabby, Ben-Gay-smelling old bat!"

"Well, yeah," Erica agreed. "Anyone would be better than old Crabby Tree!"

"I wouldn't say anyone," Xavier muttered spitefully.

But, Court and Erica didn't hear him and continued their babbling as they climbed the stairs to the main entrance. Xavier followed his friends in silence stewing over his father's budding relationship with Catherine Stokes. She had her claws in him, and she had no intention of letting go. What if they got serious? What if they got married? Oh, God! She'd be his step-mother! Well, he wouldn't, he couldn't let that happen!

"All right there, Xavier? You're a bit quiet," Court asked.

Xavier nodded as Robbie joined them, waving at her father as he drove away to take her little sister, Brittany, to grammar school.

"Hey," she gasped. "Did you hear who the new Latin instructor is?" She didn't wait for an answer. "It's Catherine Stokes, Governor Yaman's niece."

"Seriously?" Court gasped. "Oi! It's better than I thought! She's beautiful! Seriously, I believe Latin has just become my favorite subject."

The girls rolled their eyes at him. "Figures! Boys are all alike! They'd rather have a pretty face than someone who actually knows the subject they teach," Erica groaned.

"She knows what she teaches. Why else would Headmaster Spencer have hired her?" he urged.

"Because he's a man! Men are worse than boys when it comes to a pretty face," Erica retorted unscathed.

"Do you realize how sexist that sounds?" he asked irritably.

"Maybe." she shrugged. "But can I help it if it's true?"

"You're impossible, Jefferson!" he said, rolling his eyes. "X, my mate, back me up here!"

"Sorry, you're on your own," Xavier muttered and sauntered past them toward the enormous archway where Headmaster Spencer stood greeting students.

"Mills! Take that hat off! If I see it again, I'm confiscating it!" Spencer called over to a boy wearing a ridiculous pink bunny-eared cap. "Morning, Your Highness. Did you practice your telepathy this weekend?" he asked as Xavier approached him. Xavier was the only student who had the ability to read minds. It was a rare ability that could only be found in royalty, and Headmaster Spencer was the only teacher who could teach it. This was because Michael Spencer was his father's half-brother.

"Uh, no, sir. I didn't have time," he muttered.

"You need to make time! I thought after the incident in the ruins, you would have realized how dangerous it is to be open to the telepathic abilities of others. Maybe detention during your lunch break for a week practicing impediments will make you more responsible," Spencer told him.

"Uh, no, sir. I'm sorry. I'll practice tonight. I promise I'll do better."

"It wasn't a request, Your Highness. You will be there!" Spencer snapped.

Xavier stormed away, muttering under his breath. He stomped down the hall and into his mathematics class. He threw his book bag onto his seat with a loud bang, pulled out his textbook and notebook, and slammed them on top of his desk.

"Sire Wells! Please don't slam your things around," Sir Underwood scolded.

"Sorry, sir," Xavier replied, placing his bag on the floor by his desk and sinking into the seat.

"Hey, X. Why did ya' run off in such a hurry?" Robbie asked.

He studied Robbie for a moment. He had to tell someone! He had to find someone who agreed with him and his feelings, to validate them. "Okay look, Robbie, you can't tell a soul. Promise me! Promise me you won't tell anyone, not even Erica."

"Okay, okay, I promise! Now what's got you all worked up?"

"It's Madam Stokes," he muttered with disgust. "Father and..."

"Okay class, let's get started," Sir Underwood called

above the idle conversations and clowning around. "We will be starting a new unit on multiple operations and multi-step problems. Everyone open your textbooks to page 120."

As Sir Underwood continued, Robbie pointed to his notebook and mouthed the words, "Write me a note."

Against his better judgment, Xavier wrote down everything that happened last night, from how his father kissed Catherine Stokes, to how he bombarded them with vases, books, and paintings.

But, when he held the note out to Robbie, Sir Underwood demanded, "Sire Wells, bring me that note, please."

"What note, sir?" he asked, sweeping the slip of paper into his pocket.

Sir Underwood beckoned him to the front of the room with a stern glare. "Don't play games with me, young man."

Feeling dread coupled with inevitability, Xavier stood and approached the teacher. The students around him snickered and whispered as he handed the note to Sir Underwood, who promptly opened it.

"Let's see what was so important to warrant your undivided attention." He read the note quickly and looked at Xavier. "Headmaster Spencer will receive this; you can discuss it with him. You may sit down."

"Yes, sir," he muttered and returned to his seat. Boy, Xavier would have said that his day couldn't possibly get any worse, except he had Latin right before lunch.

When he arrived at Latin two periods later, the room was absent of a teacher and most of the students were wandering about, happily discussing the prospects of a new professor. Without a word, Xavier quickly found his seat and prepared himself for what he knew would be a long class period. Moments later, Madam Stokes entered the room wearing white silky blouse and a navy pencil skirt cut a few inches above the knee, exposing her beautifully shaped legs. Every voice trailed away as they watched her enter and stand in front of the room with a bubbly smile.

"Abyssus discipulus," she chirped.

"Hello, Madam Stokes," the class muttered sporadically.

"No, no, in Latin, please," she corrected sweetly.

"Abyssus Magister Stokes," the class repeated.

"Eu, discipulus," she smiled. "Now, I realize that the first term reports have already gone out to your parents," she announced, picking up a printout lying on the desk. She slid onto the desktop and crossed her legs as she studied the paper. Several boys snickered nervously, but if she heard them, she ignored it. "Tsk, tsk, tsk. It seems that some of you have had a great deal of trouble with your Latin. So I think the best way to start a new term with a new teacher is to take an assessment of sorts." She stood, walked around the desk, and pulled a thick stack of stapled papers from the bottom drawer. A loud collective moan filled the classroom.

"On the first two pages, you're to translate two Latin passages: one by Horace, the other by Catullus. For the next five pages, simply write the English word or phrase for the Latin word given, and on the last three pages, translate the English terms and passages into Latin. Correct spelling is essential."

"Is this for a grade, Madam Stokes?" a student interrupted.

"Well, of course! If I bother to create a test and check it, then yes, it will be for a grade! However, if you worked hard with Madam Crabtree, I imagine that you'll find this assessment to be quite simple. But for those of you who didn't apply yourself to your studies last term," she smiled dryly at Xavier, "I'm afraid you'll find it very difficult indeed."

Several students looked curiously at Xavier, and he felt a wave of warmth flood his face.

"You should really take a lesson from Sire Wells, here," she said sweetly, nodding at him.

"Oh, God!" Xavier thought as the heat in his cheeks intensified.

"He's been having difficulty with his Latin, but Jere...ah...King Wells has been tutoring him. And, I must say King Wells is a superb linguist and speaks flawless Latin. Isn't that right, Xavier?"

Xavier's face was scorching and felt like it might combust into flames at any moment. Whether or not Madam Stokes had intentionally started to call his father by his first name was unclear, but it had an immediate effect on the class. Twenty pairs of eyes borrowed into him from every direction as whispers ping-ponged around the room. Mac and Ken smirked all-knowingly from the front row. No doubt, he could expect endless ribbing and teasing from them. It was too much, he was embarrassed beyond words.

He glared up at the smug woman sneering down at him. "I wouldn't know," he snapped resentfully. "I continue to tell Father that it's not normal, but he insists on speaking to me in English! Imagine that!"

The class erupted in barely stifled snickers.

Xavier was amazed by the quick transformation of Madam Stokes's face from something of beauty into something ugly and twisted.

"I think you and I need to have a little chat after class, Sire Wells," she told him quietly.

"Whatever," Xavier muttered with a shrug.

Madam Stokes began passing out the tests, eying him. The test wasn't nearly as difficult as he initially thought, but after the confrontation with Madam Stokes, he no longer cared to do well and began jotting down answers on a whim.

"Define the Latin words in English," Xavier read from his test, "number twenty, malum." Now, he knew that malum meant evil, but instead of writing the correct response he wrote "Madam Stokes" in the answer blank provided. For problem twenty-five, he wrote, "Catherine" as the answer next to the Latin word for dog. He wrote, "Madam Stokes' face" for the Latin word ugly. Xavier completed the entire test in this way, and for the words he didn't know, he simply left blank. Xavier was the first to finish the test and lay it on Madam Stokes' desk. She immediately picked it up with red pen in hand and a small smile on her face. As she skimmed each page and read over his answers, her smile dropped, and she looked up at him, red-faced and outraged.

"Sire? May I speak to you for a moment at my desk, please?" she requested forcibly. Every student's head lifted and watched with confusion and curiosity as Xavier unflinchingly approached Madam Stokes.

"Yes, ma'am?" he replied sweetly.

She scowled at him. "Do you mind explaining this?" she hissed, holding up his paper.

"Ah, well, that's my test, ma'am," he responded slowly as if he were speaking to a toddler.

"I know it's your test!" she shrieked. "Do you mind telling me why you answered the questions in this manner?"

He leaned over her desk and looked at his paper. "Because it's true. Malum means teacher, right?" he lied innocently.

The sudden burst of snickers behind him was quickly snuffed out by Madam Stokes' glare. Then, she turned back to the prince. "I don't think so. I think you know perfectly well that the word means evil." There was a sudden shuffle of papers behind him as several students searched for the word on their tests to correct their answers. "If it were just one word that you used to insult me, it might be more believable, but female dog, ugly, useless, pig? I think not!" she hissed.

Xavier smiled sweetly down at her and said, "Really? Imagine the odds of that! Though, I guess I wasn't too far off with the female dog bit, huh?"

"Excuse me?" she snapped.

"You heard me!" he growled, no longer mockingly sweet.

Her eyes flickered and she whispered, "I demand an apology at once, young man!"

"Demand until you're blue in the face, *Catherine*, but you won't be getting one," he told her.

"Get out!" she screamed, jumping to her feet and pointing to the door. "Get out of my classroom this instant! The headmaster can deal with you! And you can bet I'll be talking to your father about this!"

Xavier gathered his books and walked out of the room without a backward glance. He took his time going to the headmaster's office. Her last threat got to him, just as she knew it would. His father would thrash him thoroughly for this.

"Well done, Xavier. Now what?" he muttered to himself. He detoured to the courtyard and sat under the oak tree for several minutes trying to cool his temper. He took several long, shaky breaths before realizing that he was only postponing the inevitable. Finally, deciding he had better go and face Spencer, he stood and made his way toward the office. When he entered the office, Madam Stokes stood next to the counter complaining loudly to Spencer, and Jeanette was on the phone looking grave.

The three adults turned to him the moment the office door slammed shut.

"Yes, sire. He just walked in," Jeanette said into the receiver. "Okay, we'll see you in a couple of minutes. Thank you."

Xavier felt a lump lodge itself in his throat as three daggering stares bore into him. He had no doubt that it had been his father on the phone, and he gulped.

"Where have you been?" Spencer snapped, stomping toward him. "Madam Stokes sent you to my office over fifteen minutes ago!"

"Around," he answered brazenly.

Spencer's eyes flashed thunderously, and Xavier was immediately reminded of his father. Both men had the knack of making him gimpy in the knees with just one glance. He tried to swallow the dread that suddenly clung at his throat, strangling him and making it impossible for him to breathe freely.

"Get into my office, boy! Now!" he thundered, and Xavier did just that in a near sprint.

He sat in Spencer's office for several minutes before finally, the door opened and Spencer, Madam Stokes, and a stone-faced king stalked into the room. Again, Xavier gulped.

"Now," Spencer began with a heavy sigh, "Xavier, can you start by explaining this?" He held up his Latin test.

Xavier shrugged.

"May I see that, Mike?" Jeremiah asked.

Without a word, he handed the king the test.

As he scanned through the test, Jeremiah's frown deepened. "Son, it seems I must agree with Madam

Stokes..."

"Madam Stokes? Don't you mean *Catherine*?" Xavier spat insolently.

"Excuse me?" his father questioned with his brow raised.

"Nothing," he grumbled.

Jeremiah studied him a moment before finally continuing, "You've intentionally used Madam Stokes' name as answers on this test to challenge her. Isn't that right, son?"

"No, I really thought malum meant..." his protest was cut short when his father stormed toward him and slammed his hands on the armrests of his chair.

"Don't! Don't start lying to me!" he spat, sending the boy huddling deeper into his chair. "You knew what you were doing; didn't you, son?"

"Yes, sir," he mumbled, and Jeremiah stood upright.

"Okay, Xavier," Spencer intervened, "why didn't you come straight to my office like you were told?"

He replied simply, "I knew it would tick her off, and I have no intention of making life easier for her."

"I see." The headmaster nodded. "Would your resentment toward Madam Stokes stem from your father's relationship with her?"

Xavier's head snapped up. "How do you know about that?" he asked in a small wounded voice.

Spencer held up the note he'd written to Robbie in mathematics. Then without a word, he handed it to his father who quickly read it.

Jeremiah looked inquisitively at Xavier, his face softening as the realization of what was truly going on dawned on him. He knelt in front of the boy and regarded his hurt-filled eyes a moment. "This isn't about Catherine, is it?"

Xavier looked at his father and whispered, "Yes it is."

"No, son. It's not. This is about your mother," he persisted.

"No." Xavier choked, but no one seemed to believe him. He wasn't sure he even believed himself. His eyes blurred and heavy tears teetered on his eyelashes. God, he was going to cry like a baby in front of all of them. He blinked, tears plopped heavily onto his cheeks, and he buried his face in his hands.

Sighing, Jeremiah stood and turned toward Spencer. "If you don't mind, I think I'll take Xavier home. We need to have a father-son talk," he noted softly, and the headmaster nodded. Then, he turned to Catherine and whispered, "I'm sorry about Xavier's behavior in class today. He'll be ready to apologize to you and the class tomorrow."

Catherine nodded. "That's quite all right. I know he's been through a lot the past few months..." She paused, glancing down at the boy before looking back to his father. "We'll have dinner out another time. Just call me later, okay?"

Jeremiah nodded and turned to Xavier. "Son? Let's go home," he announced, touching his shoulder.

Xavier stood and allowed himself to be led out of the school to where Loren stood next to an awaiting limo. As the vehicle pulled away from the school, the king called the Governing Hall and explained he would be taking the rest of the day off, but for the rest of the short drive to the palace, they rode in silence.

When the car came to a stop in front of the palace, Jeremiah reached for the boy's hand and guided him out of the car and into the building. They walked without speaking until they reached the door to the royal residence. The king opened the door and nudged the boy inside.

"Go on upstairs, son. Wash your face and lay down for a little while, we'll talk later," he told him gently.

Nodding, Xavier climbed the stairs to his room, leaving his father and Loren at the door.

Jeremiah watched the boy close his bedroom door and groaned. "I should have seen this coming. I should have talked to him before I asked Catherine over for dinner."

"Jer," Loren started softly, "don't blame yourself. This isn't your fault; you have the right to move on and do what makes you happy."

"At the expense of my son?" he snapped, spinning to face Loren.

Loren studied him a moment. "Wait a minute, friend. This isn't just about Xavier, is it? It's you! You're feeling guilty. You're thinking that you betrayed Julia by having feelings for this woman, aren't you?"

"You don't know what you're talking about, Jefferson," he muttered, stalking across the room to the wet bar.

The general followed. "Thank God I don't, but you and I both know that it's true. Jer, Julia wouldn't want you to live the rest of your life grieving for her. You know she wouldn't."

He turned and faced his subordinate swelling to his full height. "Loren, I don't recall asking for your opinion on this matter. Whatever my son or I need to do, that's for us to decide. Not some out..." Jeremiah stopped short of finishing.

"Outsider?" he hissed, confronting the king. "You weren't about to call me an outsider, were you? Who always stood by you when we were kids? Who took the blame for that catastrophe in the Wood so your father wouldn't beat you unconscious? Who looked after your son and kept LeMasters from killing him? You dare to call me an outsider!"

Guilt jabbed into the king's chest. Loren was right. He was never an outsider, and treating him like one was disloyal to their friendship.

Jeremiah sighed. "I'm sorry, Loren. I do feel guilty for having feelings toward another woman. I feel like I'm cheating on Julia somehow. Maybe it was too soon; maybe it was too soon for me to start this relationship," Jeremiah concluded miserably.

Loren expelled a breath and replied calmly, "Maybe, maybe not. Look Jer, don't let anyone, including yourself, make you feel guilty for reacting to a beautiful woman the way any hot-blooded, single man would. You have every right to feel attracted to a woman. You have every right to fall in love. You should love again." Loren studied his friend's downcast face. "That is, if some poor desperate soul is willing to take you," he added with a grin.

Jeremiah chuckled and gave his friend a playful shove. "Gee thanks! If a woman would have to be desperate to be with me, then what would that make poor Lucy for marrying you?"

He grinned broadly. "She'd be stark raving mad. Wouldn't she?"

Chapter 6

The Prophet

Xavier took a long shower and allowed the steaming water to wash away his tears and grief. Afterwards, he climbed in bed, but he wasn't able to sleep at all. He stared at the ceiling for nearly an hour waiting for his father to come and punish him. Finally, Jeremiah opened his door and peered in.

"Feeling better?" he asked.

Xavier nodded though he wasn't sure if he did.

Jeremiah crossed the distance between them and sat on the edge of the bed. He sighed and stroked a lock of wet hair from his son's forehead. "We need to talk," he said softly.

"I know," he murmured his voice catching in his tight, raw throat.

His father looked down at him, drew in a breath, and asked, "Let's start with how all this makes you feel. How do you feel about me seeing and possibly dating Catherine? How did you feel when you saw us...well, when you saw us kissing?" he asked.

Xavier blushed and looked away before answering. "I felt...angry and hurt. I felt like you'd forgotten all about Mom, and you were replacing her. She's not my mother, and she never will be," he finished harshly, glaring into his father's face.

"Catherine doesn't want to replace your mom, and she's not asking you to treat her like a mother. She only wants to be your friend," he reassured him, stroking his cheek. "Son, I could never forget your mother. I see her every time you smile or laugh. I loved your mother; I still do. But she's no longer with us. Eventually, we must move on with our lives, and that may mean I'll go out on a date once in a while or invite a woman to dinner. However, it doesn't mean that I'm planning anything serious. I don't intend to remarry; I don't know if I ever will. But, if the day comes that I feel like I'm heading in that direction, you'll be the first person I'll discuss it with. Okay?"

"Okay." Xavier nodded, smiling feebly up at his father.

"Good. What do you say to an early dinner since you didn't eat lunch? There's a small seafood diner in a fishing town not far from Warwood. What do you think? Should we take a mid-afternoon holiday and get away from the kingdom for a couple of hours?"

"Can I wear jeans and a sweatshirt?" Xavier asked, his eyes brightening excited with the prospect of spending some time alone with his father.

"You bet! We'd stand out if we didn't." He grinned and patted the young prince's leg.

Several minutes later, father and son exited the palace. It was the first time since the picnic a couple of months ago that he'd seen his father out of his formal attire. He looked like an ordinary guy, definitely not like a king, let alone an empowered man.

Xavier settled himself next to his father in the coolest, fastest car he'd ever been inside: a silver Dodge Viper. Once they were out of the kingdom and on a deserted, open highway, his father gave in to his pleas to punch the accelerator. Like a powerful invisible hand, the G force threw him back against his seat. The engine growled as the vehicle accelerated from thirty-five to one hundred in a matter of seconds. The normally forty-minute drive to Razorbill Cove took only twenty-five minutes.

The moment he saw the sign welcoming them to Razorbill Cove, Jeremiah slowed to the posted speed limit. Father and son laughed exuberantly as they pulled up to a small diner nestled among numerous fishing and bait shops. The salty, icy air swept across their faces the moment they stepped from the vehicle, and they hurried into the building. The diner was quite busy for three o'clock, and the crowd of patrons turned curiously and watched them enter. Jeremiah led Xavier to a booth overlooking the harbor, and Xavier, avoiding the prying eyes, watched out the window as a forty-foot wooden schooner, its deck loaded down with lobster cages, docked at nearby pier.

"Hello, I'm Darcy, and I'll be your server this afternoon. What can I get for you today?" a thin, graying woman asked.

After they ordered, father and son sat for some time in a comfortable silence watching the activity on the docks and pier. It was Xavier who finally spoke.

"Dad? Why do you and Headmaster Spencer hate one another?"

Jeremiah sighed, "We don't hate one another, son. It's just that our relationship is a bit...awkward."

"Why?"

His father squirmed in his seat and for a moment, and at first, Xavier didn't think he would answer. Finally, he did, "My mother died when I was two. Father remarried a common woman, Karissa Spencer, when I was four, and a year later, they had Michael. I guess I felt my father had not only replaced my mother, but me as well. Needless to say, I despised Michael from the start. Since we've grown, I've tried to make amends for how I treated him growing up, but I guess the damage is done."

"I don't think Headmaster Spencer likes me that much either. He's always yelling at me when I can't do what he wants during telepathy class."

Jeremiah paused and peered down at him. "He's a good man, Xavier. When he challenges you, he's trying to help you become the king you will need to be to run and protect our kingdom."

Xavier huff disbelievingly and was rewarded with a brief glare from the king.

"That is why," he added stiffly, "I've stressed the need for you to get control of your temper and to think before you act, son. I see so much of myself in you, and I don't want you to make the same mistakes I made. You will be a better man than me."

"But, if he's your brother, why is his last name Spencer? Wouldn't it be Wells too?" Xavier asked.

"Spencer was his mother's maiden name," Jeremiah explained. "Remember when I told you that William LeMasters had been a citizen of Warwood at one time?" Xavier nodded and the king continued, "Well, unknown to the kingdom's intelligence, he had formulated a plot to gain control over the kingdom. He secretly began recruiting citizens who were disgruntled with my father's bullish, tyrannous tactics and organized an attack on the throne. LeMasters and his followers stormed the castle and assassinated Father and Karissa Spencer. However, he failed to dismantle the Royal Guard, which had regrouped and forced the traitors from the kingdom. Michael was just twelve when the rebellion occurred."

"LeMasters killed your father?" he whispered.

"Yes, he did, and in doing so, I was inducted as the

King of Warwood at the age of eighteen. Mike went to live with his uncle, Quinton Spencer, in Ohio. He chose to take on his mother's maiden name then," he added dryly. "Anyway, during the first couple of years of my rule, LeMasters' men made several attempts to infiltrate the kingdom, but the Royal Guard defeated the group each time. Looking back, I realize now that the attempts were not full fledge assaults. They were simply tests to find weaknesses in the kingdom's defenses." The king gave a sardonic smile at the memory. "God, I was so young and arrogant. I thought I was untouchable. If it hadn't been for the experienced, knowledgeable Royal Guard, the kingdom would have fallen into William LeMasters' hands within the first few months of my rule. But, then, suddenly the attacks stopped. I naively thought that William had found my defenses too great and had simply given up. I grew relaxed and soft, and during my fifth year of rule, I took a holiday, perfectly confident that the kingdom was impenetrable. It was during that holiday that I met your mother. We were married within a few months, and you were born soon after. So when the prophet predicted your death at the christening, I didn't believe him. My stubbornness and ego nearly cost you your life."

"What do you mean?" he asked.

"LeMasters slipped through my lax, poor excuse for security and made his way to your nursery door before Dublin found him. Dublin was severely injured in the altercation, but he managed to scare William off. Following that incident, I took you and your mother to the beach house you dreamt about..."

"And sent us to live at my grandparents," Xavier finished.

"Yes."

The food came then, and father and son's conversation

moved to less serious matters. Xavier told his father how his mother's horse, Brewster's Coal, had bucked her to the ground and jumped a fence to join a herd of horses grazing in an adjoining pasture, and it wasn't until a few days later that she realized the horse had tossed her into a poison ivy patch. She had been covered from head to toe in an itchy, uncomfortable rash. Upon hearing this, the king's chuckle grew into a booming laughter, and Xavier couldn't help but laugh along with him.

As he laughed along with his father, Xavier felt the day's tension and frustrations melt away. He felt happy, relax, normal. He had almost forgotten what it felt like to be normal. Since the manifestation of his abilities, his life had been anything but normal, and in some instances, it had been downright freaky. However, sitting in a common restaurant across from his father, wearing jeans and sweatshirts, and sharing stories, he felt perfectly ordinary. So when his father announced it was time to head back, Xavier couldn't help but feel a bit saddened.

Thirty minutes later, as they pulled to a stop in front of the palace, Ephraim Hardcastle rushed toward them, looking extremely anxious.

"Sire! The prophet is here," he blurted the moment the king stepped from the vehicle.

Jeremiah frowned and soberly regarded the man before him. "I don't understand. I didn't contact him. Why is he here?"

"I tried to ask him that, but he bit my head off, roared that I had no place to question him, and said that he'd speak only to you. I'm telling you, Jeremiah, the man's off his head!" Ephraim declared, unable to keep the bitterness from his voice.

"Where is he?" Jeremiah asked.

"In the residence waiting for you," Ephraim answered.

Jeremiah strode into the palace so quickly that Xavier had to run to catch up with him.

"Dad? Dad, what's happening?" he asked, but his father didn't answer.

With his face set, he bound up the stairs three at a time and burst through the door. Milton and Mrs. Sommers were waiting by the door looking apprehensive.

"Where is he?" he demanded.

"In the library, sire," Milton responded.

Jeremiah nodded and turned to Xavier. "I need you to go to your room and stay there until I tell you to come out, understand?"

"No, I don't understand at all. Please, Dad, tell me what's going on," he pleaded anxiously.

"Xavier, I don't have time for this. Do as you're told!" he commanded firmly, sending the boy toward the steps with a light swat on the butt.

As Xavier climbed the stairs, he watched his father cross the room and enter the library. When he reached his room, he hesitated at the door and waited for Milton and Mrs. Sommers to leave the receiving room, before darting back down the stairs and scurrying to the library door. In his haste, his father had inadvertently left the door ajar, and a strange, slurred voice spilled out from the room.

"Sire, I understand your confusion, and your worry is well founded. However, nothing can be discussed until the divination," the stranger's voice noted abrasively.

"I don't understand! Why not just wait until April for the boy's Royal Communion?" Jeremiah asked.

"It's not for you to understand, Your Highness!" the stranger's voice insisted gruffly. "The boy's destiny is at stake here..."

"Is he in danger?" His father's voice quavered.

"King Wells, I fear this boy will always be in danger," the man muttered.

"Then I'll take him away! We'll disappear..."

"What about your kingdom, sire? Would you honestly shirk all your responsibilities, all your power and fortune, to protect the boy?"

Without hesitation, Jeremiah pledged, "In a heartbeat!"

The long, drawn-out silence that followed had Xavier questioning whether the men were still in the room. He peered through the gap cautiously. He saw his father standing with his back to the door, but the prophet stood out of sight.

Then, the prophet spoke, "As admirable as that is King Wells, you cannot take the boy from his people. Both of your destinies are intertwined here."

"Then, how am I to protect him?" Jeremiah growled.

The prophet sighed impatiently. "Sire, strengthen your telepathic abilities with the boy; both your lives depend upon it! As much as I know the boy despises it, he must develop strong impediment abilities. Michael Spencer is right about that. It's a dire skill for him. Make him practice with you every single night! Don't let him argue or whine his way out of it, make him do it!"

"Abe, can't you tell me what's going on?" Jeremiah pressed.

"No, I cannot. The divination will give you the answers you need. Both your generals must attend the ceremony as well as their children, Erica and Courtney. Dublin Minnows and Robbie must be there as well, but no one else is to know! I know that Father O'Brien has requested for the High Counsel to be present for the boy's divination, but you must forbid it, sire! We may not be able to prevent Father O'Brien from attending a divination in his own church, but we can forbid anyone else from attending that shouldn't be there. It's imperative no one knows about the divination until moments before the ceremony. Don't tell the Premier Guard, Father O'Brien, your servants; don't even tell Loren and Ephraim until you're on your way to the church! Do you understand?"

Jeremiah wasn't accustomed to receiving orders and found it difficult to stomach now, but he nodded obediently knowing the prophet's advice shouldn't be questioned.

"When? When do you want to perform it?"

"Tonight at midnight."

"Tonight? You've got to be joking!"

"I do not joke, sire," the prophet announced calmly. "I will bring the key and the prophecy myself..."

"You'll need clearance for that. I'll need to inform the guards that you'll be taking them," Jeremiah interrupted.

"No, damn it! You cannot say a thing!" the prophet's voice barked. "Haven't you been listening to anything I've said?"

"Look, Abe, I'd appreciate it if you wouldn't speak to me like that. Although I greatly respect you, I am still your king," Jeremiah demanded.

"I'm sorry, Your Highness. You just don't understand the delicacy of the situation. NO ONE must know! No one!" he implored gruffly. "Do not concern yourself about the security around the vault. I will retrieve the key and the prophecy with your guards none the wiser." The prophet sighed and continued more calmly, "Now, will you please invite young Xavier, who's eavesdropping at the door, into the room so that I can meet him?"

Xavier hissed a string of curses and opened the door, glancing up at his father with a small grin. "Sorry," he muttered.

"Come here, boy," the old man commanded.

Xavier looked directly at the prophet for the first time and was taken aback. He was a very big man, nearly as tall as the king, but it wasn't the man's size that shocked him. It was his face. One side of his face was grotesquely deformed. The skin drooped down a couple of centimeters, looking as though it had been doused in acid. His mouth hung at a perversely obtuse angle on one side with a string of spittle dangling from the corner. His snowy hair was tied into a knot at the base of his neck. From Xavier's perspective, the man seemed quite elderly, but he stood straight and proud which belied this impression. And, he was frighteningly powerful. Xavier could feel that power vibrate in the air all around them. But as scary and ugly as the man's appearance was, he saw something gentle and oddly familiar in those gray eyes. Slowly, he approached the man.

The prophet studied him with silent intensity, making him feel like a rare artifact. Then, he spoke.

"Hello, Xavier. I'm Abraham Vincent. Now, I know you've heard every word your father and I said, so let's just cut through the formalities, shall we? You mustn't tell anyone, not even Robbie, that the divination is planned for tonight. Do you understand?"

Xavier nodded his head vigorously, intimidated by the man's raw power and appearance. Abraham gave him a horrific lopsided smile. At least, he thought it was a smile although it looked more like a snarl.

"Sire? May I speak to the boy alone?" he asked the king.

Jeremiah hesitated briefly before replying, "Ah, sure." He looked down at Xavier. "I'll be just outside the door in the receiving room."

Then, he marched out of the room, leaving Xavier

alone with the hideous man.

Abraham studied the timid boy a moment before speaking. "Your father is a good man and a superb king, boy. Watch him and learn from him, so that when your day comes, you will be just as honorable." Abraham moved to stand within inches of him, and he could smell the old man's sour breath. "But, if your divination goes as I know it will, you will develop into a far greater, more powerful king than your father could ever dream of becoming."

He looked up at the prophet in disbelief. More powerful than his dad? It was hard to imagine!

"Xavier, there's another reason why I am here now, and why I didn't wait for your thirteenth birthday to perform the divination. You may not believe me. In fact, I'm certain you will not, and that you won't take the divination or anything I say seriously at all, but you must be warned." He hesitated before continuing in a low, strained tone. "There is great evil oozing its way into the kingdom. The dark seeks to return, and you, your father, and all you value is in grave danger, boy. The Dark Lord will come and you and your father must take heed!"

Xavier coughed out a nervous laugh. "What are you talking about? You're not making sense? Do you always talk like a fortune cookie?" he blurted, trying to sound more secure than he felt.

Abraham grabbed him roughly by the collar and hissed irritably, "Don't presume to mock me, boy! Your jokes don't make it any less true. It will happen! Even you have begun to sense what lies ahead."

"But I haven't..."

"Yes, you have!" the prophet barked, shaking him. "You've already envisioned the fall of the king, and yet you and your father have chosen to ignore it!"

"What are you talking about?" he whispered, his anxiety toward the man escalating into fear.

"The dream, boy! The dream! You dreamt of your father's fall two nights ago. You dreamt of Father O'Brien ordering your father's most trusted assistants to beat him while his enemies looked on, buying time to attack."

"How do you know about that?" he questioned, his entire body shuddering.

"It doesn't matter how I know!" the prophet snapped impatiently. "What matters is that you believe it will happen and..."

"No! No, you're lying! It was just a dream! That's all! It was just a dream!" Xavier cried, struggling against the old man's surprisingly strong grasp.

"If you need evidence of what I say is true, then remember this: the Dark Lord's servants are in place, and they will take the life of someone you care about. I'm afraid that she'll be just one of many. Children will begin to die right under their parents' noses, and terror and suspicion will follow. This will set the stage for the uprising, and I'm afraid your father and his Royal Guard will not be able to stop it. The Dark Army will overrun the kingdom, and the much of the Royal Guard will be massacred. The only option for those loyal to the throne will be to flee the kingdom."

"No, no! It can't be true! It can't! You're lying!" he yelled.

The prophet painfully tightened his grip. "Listen to me, boy! There's more!"

"No!" he cried, trying to squirm free. "I don't want to hear any more! Please!"

"But you must hear it. You must!" The man's yellowed, long nails dug painfully into his arms, and Xavier instantly stilled. Abraham continued with rushed, urgent words that sprayed across the boy's face. "When the Dark Lord rises, he will come for the throne. Death and sorrow are his bedfellows. He will be more powerful than your father, and he will kill him."

"NOOOO!" Xavier screamed. He tore from the prophet's clutches and raced across the room.

The prophet was more agile than he looked and before the young prince could reach the door, he had Xavier in his hands, spinning him around and pinning him against the wall. "Listen to me! Jeremiah will sacrifice himself for you. You and only you can stop him. If you fail, your father will die, and you will grow into a man without his guidance. You must stop him! You must prevent him from sacrificing himself."

"NO! God, please! Let me go!" Xavier wailed.

"That's enough! Release him!" Jeremiah boomed, stalking over to the older man and pushing him away from the visibly shaken boy. "Don't you ever put your hands on my son again!"

He pulled Xavier's quivering body against him and stroked his head soothingly while glaring murderously at Abraham.

"It's all right, son. I'm here," he reassured the boy.

Xavier wrapped his arms around his father as a cold chill raced down his spine at the memory of the prophet's words, "...your father will die..." It wasn't true! It couldn't be, right?

"Son," his father interrupted, caressing his cheek until he looked up at him. "Go up to your room. I'll be up in a couple of minutes after I see to the dismissal of our *guest*."

He hesitated, suddenly anxious of leaving his father's side for even a moment.

"Go on, Xavier. I'll be there in a minute," he reassured as he guided him toward the door.

Xavier left the library and climbed the stairs to his bedroom. Suddenly feeling very tired, he collapsed onto his bed. But, the old man's gnarled face flashed into his mind every time he closed his eyes, and his words kept replaying in his mind. "Even you have begun to sense it...children will begin to die...the Royal Guard will be massacred...your father will die..." He fought against the fear freezing his insides, and he shivered violently.

Nearly ten minutes later, Jeremiah entered the room, looking drained. "Are you all right?"

He nodded. "Yeah. He just scared me," he replied, trying to sound unbothered, but failed. "Will I have to see him again? He gives me the creeps."

His father crossed the room and sat on the bed next to him. "Yes, son. You'll be seeing him again tonight for the divination."

He grimaced. "Do I have to?"

"Yes, son. You do," Jeremiah insisted gently.

Fear clutched at his chest, and his breathing became erratic at the thought. "Father?" he squeaked. "Just promise me something. Promise me you won't leave me alone with him again."

The king's gaze jerked to the boy, and he frowned. "What did he say to you, Xavier?"

"I...nothing. I just... he looks so...he's scary," he muttered.

His father studied him a moment before responding. "All right. I promise I won't leave you alone with him again." He patted Xavier's knee and stood. "You should get some rest. It's going to be a very long night."

Chapter 7

Divination

All too soon for Xavier's preference, his father was shaking him awake to prepare for the divination. Next to LeMasters, there weren't many people he feared like he now did the prophet. Shortly before midnight, Jeremiah led him out of the palace with Ephraim and Loren and a very sleepy Courtney and Erica shuffling behind them. Both men had obeyed Jeremiah's instructions without question, even though a midnight meeting was highly unorthodox.

"Milton, we must stop at the Minnows for Dublin and Roberta," Jeremiah informed him as they piled into the limo. Milton drove directly to the Minnows' residence and Jeremiah, not waiting for Milton to open his door, bounded out of the car and up to the dark house. A moment later, a sleepy-eyed Dublin answered the door, and after a few brief words from Jeremiah, Dublin nodded and went back inside the house. Jeremiah returned to the car and slid into the seat next to Xavier.

"He's getting Robbie," he told him before looking at the bewildered men sitting across from them. "I know all of this is quite unusual but when Dublin and Robbie arrive, I'll explain everything. I truly appreciate your unconditional loyalty, gentlemen."

Several minutes later, Dublin came hurrying out of the house, nudging a yawning Robbie in front of him. Once they were all loaded in the car, Jeremiah opened the small window that separated the back compartment of the limo from the driver.

"Milton, take us to Saint Christopher," he ordered.

"Yes, sire," Milton answered dutifully.

Jeremiah closed the window, turned, and regarded the group. "The prophet has called for Xavier's Royal Divination to be done now, in secret." As Jeremiah went on to explain everything the prophet had said, Xavier stared out the window at the darkened streets, avoiding the puzzled and questioning stares from his friends.

Once the king had finished filling in the group, there was a long drawn out silence. Xavier felt every eye on him and his shoulders gave under the weight of the tension in the car.

Finally, Dublin broke the silence, worry spiking his voice up an octave. "But, why has he asked for the children to attend, sire?"

"I don't know, Dub," Jeremiah answered quietly. "I guess we'll all find out soon enough."

When the group entered the church, Father O'Brien rushed toward the group looking frazzled and perplexed. His white hair stood on end, and his religious robes were disheveled and wrinkled.

"Sire! Sire! What's going on? Abraham Vincent tells me that he is here to do the divination *now*! I told you that the High Counsel wishes be present for this! I could round them up and have them here within a half hour," he blurted.

"No, Father. You will do nothing of the sort. The people permitted to attend the divination are present. There will be no one else," the king ordered. "Now, just relax and prepare the altar for the ceremony."

"But, sire..."

"Father O'Brien. That was an order not a request!" Jeremiah's voice was low and authoritative, and with a begrudging nod, Father O'Brien did as he was told.

Jeremiah turned to the others. "Xavier must change and prepare for the ceremony. If the rest of you will go the pulpit, I'm sure Abraham will explain the process and your responsibilities."

His father placed a hand on his shoulder and led him up the aisle to the robe chamber. The moment the door shut behind them, Xavier whispered, "Father? What do I do?"

"Very little, son. Just try to relax," he told him softly, setting a small black bag on a table.

"What's that?" he asked, noticing the bag his father had carried from the palace for the first time.

"It's a ceremonial robe." He pulled a white silk robe and pants from the bag. "It was mine, my father's, and his father's, and...well, I think you get the idea. I wore this for my Royal Communion and Divination."

Once Xavier was changed, Jeremiah led him from the room and out into the pulpit where the others were gathering around an altar covered with a navy velvet cloth. A large trivet with a basin of water stood off to one side, and the King's Key and a small black vial sat on one end of the long altar. Xavier's pace stuttered the moment Abraham Vincent stepped into view and peered all-knowingly down at him, but his father was there to guide him forward with a gentle push. When they reached the others, Father O'Brien asked for the group to join hands and bow their heads in prayer.

Then, Abraham spoke in his slurred, gruff voice. "Sire? Please place the boy on the altar."

Jeremiah lifted Xavier and placed him on the hard surface. "Lay back, son," he instructed softly. Xavier did as he was told, his eyes wide with apprehension. Jeremiah grasped his hand and gave it a reassuring squeeze. "Relax, son. I'm here. I won't let anything hurt you. You're safe."

Abraham circled around the altar to face the group and Xavier. "Would everyone gather close to the boy and touch him, please. Each of your destinies is intertwined with this boy's. It's unclear what exactly your role will be... only the divination can give each of you that answer. Father? Please bless the boy."

The overwrought priest staggered forward, muttered a prayer as he anointed Xavier with holy water, before quickly backing away.

"Let's begin, shall we?" Abraham muttered and shakily lifted the King's Key. He stared hungrily at the luminescent object in his hands as it glowed brighter. He closed his eyes as if in prayer, but he didn't look calm or peaceful. He appeared to be battling with some internal struggle, but it quickly passed, and when he opened his eyes, his hands no longer shook and his eyes were calm and resolute. He met Xavier's curious stare before looking at the group.

"Lord, provide us with the power and might of the King's Key so that we may have the strength to intercept and understand the messages we are about to receive. Give us courage and steadfastness to do our duty even if that duty means abandoning everything we hold dear and love. God bless the key, this boy, and his destiny."

Xavier's heart felt as if it had lodged itself in his throat, and he watched as the prophet swirled the King's Key in the basin of holy water, muttering under his breath something about purifying the key. With the dripping tip of the key, he traced the sign of the cross on Xavier's forehead as he called out, "Reveal the truth, the knowledge, and the destiny of Prince Jeremiah Xavier Wells V." He placed the key perpendicularly above Xavier's head on the altar. Then, he picked up the small vial and threw it into the basin of holy water, shattering its onyx-colored casing. A rumbling echoed throughout the room. The group looked around nervously with bated breath. Finally, Abraham turned with a ladle of water that had a fascinating iridescent quality to it.

"Open the boy's robe," he ordered.

Jeremiah complied without a word. Xavier watched with dread and, oddly, excitement as the prophet approached him and slowly poured the water over his chest.

At first, Xavier felt only the water, but within seconds, a small seed of warmth formed in the center of his chest and slowly began to creep throughout his body. Soon, his entire body felt flushed and feverish as the warmth pulsating through him like a soothing heartbeat. He closed his eyes and sighed, feeling utterly content. But when he opened his eyes again, a blinding, blue light flashed over him and wrapped around him like a blanket. Xavier stiffened as he watched the light grow in intensity. But, within moments the light and its warmth evaporated, leaving Xavier with wretched emptiness. Was that it? Surely not! He looked around at the others, who were just as puzzled by the light's briefness. Then, suddenly, a reporting boom shook the temple as the blue light reappeared above them.

"Oh, my God," Jeremiah muttered softly as he watched the swirling light above them, his face cast in its blue hue.

Father O'Brien dropped to his knees and crossed himself repeatedly, muttering prayers. The air pressure around them dropped rapidly, and the light above droned louder and louder like a jet engine until finally it split into seven streamers of light and descended upon everyone except Xavier, the prophet, and Father O'Brien.

After the light vanished, there was complete silence, and Xavier looked around. Dublin Minnows was climbing to his feet where the light had knocked him to the floor. His face was ashen as he staggered down the aisle away from the group before collapsing in the last pew and burying his face in his hands. Xavier looked at Robbie, who blushed and quickly glanced away. Xavier sat up and peered up at his father, who simply stared at him. Ephraim's shock wore off first, and to Xavier's chagrin, he dropped to one knee and bowed his head. One by one, the others followed suit and knelt, including his father!

"Father! Don't! Stand up. What's going on?" he implored.

Jeremiah slowly stood, still staring at Xavier with the same shocked expression.

"What?" Xavier croaked, jumping to his feet. "What is it?"

He looked frantically around at the wide-eyed group until his gaze fell on Abraham, who watched them with an all-knowing smile.

"What did you do? Why did you make them afraid of me?" Xavier yelled, rushing at the old man and grabbing him.

"Xavier! We're not afraid of you," Ephraim whispered. "We...we're in awe." He looked apprehensively at Jeremiah, who hadn't taken his eyes from the boy.

"Dad?" Xavier questioned, going to his father and taking his hand. "What is it? What's wrong?"

Jeremiah shook his head slowly. "I don't think...I can't tell you everything, but I can tell you this, son. You will be a great king, greater and more powerful than me, or my father, or any of your ancestors for the last thousand years! You will develop many, many empowerments in the next couple years...I just...wow," he concluded softly, looking down at him with more admiration and respect than Xavier had ever experienced before!

Xavier glanced at the rest of the group and found the same awed, stunned expression.

The ride home was so quiet that only the hum of the engine and the crunching of gravel could be heard. Xavier realized his life had just made a giant leap forward, surpassing all those around him, and he felt enigmatic and alienated. He had never felt so alone in his life.

After dropping off the Minnows, the car finally pulled to a stop in front of the palace. Xavier followed the group as they climbed out of the limo and entered the building.

"Ephraim, you can take the rest of the night off. Timmins will cover your duties tonight. Good night, gentlemen," Jeremiah announced wearily.

Neither Court nor Erica looked at Xavier as they left and that bothered him a lot. Not waiting for his father, he trudged up the stairs, feeling drained and depressed. With the reaction he received at the divination, the prophet might as well have told everyone he was a leper. Tears stung his eyes as he opened the door to the royal residence and climbed the steps to his room. Without turning on the light, he stumbled across the blackened room, fell onto his bed, and began sobbing.

Light spilled over his bed as his bedroom door opened, and his father was at his side in an instant. He pulled the weeping boy into his arms and held him, gently rocking him.

Chapter 8

Repercussions

Father O'Brien glared down at the king with something close to a smirk, as Jeremiah, leaning on a blood-smeared, white pedestal, stared brazenly back. Xavier watched this silent confrontation with his stomach twisting and retching. Two strong, unyielding arms held him tightly, keeping him from running to his father's aid, and he turned to peer up into Dublin Minnows' strained face.

"Please, Mr. Minnows! Stop them!" he pleaded, but Dublin didn't respond. He continued to watch the tense exchange between the king and Father O'Brien. Xavier followed his gaze back to the square and the nightmare unfolding there. Loren and Ephraim looked exhausted and neither seemed capable of standing upright.

"Continue!" O'Brien screeched. "Continue or be replaced!"

Weightily, Loren straightened and approached his bloody, battered friend with tears pooling in his eyes. Silently he pleaded with the king to end the torture, but Jeremiah shook his head. The general closed his eyes in frustration, dropping tears heavily onto his face. Then, with a despondent groan, he swung the rod and struck the king with every ounce of strength he could muster.

Jeremiah instantly dropped to the ground and cried out in pain as Father O'Brien looked on, sneering and victorious.

Xavier struggled frantically against Dublin's arms. "Stop! Please, stop! Please," he bellowed. Finally, he wiggled free of Dublin's grasp and raced to Loren, who was preparing to strike again.

Xavier sat up in bed, his face and pillow soaked with tears and his heart thumping against his chest. There was no moonlight and his room was black. Panting, he flicked on his bedside lamp and peered around the room, working to calm himself. He looked at the clock on his nightstand; it was five in the morning. Slowly, Xavier peeled back the covers and stood. Taking one last look around, he tiptoed to his father's room. The door opened with a soft moan, and he quietly crossed the room to his sleeping father.

"Dad?" he whispered, shaking him. "Dad?"

"Hop in," he mumbled, still mostly asleep.

Relieved, Xavier clambered over his father's body to the opposite side of the bed and burrowed under the covers next to him. He wasn't exactly sure when he fell asleep, but he was fairly certain it was the moment his head hit the pillow.

The next morning, Xavier was awakened by pale daylight spilling through the windows. He turned to find his father sitting up in bed watching him. He smiled. "Morning. Sleep well?"

Xavier struggled out of the covers to sit up. "Yes, sir."

"When did you become my slumbering pal last night?" Jeremiah asked, kissing his forehead.

"Around five. What time is it now?" he asked, searching around for a clock.

"Almost ten." His father smiled.

"Ten! I'm late for school!" he blurted, trying to

untangle himself from the blankets.

"It's all right, Xavier. I called Sir Spencer and explained. Besides, I want to accompany you to your Latin class at 11 o'clock."

"My Latin class?" He was bemused. "Why?"

Jeremiah gave him a reproachful glance before standing. "So you can apologize to Madam Stokes, of course."

"Oh," Xavier remarked dryly. "I forgot about that."

"Well, I didn't. Now, go get a shower and get dressed. I'll meet you in the dining hall in twenty minutes for breakfast," Jeremiah told him, lifting him out of the bed and sending him to the door with a light smack on his bottom.

Xavier wanted nothing more than to shrink into the shadows of the academy's hallways as his father and Headmaster Spencer led him to his Latin class. Then, to make matters worse, the bell rang, and the normally chattering students fell silent when they saw King Wells. Jeremiah and Spencer seemed oblivious to the attention and continued their discussion as they led Xavier down the hall, up the stairway, and onto the second floor where Madam Stokes' Latin class was about to start. Jeremiah guided Xavier into the room where they found Catherine sitting at her desk grading papers.

"Catherine?" Jeremiah called quietly.

Catherine looked up and grinned at the sight of him. "Jeremy, what are you doing here?"

Jeremiah looked down at Xavier and nudged him forward. "My son has something he needs to say to you and the class."

Xavier jerked his head up to his father. "I have to apologize to her in front of the class?"

Jeremiah didn't respond verbally. Instead, Xavier heard his father's stern voice encroaching into his thoughts. *"Yes, son. Since you embarrassed her in front of the entire class, I think she deserves an apology in front of your classmates. Don't you?"*

Before he could protest, Headmaster Spencer's voice crowded into his mind as well, *"Your father is right, Xavier. It's either this or a week suspension."*

Xavier sighed heavily and muttered, "I think I'd rather take the week suspension." Jeremiah glared down at him. The classroom was nearly full when the tardy bell rang and Court and Erica scurried into the room.

"Mr. Hardcastle, Miss Jefferson, I sure hope this isn't a normal habit," Spencer commented.

"No, sir," Court answered meekly as they scrambled to their seats.

"Class," Spencer began, and instantly the chatter died away. "We have a visitor." He motioned to Jeremiah, but it was completely unnecessary as the entire class was quite aware of their visitor. They had been whispering excitedly the moment the king had entered the class.

"Good morning, King Wells," the children chorused.

"Good morning, children. I've accompanied Xavier to class this morning because he has something he needs to say to all of you and especially to Madam Stokes. Xavier?"

Xavier hesitated as every eye in the class settled on him.

His father squeezed his shoulder and nudged him to face Madam Stokes. "Son?" he prompted again.

"I'm sorry," he squeaked quickly, not looking at her.

"Xavier, there's more to an apology than that! You need to tell her why you're sorry and that you won't repeat it," Jeremiah told him. "Now, do it properly."

Xavier cleared his throat nervously. "Ah, Madam

Stokes, I...I'm sorry for speaking to you the way I did yesterday. And I'm sorry for being disrespectful and using your name on the test. I'm sorry for not doing as I was told and not going straight to the office." He turned to the class. "And I apologize to the class for being disruptive and making it difficult for you to pay attention and complete your work. I'll try to do better."

"Thank you, sire. I appreciate your apology. I only hope that you've learned a lesson from all this," Madam Stokes noted.

He bowed his head and muttered, "Yes ma'am. I did."

"Can we come to a mutual understanding that this class won't suffer whenever you and I have a personal issue?" she asked sweetly enough, but Xavier could feel the iciness of her words. He looked up into her triumphant, cold eyes, as she smiled down at him. He knew that to anyone watching, the smile would seem friendly, encouraging, but to him, it was a smile of conquest and provocation. He despised this woman more than words could ever express.

He felt his father's hand tightening on his shoulder again, and he smiled mockingly back at his new nemesis. "Yes, ma'am. I totally agree." He was surprised by how calm and sweet his voice sounded while his entire body shook with hatred.

"Good!" Spencer's boisterous voice said with relief. "Now that we've settled that, King Wells and I will leave you to your lesson."

"Xavier," his father's voice was less enthusiastic. He turned and met the king's eyes, trying to mask the overwhelming desire to smack the woman next to him. "We'll talk at home," his father promised ominously.

Xavier nodded and made his way to his seat between Court and Beck.

Latin seemed to drag by but finally at noon, the bell rang, and Xavier hurried out the door before Madam Stokes could stop him to gloat in his face.

"Jeremy? Jeremy?"

Ken's smug voice sneered from behind him. Xavier continued to walk on, refusing to be goaded into a fight, but what Ken said next sent him over the edge.

"Is your daddy *doing* the teacher so you won't fail Latin?"

Without hesitation, he spun and punched Ken solidly in the face. Ken fell to the floor with a thud, and when Xavier moved to finish the job, Court and Beck grabbed him and hauled him away.

"Come on, mate. You don't want to do that!" Court coaxed.

"Just you wait, Prince of Cream Puffs, I'll get you. One of these days, I'll even up the score, and you'll have no one around to save you!" Ken bellowed.

"Piss off, Calhoun!" Court yelled as he and Beck pulled Xavier down the hall toward the cafeteria.

"Man! Why do you let him get to you with all that rubbish? You know he only does it so you'll lose your head and get into trouble!" Court muttered as they quickly got their lunches and sat down with Erica and Robbie.

"I know. God, I can't stand him," Xavier groaned, but then he grinned. "Well, at least he'll think of me every time he looks in a mirror for the next couple of weeks."

"You know it! Awesome punch, Your Highness! He'll have a shiner for sure!" Beck hooted, clapping Xavier on the back. After a brief chuckle, the table fell into a profound silence.

Robbie avoided looking at him, but whenever she did, she'd quickly look away, her face turning scarlet. Erica sat unusually quiet next to Robbie, and even Court sat without talking, toying with his food. Their behavior worried him. What had they seen at the divination? What did they learn that caused this change, this deterioration in their friendship?

The thick, tense atmosphere didn't escape Beck's attention, either. He shifted uncomfortably in his seat and studied the group. Finally, he remarked, "Hey? What's going on? Did you lot have a fight or something?"

"No, of course not!" Robbie answered. "We just...we..." And once again, silent tension built in the air around them.

Finally, Court blurted to Beck, "So, what are you planning for Mummering?"

"Mummering?" Xavier questioned.

"Yeah, Mummering! It's great!" Beck announced gleefully. "Mummering is a Christmas tradition all over Newfoundland, but it's particularly special here. Grown-ups hate it, but they can't give us too much of a hard time because they did it when they were kids."

"That's what you think!" Robbie warned, but the boys ignored her.

"What is it, exactly?" Xavier asked.

"Basically, it's a practical joke night. It's usually celebrated the week before Old Christmas," Court told him.

"Old Christmas? You have more than one Christmas?"

"Yeah. Well, here we have Christmas Day like everyone else, but we also celebrate Old Christmas. Christmas used to be celebrated on January sixth before the calendar changed, and I guess our people could never really let go of our old traditions. So, on the sixth of January we have sleigh rides, a huge bonfire by the lake, a Christmas Rugby Tournament, a huge banquet, and a dance. So, if you have an idea who you'd like to take as your date to the dance, you better ask her soon before someone else does," Beck told him, before turning to Court. "It's your year to host the mummering celebration, Hardcastle. Which day are we having the sleepover?"

"Let's do it a couple of days before Old Christmas. That way, we'll have a day to recover from our late night festivities," Court announced. "Don't forget to bring masks."

"We know! We know! We're not idiots!" Beck retorted.

Following lunch, Xavier, Court, Erica, and Robbie sat stiffly next to one another on the gym's bleachers during lunch break. The uncomfortable atmosphere had returned, and Xavier felt as though he would explode from the tension.

"You guys!" he spat. "Come on! Can't we just pretend that the divination never happened? The way you guys are acting is freaking me out. Please?"

"Sorry, Xavier. We're trying, but it's hard to do," Robbie told him, still not quite meeting his eyes. "Just give us a little more time. We'll get over it."

Xavier nodded and muttered, "Yeah, fine. No problem."

They fell into another uncomfortable silence until Court asked, "Got any ideas who you're going to ask to the Old Christmas dance?"

"Oh, I don't know. How about you? Any prospects?" Xavier asked.

"A couple potential lucky girls," Courtney teased.

Robbie and Erica rolled their eyes in disgust.

Then, Court turned to Erica. "Well, what do you say, Jefferson? Want to go?"

Erica blushed, and for a moment, she seemed speechless. Finally, she shrugged. "Sure. I don't have anything better to do, so why not? But listen carefully, Hardcastle! There's to be no handholding, no corsages, no kissing, and absolutely no fooling around! Got it?"

Court gaped at her in something just short of shock before turning to Xavier. "She's crazy about me! Can't you tell?"

Xavier snickered as Erica began pounding on him.

"Ow! Erica, stop flirting with me! You're giving mixed messages about fooling around!" Court sputtered between laughs.

"God! You're an idiot, Hardcastle!" Erica growled rolling her eyes.

"Hey, Robbie? Do you have a date for the dance? If not, maybe you and..." Xavier began.

"I already have a date. Beck asked me ages ago, and I...I...well, I said yes. You're not mad are you?" Robbie blurted, blushing.

"Nah, he's not mad, Rob," Court told her. "I mean he's the Prince of Warwood! I'm sure there are at least a dozen girls just waiting for him to ask them. Hey, Xavier! What about Maggie Applegate? She's hot, and she seems to like you!"

"Yeah, okay. The next time I see her, I'll ask her then," Xavier replied with more confidence than he felt. The truth was, Xavier was a little angry that Robbie and Beck were going to the dance together and that surprised him.

"No time like the present," Erica teased, pointing. "She's right over there making love sick cow eyes at you. Ask her now before someone else does."

Xavier looked behind him at Maggie, who was surrounded by her friends, like a chattering, giggling force field. God, he hated it when girls did that; it made it twice as hard to talk to one of them because the other girls would giggle and make him feel like a bumbling idiot.

"She seems busy, maybe later," Xavier muttered.

"Later? Are you chicken, Prince of Warwood?" Erica teased.

"No, it's just..."

Xavier looked back at Maggie smiling, laughing, and looking absolutely beautiful. She glanced over and caught him watching her. When she smiled and waved at him, Xavier turned back to his friends, blushing.

"Fine. I'll do it now."

Mustering up as much courage as he could, Xavier stood and made his way over to her. The short walk to Maggie was painfully awkward. He felt as if he was wearing large clown shoes, and he kept stumbling. He didn't know what to do with his hands. He tried tucking them in his pockets but when he stumbled again, he nearly fell on his face before he managed to pull out his hands to regain his balance. He decided to keep them awkwardly at his sides as he approached Maggie and her entourage. The group of giggling girls went silent the moment he reached them.

Xavier cleared his throat and squeaked, "Ah, Maggie? Can I talk to you for a moment?"

"Ah, sure." Maggie stood and followed Xavier.

The frenzy of whispers that immediately followed drew Xavier's eyes back to the group of girls and the whispers transformed into high-pitched squeals and giggles. Blushing, Xavier led Maggie to an empty area of the bleachers. They sat in silence as Xavier fidgeted with his pants leg, trying to find the courage to ask her.

"Ah, Xavier? What is it you wanted to talk to me about?"

Xavier looked at her enormous pale gray eyes and his heart nearly jumped from his chest. "Ah, ah, I..." he stammered. God! Why was he so nervous? This girl liked him! After all, she had kissed him once on the cheek! "Well, I was wondering. Has... anyone asked you... to the Old Christmas dance yet?"

Maggie smiled, and Xavier's heart felt like it exploded in his chest. "No, sire. No one has asked me."

"Well, would you like to go... with...me?" he whispered timidly.

Oh, there was that smile again. Lord, did girls know the power they had over boys with a simple smile? Xavier's body tingled.

"I would love to!" Maggie replied softly, and Xavier beamed. "I'll let you know what color my dress will be next week."

Xavier's smile fell marginally. Okay, now he was lost. Why would he need to know that? His confusion must have been apparent on his face because Maggie patted his hand and explained, "The guy is supposed to wear a matching tie and vest."

Xavier barely heard her answer. The moment she touched his hand, a strong energy drummed through him and the pounding of his heart was nearly deafening. He wanted nothing more than to kiss this girl.

"Ah, okay," he squeaked, jumping to his feet. "Thanks. Ah, I better...ah...get my stuff; the afternoon classes are about to begin. See ya." He hurried away from a slightly baffled and bemused Maggie Applegate.

Chapter 9

Mummering

The next couple of weeks went quickly and before Xavier knew it, Christmas break was well underway and the night for Mummering had come. Although he still wasn't sure what Mummering was, he was excited to be attending a sleepover and hanging out with the guys. With a duffle bag in one hand and his dad's sleeping bag tucked under the other arm, he exited the royal residence. Ephraim was standing guard outside the door and greeted him with a smile.

"Now, you tell that son of mine to mind his mother and behave himself. In fact, the whole lot of you better behave or I'll take a strap to your backsides!" he teased.

"Yes, Sir." Xavier laughed and continued down the steps to the Hardcastle residence. Court greeted him at the door and dragged him into the residence.

"About time, X. We were afraid we'd have to start without you," he whispered as he dragged him past Mrs. Hardcastle.

"Hello, Xavier." She smiled. "Please excuse Courtney's rudeness."

"Hi, Mrs. Hardcastle. Don't worry. I'm used to it," he answered, smiling back.

Courtney dragged him into his room where Beck,

Harry, Frankie, and Garrett sat goofing around. "Get out!" Court growled at his little brother, Caleb, who sat on the bed watching the older boys.

"It's my room, too!" he whined.

"I said get out!" Court repeated, hauling Caleb off his bed and pushing him out the door.

"Hey, X! Glad you could make it," Beck whooped excitedly.

The other boys instantly began chanting, "Prince Wells, Prince Wells, Prince Wells!" But the moment Beck raised his hand, everyone fell silent so Beck could announce the plans for the night.

"Okay, the best thing to do is to wait until Court's mother is asleep; it'll make our escape easier. Once we're out of the residence, we'll borrow Governor Yaman's horse and sleigh so we can have fast teleportation around the kingdom." Beck continued to describe the plans with flawless detail. They were perfect in every way except one: what would they do if they were discovered? But the boys didn't notice this enormous flaw and continued to discuss ideas in making the night the best Mummering night ever.

Finally, at midnight, Courtney led the troupe into the kitchen, threw back a large braided rug, and pulled up a hatch in the middle of the floor.

"Whoa! Hardcastle! I didn't know this place had hidden doors and passages! Awesome!" Garrett whispered excitedly.

"Yeah, it's pretty cool. The entire palace is full of them. I guess it's so that if the palace is ever invaded, the king and his closest officials can escape unharmed." Court shrugged, already climbing down the ladder into the passageway. The boys followed him one by one, descending into the dark cramped space.

"God, Hardcastle! It's pitch black down here! How are

we going to see to get out?" Beck's voice chastised.

"Damn! I forgot the sodding flashlight," Court spat.

A collective groan and complaints echoed down the passage.

"Jeez, Court!"

"What are we supposed to do now, Hardcastle? Bounce off the walls until we find our way out?" Garrett belittled.

Suddenly, the tunnel filled with a brilliant white light. Every voice fell silent, and the boys gapped at Xavier and the small sphere of light cupped in his hand. He looked at each stunned face in turn.

"What?" Xavier questioned. "We need light, right?"

The boys burst into laughter.

"Okay, disguises on!" Beck announced. Xavier pulled on the full head clown mask complete with wild orange hair that Court had loaned him. After a brief heckling at one another's masks, the group made their way through the passage and slipped out into the night through a cellar door at the rear of the palace.

They had no difficulty "borrowing" Governor Yaman's horse and sleigh. Xavier discovered that Garrett was quite knowledgeable about horses, and with Xavier calming the beast with his anima-lingua, Garrett soon had the horse harnessed and strapped to the sleigh. The boys tumbled into the sleigh in one tangled, giggling heap. Garrett took the reins and the group was whisked out of the palace grounds and into Wellington's residential streets. Soon, they were racing from house to house collecting lawn furniture, lights, Christmas decorations, mailboxes, and even street signs.

"What are we going to do with all this stuff?" Harry asked.

"I've got an idea," Xavier announced, laughing. "Let's put it all on Headmaster Spencer's front lawn."

At first the group just stared at him like he was insane, but slowly, enormous grins spread across their faces.

"You know something, Your Highness? If I didn't have any respect for you before, I sure do now! You've got moxie, man." Beck laughed, clapping him on the back and turning to the others. "Well? You heard your king, the headmaster's house it is! May the Lord protect us if he catches us!"

Xavier had no idea what to expect when seeing Spencer's home for the first time, but what he saw surprised him. Michael Spencer didn't live within the palace's walls as a royal. Instead, Garrett guided the sleigh onto the streets in the Merchant Area. Spencer's house was a well-kept, modest home not much different from the house where he had lived with his grandparents.

"*Spencer* lives here?" Xavier whispered as he climbed out of the sleigh.

"Well, not everyone can live in a palace, Your Highness," Garrett pointed out softly.

"Oh, no, that's not what I meant. I guess I just figured that since he's royalty, he'd have to live inside the palace walls or something. I didn't mean anything bad by it! I lived in house like this before my mom...well, before I came here."

"I'm just teasing ya, X." Garrett smiled as he jumped down from the buckboard and pushed the prince playfully.

"Dude! You didn't just push me," Xavier spat good-naturedly, pushing the smaller boy back.

"Shut it, you two." Beck hissed. "We don't want to wake him up before we're finished."

Nearly twenty minutes later, the boys had several complete sets of patio furniture, three erected street signs, several strings of Christmas lights, and four mailboxes strung across the lawn.

"Do you think he'll even notice?" Xavier blurted, stifling a chuckle.

The boys burst into laughter, and Beck gestured wildly with his hands to quiet them down. "Hush! You'll wake the dead."

"It's not the dead I'm worried about," Court retorted, before bursting into loud laughter with the rest of the boys.

"Jeez! Shut it, you idiots! Come on! Let's get out of here! I've got plans for the rectory."

The group tumbled into the sleigh, giggling. Garrett snapped the reins and began to bellow out "Silent Night." For some reason, the group found the song hilarious beyond words and collapsed into hysterical laughter while Beck persistently shushed them.

By the time the troupe arrived at the church's rectory, they were all bellowing out the lyrics to "Silent Night." Garrett pulled the sleigh to a stop and grinned at Beck, who was shaking his head.

"You guys are thick! Now, will the lot of you respectfully shut it so we don't get caught vandalizing sacred ground!"

Again, everyone burst into barely contained laughter. Beck rolled his eyes and hopped out of the sleigh.

"He's right, guys. Settle down. Here, choose your weapons," Court announced as he dumped the contents of a sack onto the bed of the sleigh.

Court had come prepared! There were rolls of toilet paper, several bars of soap, bottles of food coloring, and four cartons of eggs. Each boy took his fair share of supplies and set to work "decorating" the rectory. Xavier and Garrett busied themselves stringing toilet paper over all the shrubs and trees in the front lawn, while the others soaped the windows and rectory walls and wrote crude messages in food coloring in the snow on the front lawn. When they were finished, they stepped back and admire their work.

"It looks jolly good, mates," Court grinned.

"Ah, but, it's missing something," Beck announced, studying the rectory closer.

Then, Xavier noticed the eggs on the front seat of the sleigh. "What are the eggs for?"

Beck turned and smiled devilishly. "That's it! That's what's missing!" He marched over to the sleigh and grabbed the eggs. "Okay everyone, load up on ammunition," Beck called, holding out the cartons to the other boys. "This game is called Pelt the Priest. Now, everyone will need to find a good hiding place. I'll ring the doorbell, and when Father O'Brien comes to the door, we'll pelt him with eggs. Whoever gets him in the face wins!"

The boys snickered and scrambled behind shrubs and trees as Beck marched up the sidewalk. Then, after glancing over his shoulder to see if everyone was hidden, he pressed the doorbell and raced off behind a bush. Several moments later, a yawning Father O'Brien came to the door. He opened his mouth to say something when an egg splattered on his chest. The priest blinked stupidly as two more eggs zipped past him and splattered on the rectory door. Xavier stood and threw his egg, hitting Father O'Brien squarely in the face just as three more eggs splattered across his chest. The other boys immediately raced away from the rectory, abandoning the horse and sleigh, but Xavier made the fatal error of hesitating to watch a yelling O'Brien tumble off the porch and into a shrub before finally sprinting off into the darkness.

He didn't get more than half a block from the church

when he heard heavy footsteps behind him, running. Surely it couldn't be the pudgy priest chasing after him! Without a hesitation in his pace, he turned and squinted into the darkness. Someone was indeed following him, but it was definitely not Father O'Brien. This man was athletic, fit, and very fast, and he was gaining on him with very little effort. Xavier sprinted as fast as his legs would carry him, but several strides later, he felt the man's hands on him, pulling him to the ground.

"Okay, you little delinquent, let's find out who you are!" a deep voice growled as he flipped Xavier onto his back and tore the mask from his face. Xavier looked up into the steel eyes of his uncle, Michael Spencer.

"Xavier? What the... You did this? You're responsible for all this mayhem?" he spat out.

"Yes, sir," Xavier responded meekly.

Although he could never be certain, Xavier thought he saw humor in the depths of his uncle's eyes, but with a blink, all humor disappeared and a precarious chill took its place. Spencer stood and pulled him to his feet.

"Let's go. We're going back to the rectory for Father O'Brien. Then the two of us will take you home," he announced, grabbing him by the collar and steering him back toward the church. "Do you mind telling me who the horse and sleigh belong to? I'm certain the owner will want them back."

"They're Governor Yaman's," Xavier muttered.

"Ah, yes. I thought I recognized the horse."

Father O'Brien was not a very forgiving man. If Spencer hadn't been there, he would have beaten Xavier to a pulp. As the men escorted him back to the castle, O'Brien tried to pressure him into revealing his accomplices, but he stubbornly refused to talk. He knew his loyalty was useless because once his father and

Ephraim found out what happened they'd know that the others had been involved as well. No, he wouldn't need to say a word. The others were just as busted as he was. He sighed dejectedly as they entered the palace.

Spencer and O'Brien followed Xavier into the antechamber. Ephraim went rigid at the sight of them, and his eyes narrowed knowingly at the sight of Father O'Brien's egged robe and face.

"Where's Courtney, Xavier?" he asked stiffly, as the trio climbed the steps to the royal residence.

"In your residence, I think," Xavier muttered.

"We need to speak to the king, Ephraim," Spencer announced calmly.

Ephraim led them into the receiving room and then climbed the stairs to Jeremiah's room. Moments later, Jeremiah appeared in his pajamas, looking sleepy-eyed and very grumpy. Xavier tried to blink back the tears already forming at the edges of his eyes.

"Your Highness!" bellowed Father O'Brien, not even waiting for Jeremiah to finish climbing down the steps. "This boy has been out vandalizing the kingdom! He and his cohorts soaped and toilet papered the church's property! They wrote crude messages on the lawn and on the rectory walls! Not to mention the personal assault they directed toward me! Just look at me! One little deviant even hit me in the face!"

Xavier had been staring at the floor throughout O'Brien's tyrant, but at the priest's last words, his head and shoulders sank. He felt a light, reassuring squeeze on his shoulder and looked up at Spencer's softening expression.

"There were others there, but the boy will not divulge their identities! I want you to invade the boy's mind and tell me who the other boys are," Father O'Brien demanded.

"There's no need to do that, Father O'Brien," Ephraim answered.

"Then you know who the other culprits are?" Father O'Brien asked.

Ephraim sighed and nodded. "I'm afraid we have a bloody good idea."

"It doesn't take a genius to figure it out," Jeremiah added gruffly. "Mike, why are you here?"

"Well, it seems the boys left me a front yard full of presents that I'm fairly certain weren't theirs to give," he explained, trying not to smile. "And the boys seem to have *borrowed* Governor Yaman's horse and sleigh as well, but I'll make sure they get back to the stables when we're done here."

Jeremiah nodded. "Ephraim, would you round up Xavier's conspirators and bring them here."

"Yes, sire," Ephraim muttered, leaving the residence.

Jeremiah looked at the downcast head of his son. "Xavier? What do you have to say for yourself?"

Xavier looked briefly into the stern eyes of his father and shrugged. "I guess nothing, sir. I was just celebrating Mummering."

"Well, that's the understatement of the year! It's quite obvious you were celebrating Mummering, but did your friends tell you that Mummering is frowned upon by the community, not to mention illegal?" Jeremiah asked.

"No, but didn't you do it when you were a kid?" Xavier muttered.

"Yes, I did, but if you had asked me that beforehand, I would have also told you that my father reddened my backside for it," Jeremiah responded roughly.

"Yes! A worthy punishment if you ask me! One that I want to administer myself!" Father O'Brien spat.

Jeremiah stiffened noticeably. "I don't think that's necessary, Father. I will punish the boy appropriately."

"I think not, Jeremiah! You're too soft on the boy! That boy," he spat, jabbing a finger at Xavier, "needs a good old-fashioned spanking that will make him think twice before he does something like this again," Father O'Brien demanded, stepping toward Xavier.

"I can guarantee he'll think twice before doing something like this again," Jeremiah spat back, moving aggressively toward the priest and blocking him from Xavier. "But you're not touching my son, O'Brien!"

Spencer pulled Xavier away and protecting him from the sparring men as their argument escalated.

"Now, look here, Jeremiah! I have the right to..."

"No! You have no rights where my son is concerned! You will not touch him! I am not my father!" Jeremiah countered.

"I'm painfully aware of that, *Boy*," O'Brien hissed.

Jeremiah's entire body seemed to swell at the word "*Boy*", and he stepped aggressively forward, towering above the older man.

"Oi!" Ephraim called, stomping into the room with a timid troupe of boys behind him. He pushed between the two angry men. "Your Highness, Father O'Brien, this isn't going to help. I think both of you need to take a step back and calm down!" he interrupted firmly.

"Ephraim's right! This isn't solving anything," Spencer added. "Surely we can come up with a punishment you both can agree upon."

Jeremiah sighed raggedly, visibly reigning in his fury. "Father," Jeremiah began with forced calmness, "I will punish the boy, but you can gain retribution by bearing witness if you'd like, and all six boys will report for clean up duty tomorrow morning at seven."

"Seven? Ah, man!" Garrett whined.

Jeremiah turned on the boys. "Yes! At seven, Garrett Bracus!"

Garrett immediately cowered and muttered meekly, "Yes, Your Highness."

"Rebecca is calling their parents," Ephraim murmured to the men before turning to the boys. "Of all the stupid, idiotic ideas...whose idea was this?" Ephraim demanded, glaring at his own son. When the boys didn't respond right away, Ephraim repeated more harshly, "Whose idea was it?"

"Mine, sir," Xavier murmured softly. All four men spun toward him.

"Your idea?" Jeremiah repeated, clearly unconvinced.

"Yes, sir. It was my idea to put all that stuff in Headmaster Spencer's yard, and I was the one who hit Father O'Brien in the face with an egg. It was me."

Jeremiah and Spencer looked at one another and shook their heads.

"No, it wasn't," Jeremiah retorted. "It may have been your idea to decorate Mike's front lawn, and you may have thrown an egg at Father O'Brien, but this entire escapade wasn't your idea, was it, Beckley?" Jeremiah turned to the red-haired boy.

"No, sire," Beck agreed resigned. "It was mine."

"Okay, have a seat, boys. Your parents will be here shortly," Jeremiah insisted firmly, gesturing to the sofa and armchairs next to the glowing ash in the hearth. The boys obediently did as they were told.

"Geez, X! How did you get caught?" Garrett hissed once they were all seated next to the fireplace.

"We must've woken up Spencer when we did his lawn. You know, he's a lot faster than he looks," he muttered. "You don't think we'll be grounded for the Old Christmas

Celebrations, do you?"

"Don't even think of that, Xavier! Crikey! I'd rather be caned within an inch of my life than for that to happen!" Court gasped, horrified.

The boys fell into a strained silence, contemplating their fates and the repercussions they would undoubtedly face.

When the doorbell chimed several minutes later, all six boys went rigid as two men stomped into the palace.

"Oh, no! We're dead men, Bracus!" Beckley whispered, punching Garrett beside him. Both boys peered over the back of the sofa as their fathers shook hands with Jeremiah before listening intently to Spencer and Father O'Brien. The tall redheaded man was obviously Beck's father, and the shorter, burly man with a thick beard had to be Garrett's dad.

"Beckley Adam Wilcox!" Beck's father barked. "Get over here, boy!"

"Garrett, you too, son," Mr. Bracus called, more calmly.

Garrett and Beck stood and went to the men, and Xavier couldn't help but watch the exchange. Although he couldn't hear what was being said, Father O'Brien seemed to be monopolizing the conversation, and Beck and Garrett looked to be on the verge of tears. After a moment, Father O'Brien led the group into the library and closed the door behind them.

Xavier turned and stared into Court's pale, terrified face.

"What do you imagine will happen to them now?" Frankie asked in a quiet, shaky voice.

"I don't have to imagine," Court croaked. "I *know* what's happening, and you will too when your mum gets here!"

But Frankie didn't have to wait for his answer. A

moment later, muffled thuds and whimpers seeped from the library. Frankie's face went crimson and his eyes widened.

"Surely... they're not...Father O'Brien wouldn't dare touch me! Mom wouldn't let him!" Frankie declared with shaken confidence.

"I wouldn't count on that," Court muttered.

Finally, Garrett and Beck exited the library with runny noses, red eyes, and moist, flushed faces. Garrett glanced over at Xavier with an embarrassed, meek smile. Beckley, on the other hand, stomped out of the palace without a glance at the other boys.

After Mr. Wilcox and Mr. Bracus left the residence, Ephraim looked at his son. "Courtney? You're up."

"Dad...don't...uh...just don't let Father O'Brien do it. Please?" Court whispered.

"He's not administering the punishment. The king is," Ephraim replied.

"Oh, Crikey!" Court muttered and followed his father into the library.

"The king? Oh God, oh God, oh God!" Frankie cried.

Frankie's mother finally arrived, and soon, only Xavier was left. He wasn't sure which was worse, listening to his friends being punished or waiting for his turn.

Finally, his father came to him and knelt in front of him. Xavier's stomach lurched with anxiety. "Son, you know what you did was wrong. I'd dare to say it crossed your mind while you were playing your part in this evening's pranks. Am I right?"

Xavier nodded, reluctant to meet his father's eyes.

"When you victimize others, they have a right to decide and witness your punishment," Jeremiah explained softly. "Do you understand?"

"Yes, sir," he croaked as tears finally spilled over his

cheeks.

"Even though I've asked Father O'Brien not to spank you, it doesn't mean that you don't deserve it and won't be getting it. I will spank you, son, and Father O'Brien and Headmaster Spencer will bear witness," he concluded and stood. "It's been a very long night, and I'm just as anxious as you to get this over with so we can both go to bed."

"Remember our agreement, sire," Father O'Brien reminded him testily.

"I remember, Father," Jeremiah grumbled, bitterly.

"If I feel you're being too lenient..."

"Yes, Father! I know! I remember our agreement!" Jeremiah barked, glaring at the priest as though he would rather pummel him.

After another heavy sigh, Jeremiah turned back to Xavier. "Stand up, son," he sighed, grasping Xavier's arm and pulling him to his feet.

With a shuddering moan, Xavier found himself pinned against his father's left hip, and suddenly, Xavier wanted to bawl.

Maybe it was because Father O'Brien was watching with a critical eye, or maybe it was the fact that it had been months since his father truly gave him a spanking, but when his father struck him, Xavier realized that Father O'Brien needn't have worried about his father being too lenient for this punishment would be quite the contrary. The priest must have been satisfied because he didn't say a word as Jeremiah finally released Xavier and straightened.

After a moment of uncomfortable silence, O'Brien's announced smugly from behind Xavier, "I'm sorry it came to this, young sire,"–though, he didn't sound at all sorry–"but will this punishment help you to reject obviously poor schemes your friends dream up? Will it help you think for yourself?"

Seething, he didn't trust himself to speak.

"Xavier?" Jeremiah questioned, gently grasping his chin and lifting the boy's gaze to his. "Father O'Brien asked you a question."

Xavier hastily wiped the tears from his face and turned to face the priest. "Yes, sir," he muttered.

"Good," O'Brien announced with a satisfied smile.

"Son, you and your partners in crime will spend tomorrow morning taking everything you stole and left in the Headmaster's yard back to their rightful owners, and you will clean up the mess at the rectory."

"Yes, sir," he answered quietly.

Jeremiah rubbed his face and raked his fingers through his pale hair. "Okay, it's late, son. Go on up to bed."

Xavier left without looking back and a moment later, the door to his room slammed shut.

Chapter 10

First Love

The boys were lucky in that they had not been grounded from the Old Christmas Celebrations. So the next morning, "the morning of restoration" as they came to call it, they spent cleaning the exterior of the church and its grounds. In order to get things done quickly, they divided themselves up into task groups. Garrett and Frankie used the king's sleigh and horses to return the stolen lawn furniture, Christmas lights, decorations, and street signs they had used to decorate Headmaster Spencer's front lawn. Courtney and Harry busily raked snow so that the words written in food coloring were erased. Xavier was paired with Beck to clean the rectory windows and door. The bar soap was caked heavily on the door and windows and it took a good bit of scrubbing to get it all off.

"X? Sorry I got you in trouble with your dad. Going Mummering was a stupid idea," Beck said.

"Don't worry about it. It's not your fault. I could have said no. I wanted to go Mummering," Xavier responded, not looking at his friend as he continued to scrub at the door. "I can't stand Father O'Brien. He was so..." Xavier groaned, not sure how to finish the sentence. "I just hated it that he got what he wanted from our dads. You know?

That we all got punished like we did."

Beck was shaking his head before Xavier finished. "He didn't exactly get it his way. When Garrett and I went back into the library, Garrett's dad asked King Wells what he believed was an acceptable punishment. Father O'Brien started to answer, but Mr. Bracus completely dismissed him and told him that he wasn't interested in his opinion, that he was speaking to the king. The look on Father O'Brien's face was priceless. King Wells said he felt corporal punishment was a fitting punishment, but he didn't recommend Father O'Brien do it. He said it was inappropriate for the priest to spank us because he was the victim of our prank. His anger might get the better of him, and he might go overboard. You should have seen Father O'Brien! He looked like he wanted to pummel King Wells. It was all I could do not to laugh, but then, my dad says since what we did was technically against the laws of the kingdom, our punishment should be done by the king anyways. I about swallowed my own tongue! I thought my dad was a hard hitter, but your dad beat him, hands down. I don't know how he does it, but he sure knows how to make it sting like a mother!"

"Yeah, he's good at that. Sorry."

"Don't be. I'm not. I'm just happy that O'Brien didn't lay a finger on me, the wanker!" Beck told him.

The boys worked in silence for several minutes before Beck added, "Ever wonder if Spencer would hit as hard as the king?"

Xavier stopped cleaning to look incredulously at Beck beside him. "You're completely nuts, Beck!" Xavier laughed.

Beck laughed with him. "Yeah, I know. Sorry, the thought just popped in there. Like just now I'm wondering if Loren would hit as hard as he looks like he would. That bloke is big. His biceps are as big as my entire waist!"

The boys laughed harder.

"I don't know. Loren's kind of like a big kid, you know. I don't think he'd hit as hard because of that," Xavier observed.

"Yeah, you could be right. He'd probably hit like a little old lady," Beck responded, snickering. "Now, Ephraim Hardcastle, I bet that bloke hits hard. He's not as big as Loren, but he's got this just-try-to-mess-with-me thing going on that's scary as hell. I guess I could always ask Court who hits harder, the king or his old man."

"Beck," Xavier coughed, laughing. "You're totally mental!"

After they finished with the clean-up from their night of Mummering, Xavier entered the royal residence exhausted and filthy. He trudged up the steps to his room and collapsed onto his bed with an exaggerated moan. Moments later, there was a knock at his door just before Mrs. Sommers swayed into the room.

"Xavier, honey. Miss Applegate called while you were out to discuss the dance. So I invited her over for lunch."

Xavier's head jerked up from his pillow. "What? Maggie's coming to lunch? What time?"

"At noon," she answered, crossing the room and opening his curtains.

He blinked at the sudden explosion of light. "Noon? That's in fifteen minutes! That's not enough time! I stink! I need to shower!" He whined as he jumped up and raced around his room, picking up his dirty clothes and strung out toys. "God! And, look at my room! What if she wants to come up here after we eat?" He huffed exasperatedly and threw his arms into the air. "I'll never be ready in time! Just tell her I couldn't make it. Tell her I'm still cleaning the church! Tell her anything!"

"Now, Xavier. That's enough. Calm down. Go and get your shower. I'll straighten up here and set out some clean clothes for lunch. Don't worry. Everything will be fine," she cooed, shooing him into the bathroom and closing the door behind him.

Ten minutes later, Xavier raced from the bathroom with a towel wrapped around his waist to find his room straightened and vacuumed. Mrs. Sommers had even lit a small candle that filled his room with a sweet, spicy aroma. He was immediately relieved that she hadn't chosen a flowery-scented candle. He couldn't help but smile as he quickly dressed in cargo pants and a dark blue sweater. Then, he combed his fingers through his hair and looked at his image in the mirror.

Not bad, he thought, giving his image a devilish grin.

"Hi, Maggie." He practiced the greeting and winked into the mirror.

He turned and studied his reflection from a different angle. "Hey. What's up?" He attempted with a nod and a waggle of his eyebrows. No, too sleazy.

Shaking his head, he tried again. "Hello, Miss Applegate. It's very nice to see you again." No, that was too stuffy.

"Son?" Jeremiah's smiling voice called from the doorway.

He spun and glared at his father accusingly. "Dad! Do you mind knocking?"

"I'm sorry," he said, trying not to grin. "It's just that your guest has arrived, and lunch will be ready in ten minutes. I think she could use your company."

Xavier stiffened. "She's here?" he asked, his voice cracking. "O...Okay, I...I'll be down in a second."

"All right, son, but get a move on. You should never

keep a beautiful lady waiting," he told him before leaving the room.

He looked back into the mirror at the frightened face staring at him. He looked good, but something was missing. A waft of spice from the candle made Xavier smile again at Mrs. Sommers' thoughtfulness, and it gave him an idea. He should smell as good as he looked! He raced out of the room and into his father's bathroom. He opened the vanity and began searching for a bottle of aftershave or cologne. His father had two different bottles, so after sniffing them, he made a selection and splashed the light amber liquid on his neck and jaw. Hastily, he shoved the bottle back into the vanity and sprinted for the steps to the lower floor. Down below, Maggie Applegate sat in the receiving room talking to... oh great, his father! Xavier raced down the steps and into the receiving room where he slowed into a relaxed stroll just as he reached Maggie and his father.

"Ah, here he is! If you'll excuse me, I'll see how lunch is coming along," Jeremiah told her. He turned to exit the room but stopped next to Xavier. "Son? Have you been into my bathroom cabinet?" he whispered softly.

"Yes, sir," he answered, blushing.

"I thought I recognized the scent, but for future use, a little cologne goes a long way," he commented with a chuckle, patted Xavier's shoulder, and left the room.

"Hello, Xavier," Maggie greeted softly, batting her long, dark eyelashes at him.

His brain immediately went fuzzy.

"Ah...hi," he managed, strolling over to the sofa and sitting next to her.

"I was so glad when you asked me to the Old Christmas Dance. I really hoped you would. I... I really like you, Xavier. I think you'll make a great king one day," she stated shyly.

"Ah...thanks, Maggie. I...like you, too," he stammered like an idiot and fidgeted with the pocket on his pants leg.

"Will you be going to the rugby tournament too?" she asked.

"Yeah, of course," he answered.

"Is your father playing this year? He broke his arm last year and couldn't play."

"I...I don't know. He hasn't really said anything about it," Xavier answered.

"Hopefully he will, because if he does, the Royals will win the tournament for sure. Last year, the Wellings won," she continued, making a gagging face.

"Then I take it you're not a Welling?"

"No. My mother is a representative to the parliament and a member of the High Council. So I guess that makes me a Royal."

"Oh," Xavier responded.

"Well," Maggie continued, reaching into her small handbag. "I brought a swatch of fabric so you could match up your vest and tie to my dress."

"A swatch?" he asked.

"It's a little piece of the fabric that my dress is made from," she answered, pulling out an emerald velvet scrap of fabric and handing it to him.

"Children, lunch is ready," Mrs. Sommers announced, entering the room. "Ah, is that a swatch from your dress, dear?"

"Yes, ma'am," Maggie replied, smiling at Xavier.

Oh, God. Xavier felt a hot tingling sensation race through his body, and he found himself holding his breath. It was uncanny how easily this girl could turn him into mush.

"Xavier?" Mrs. Sommers called with a small laugh.

"Huh?" he grunted, jerking his head away from Maggie's intoxicating smile to Mrs. Sommers.

"I've asked you twice now to give me the swatch so I can pick up your vest and tie this afternoon," she snickered, extending her hand for the cloth.

"Oh," Xavier muttered, handing it to her.

Following lunch, Xavier and Maggie sat next to the fireplace in the receiving room, discussing the Old Christmas festivities. He was beginning to feel comfortable in Maggie's company. Okay, maybe comfortable wasn't exactly accurate, but he could now hold a conversation with the girl without constantly stammering.

"Who do you plan to go with to the rugby tournament?" she asked.

"I don't know, probably Robbie, Erica, Court, and the guys. Do you want to hang out with us?" he asked hopefully.

Maggie blushed. "Well, yeah. Of course, I want to hang out with you. Is that okay?"

"Yeah! Sure!" he replied with a broad smile.

She beamed back at him and slid her hand into his.

Xavier thought he would pass out from the sensations swarming through him. He couldn't seem to stop the small groan that slipped from deep in his throat, and he tightened his grip on her hand. Okay, this was it. He was going to kiss her! Not some wimpy kiss on the cheek either, he was going to *really* kiss her. Slowly, his head inched toward hers.

"Son?" His father's voice snapped him across the sofa as if someone had thrown him there.

He jumped to his feet and jammed his hands into his pockets. "Uh...uh... yes, sir?"

Jeremiah paused, looking between the two children. "Maggie's mother is here," he announced finally.

"O...okay," he stammered quickly and held out a hand to help Maggie to her feet. He walked her to the door where her mother stood waiting.

"Mom, this is Xavier Wells. Xavier, this is my mother, Lana Applegate," Maggie introduced.

"Ah, uh, g...good afternoon, Mrs. Applegate," Xavier stammered, gaping at Maggie's mother. She was drop-dead gorgeous! Her dark hair fell in soft curls onto her shoulders, and she had the same pale gray eyes ringed in charcoal as her daughter. "Whoa, I know why Maggie's so beautiful now!" Oh, God. Why did he say that? His face ignited with heat.

"Oh my! What a charmer you have, Your Highness!" she exclaimed with a laugh.

"Yeah, he's a little too charming," his father muttered dryly.

Lana laughed and hugged Xavier. "Thank you so much, Prince Wells. It makes an old woman very happy when a handsome young man pays her such a wonderful compliment."

"You are far from old, Ms. Applegate," Jeremiah countered. "I imagine Xavier couldn't help himself when faced with unparalleled beauty such as yours."

Xavier snorted, trying not to laugh out loud but not succeeding. His father scowled playfully and nudged Xavier with his hip, nearly sending him stumbling to the floor.

Lana laughed heartily at the exchange before commenting, "My, my, getting compliments from two handsome men is bound to go to my head. Well, Maggie, we better get going. We've got lots to do before the festivities tomorrow."

"Will you call me tomorrow?" Maggie asked Xavier.

"Yeah, of course," he replied, grinning at her.

On Old Christmas Day, it was customary for the kingdom to attend morning mass before the festivities, and throughout the service, Xavier continually snuck peeks at Maggie, who sat with her mom. It occurred to Xavier then that Maggie had never spoken of her father, and there didn't seem to be a father with her today. Maggie caught him staring at her and gave him one of her heart-wrenching smiles.

"Hey, lovebird," his father muttered under his breath. "You're supposed to be worshipping God, not a beautiful girl."

"Sorry, Father," Xavier replied meekly. "But I was wondering, where's Maggie's father?"

"Her father died of cancer six years ago. When he died, Lana returned home to Warwood where she could be around her own kind and where Maggie could learn about her people. You see, like you, Maggie had a common parent and grew up thinking she was a commoner."

"Oh."

"So, do you think you can concentrate more on worship now?"

He nodded, but he was certain he would hear very little of what Father O'Brien was preaching.

At the end of services as the congregation spilled out onto the church's front lawn, Xavier rushed over to Maggie.

"Hey," he greeted, smiling like a fool.

"Hi," she replied, slipping her hand in his.

His body exploded with heat, and his grin widened.

"Look, I'll give you a call before noon after I've had a chance to talk with the guys, and I'll let you know when and where you can meet us," he told her.

"Why don't I just have Mom drop me off at the palace before the rugby match? That way I could walk over with you?" she asked.

"Even better! Okay, I'll give you a call and let you know what the plans are," he confirmed.

"Son?" Jeremiah called from the doorway. Catherine Stokes stood next to the king, her arm interlocked with his. Xavier felt a stab of resentment. "Let's get a move on. You'll see Maggie later."

"You'd better go. I'll see you after lunch," she told him.

Xavier jogged to where his father and Catherine stood. Although he still didn't trust Catherine, he tried to put those feelings aside for his father's sake. He understood his father's needs better now that he had a... well, a girlfriend.

"Son, why don't you go on to the car? I'll be there in a minute," Jeremiah told him.

"Sure," he responded with more enthusiasm than he felt and went to the limo where Loren stood with his family.

"Hey, X," Erica greeted, bounding over to him. "I saw you and Maggie." She blew kisses at him as she continued to tease him. "Xavier has a girlfriend! Xavier's got a girlfriend!"

"Shut up." He laughed, trying to smack her, but she danced around her father just out of reach.

"Oh, Maggie," she mocked in a high-pitched voice and smacked kisses at him.

Finally, Xavier stopped and gave her a smirk of triumph. "You know, Erica, unless you plan to walk home, eventually, you will be confined to the back seat of the limo with me, and I will get even!"

The smile fell from her face, and Xavier couldn't help

but laugh.

After lunch, Xavier called Maggie, but not in the way she probably intended or expected; he used his telepathy abilities instead of a telephone. He followed the telepathic regime that Spencer had taught him. Sitting in the middle of his bed, he concentrated on quieting his mind and focusing on the noises in his room. He meditated like this for several minutes, relaxing his mind and body before opening himself up to the forces around him. Then, he concentrated on the most memorable aspect of Maggie, her eyes, and reached out to her with his mind.

"Maggie? Maggie, can you hear me?" he called, but there was no response. Taking a deep breath, he concentrated harder on her eyes and their exact shades of gray, and tried once more. Still, he couldn't connect at all!

"What's the matter? Why can't I do it?"

Maybe if he went out onto the patio, he would have less interference. Xavier jumped from his bed, raced into his father's room, and out onto the patio. He stood among the dead decaying leaves and shivered as a brisk, cold breeze washed over him. He concentrated on Maggie's eyes and tried again.

"Maggie? Can you hear me?" he called out and immediately heard her startled response.

"Xavier? Is that you? I didn't know you were telepathic!" she responded with a note of fear.

"Well, yeah. I'm the king's son. Of course I have telepathy. It's okay. Don't be afraid. No, I don't always do this, and I've never read your mind no matter how tempting it was," he told her.

"Well, you're reading my thoughts now. I don't like this, Xavier. Stop it and call me like a normal person!" she told him, agitated.

"What do you mean? Don't you think it's cool we can

talk to one another as long as we want without our parents butting in!" he replied with a laugh.

"What about your father? He'd be able to listen in."

"Not without me knowing. You see, I have the ability to feel when someone is trying to infiltrate my thoughts," he bragged. She was still very uncomfortable; he could feel it in her thoughts. *"Would it help if I told you something very personal about me?"*

"Maybe," she responded faintly.

"Well, I really wanted to kiss you yesterday, before my father interrupted us. I still do," he told her, feeling his face flush.

"Really?" she asked, more relaxed. *"Well, maybe you'll get your chance tonight at the dance."* He could feel her smiling. *"So, when do you want me to meet you?"*

"Oh," he choked out, still thinking about the promise she had just made him. *"Ah...in an hour, and Dad will be playing in the tournament. He and the rest of the Royals are practicing as we speak. If they win against the Merchants this afternoon, they'll play the Wellingtons tonight."*

"Cool," she said, *"well, I'll see you in an hour, my sweet prince."*

He wasn't sure she had meant to say that last bit, but he grinned at the knowledge that at least she had thought it.

Chapter 11

Old Christmas Dinner

The first match of the Old Christmas rugby tournament was a close one. The Merchants were well-trained and proved to be worthy adversaries for the king and the Royals. Maggie sat next to Xavier throughout the match, and each time a player on either team sustained a particularly savage blow, she would grab his hand and hide her face in his shoulder. Of course, this didn't go unnoticed by his mates.

"Xavier?" Garrett whispered in his ear. "Will you hold me too?"

A collective laughter echoed Garrett's words. Xavier swatted his friend away and tried to ignore the jeers behind him.

By the end of the match, the Royals won seventeen to fourteen, and the boisterous group made their way out of the stadium, teasing Xavier and Maggie. Maggie was in a constant state of blushing.

"Prince and Maggie sitting in a tree, K.I.S.S.I.N.G..."

"Oh, would you guys shut it!" Xavier shouted.

"Seriously, how old are you guys? Eight?" Erica spat out, rolling her eyes.

"Not even close! Want proof?" Court chided, attempting to kiss her.

But Erica wasn't having any of it and elbowed Court firmly in the stomach. He doubled over gasping for breath as a collective moan erupted from the group.

"Ouch! Rejected, Hardcastle!" Beck taunted.

Court punched Beck in the arm. "Think you can do better? Let's see you kiss Robbie."

"Hey, guys," Xavier interrupted, not liking the direction the conversation was heading in. "You guys want to hang out at the palace before the Christmas Dinner."

"Don't tell me you guys plan to waltz over to the banquet hall dressed as you are!" Robbie demanded, looking appalled.

The boys looked at her dumbfounded. "Of course, why would we get all cleaned up just to eat and go to another rugby match?" Beck questioned.

"Boys are so gross!" Robbie exclaimed.

"What? What's wrong with that? I took a shower this morning, and I plan to take another before the dance! It's stupid to keep taking showers and changing clothes all day!" Beck grumbled.

"Come on, girls! Obviously, boys don't understand that it takes a lot of work to look beautiful, so let's leave them to wallow in their filth while we clean up and pick out something to wear to dinner," Robbie suggested, grabbing Maggie and a reluctant Erica by the hand and leading them toward her house.

Maggie looked back at Xavier and smiled. Xavier felt his knees go weak, and he waved stupidly back.

"Jeez, man! She's really got you whipped!" Beck chastised.

"What are you talking about?" Xavier asked.

"Oh, X! Hold me!" Garrett squeaked, racing to him, grabbing his hand, and hiding his face in his shoulder. "I'm scared of those big bad men playing rugby!"

"Get off!" Xavier laughed, pushing the other boy away. "You guys are just jealous. I've got a complete hottie all over me and you don't!" he bragged.

Immediately, the boys responded in a loud, unified groan before charging at Xavier, tackling him to the ground, and subjecting him to noogies, wet willies, and punches. Laughing, the boys tumbled and rolled over the snow-covered ground, attracting the attention of several passing spectators, who carefully stepped around the tangled mess of boys.

"Okay, okay, enough!" Xavier declared, struggling to his feet and brushing himself off. "Are you guys coming to the palace or what?"

"Yes, Your Highness!" the boys barked, snapping to attention and saluting him.

"Jeez, you're all impossible," Xavier snickered as he led the way.

The boys barged into the royal residence, still bantering and teasing one another, though the hottest topic still seemed to be Maggie. The boys fell lazily into the sofas and armchairs in front of the roaring fire in the receiving room.

"Mate, I have no idea how you got Maggie to go out with you. She's wickedly hot!" Beck remarked.

When Xavier only shrugged in response, Frankie remarked, "I bet it's because he's the prince. Girls like a guy with power and all that."

"That's not why!" he snapped. He hated the idea that some girl would only want to be with him because he was the prince. "She said I was cute," he muttered, thinking back to her thoughts earlier that morning.

"Cute? You? I think your girlfriend needs glasses, mate," Court jeered which earned him a punch.

"So, just how far have you gotten with the

magnificently gorgeous Maggie?" Harry ribbed.

"Yeah, have you kissed her yet?" Garrett asked, now truly interested as the other boys closed in around him, eager to hear the answer.

"Have you gotten to third base, yet?" Beck asked with an enormous grin.

Xavier choked out, "What does that even mean, Beck?"

Beck shrugged.

Xavier laughed. "No way! Forget it, guys! I'm not telling any of you anything!"

At the Old Christmas Dinner, Xavier didn't sit at his usual spot at the head table with his father. Instead, he sat at the table his friends had confiscated just for them and their dates. When the girls arrived, the troupe of boys went silent. Robbie attracted everyone's attention. She looked stunning. She wore a navy skirt trimmed with white eyelet lace, cut just above the knee, and a crisp white pilgrim blouse that accentuated her slender neck and shoulders. At first, Xavier could only stare. Then, remembering his manners, he got to his feet and smiled as she approached the table. When she returned his smile, something stirred deep inside his gut.

"Whoa!" Beck muttered as he gaped at her. After a nudge from Xavier, Beck stood and moved to the side to make room for Robbie beside him.

Then, Maggie approached the table. Her eyes immediately fastened on Xavier's, and he couldn't look away even if he had wanted to.

"Hi," she whispered, taking the seat next to him.

"Hi," he whispered back, sinking into his chair. "You look great."

"Thanks," she responded, grinning and batting her eyes.

"Whoa! Jefferson, is that you?" Beck blurted as Erica moved to sit next to Court. "I didn't even know that you owned a dress!"

Erica looked fantastic, and it transformed Courtney into a bumbling, stuttering dope.

"Y...you look awesome!" he managed as her pulled out her chair for her.

Erica smiled sweetly before drawing back and punching Court's shoulder.

"Ow!" he bellowed, rubbing the aching spot. "What was that for?"

"To remind you of our agreement, Hardcastle. Keep your hands and *lips* to yourself," she hissed.

The group chuckled as Courtney shrugged and retorted, "Yep, she's crazy about me."

In response, Erica walloped Courtney hard across the chest, knocking him back into his chair, and the group exploded in laughter.

Dinner was a fantastic spread of every food imaginable, and as the attendants began serving dessert, the group leaned back in their chairs and playfully began teasing one another. Thankfully, the topic fell on Courtney and Erica, giving Xavier and Maggie a brief reprieve.

Xavier looked at the head table where his father and Catherine sat in deep conversation. They were inches from one another, and Jeremiah seemed oblivious to everyone around him. Xavier scanned the crowd. Most people were too wrapped up in their own conversations to notice, but the few who were watching the king and his date began nudging the people at their tables. Soon, the majority of the hall was watching the spectacle. Xavier glanced back at his father and watched as he caressed Catherine's cheek affectionately. Bitterness mushroomed inside his chest until he wanted to scream, and he tore his eyes away from the couple.

"Jeez! Get a room!" he muttered.

"You don't like her very much, do you? Madam Stokes, I mean," Maggie asked softly.

Xavier looked at her enormous eyes in surprise and answered quietly, "No, not at all."

Maggie looked at the head table and studied the couple thoughtfully. What she said next astounded Xavier. "I bet your dad thinks you're acting out because you're scared she'll replace your mom, but that's not true, is it?" She didn't wait for him to answer as she continued, "She seems a bit needy to me. I don't know exactly what it is, but I don't trust her! She's up to something."

Xavier's mouth dropped open. Not only did she completely understand and describe his feelings about Catherine, she also stated the one fear he had thought so many times but hadn't the guts to say aloud. Catherine was up to something!

Maggie looked at his stricken face. "I'm sorry. Was I completely off base? I shouldn't talk about them that way..."

"No," Xavier interrupted almost fiercely. "No, you're right. I'm just surprised that someone else gets it. Everyone else thinks I'm being nutty, and I was beginning to believe that they were right. Why do you think she's up to something?" he asked.

"Oh, I don't know," she stated, looking back at the table. "Well, just look at her. Even though she looks like she's enjoying being with your dad, she keeps looking around at everyone else. It's like she's trying to get everyone else's attention. If she was really into him, she wouldn't be looking around, would she?"

"Yeah. That's what I..."

"Hey, Your *Highness*!" a sneering voice interrupted, ending their conversation abruptly.

Xavier spun and found Mac and Ken standing behind them, looking very amused about something.

"I see you managed to get yourself a date!" Ken chastised, looking Maggie over with contempt. "It seems some girls are so desperate that they'll go out with anyone!"

Xavier turned away from the boys with every intention of ignoring them. "Don't listen to them," he muttered to Maggie.

Maggie nodded her agreement, but Ken wasn't going to allow that to happen.

"You know, Maggie," Ken whispered in Maggie's ear, "if you want a real boyfriend, one who's not a complete tosser, I could help you out." Then, he licked her cheek.

Maggie squealed and pulled away as Xavier jumped to his feet and pushed the boy away from her. Chairs squealed as Beck, Garrett, Harry, and Court all jumped to their feet to back him up.

Ken snickered triumphantly, "God, Wells! You're so reactive! I wonder what daddy-dearest had to do to keep you from going ballistic about his new girlfriend! And I use the word girlfriend lightly; everyone knows she's easy, but of course, that's probably why King Wells likes her!"

Xavier lunged forward, but Beck and Garrett grabbed him. "Don't, Xavier!" Garrett hissed. "Your dad's watching!"

"I don't care! I'm going to rip his heart out!" Xavier growled.

"Xavier, calm down. Don't listen to that idiot!" Maggie whispered. "He's only doing it to get you worked up."

Ken laughed. "You better listen to them, *sire*. Daddy's watching, and we wouldn't want you to get another spanking after the one you got for wrecking the church."

Maggie shot him a disbelieving look. "You're such a liar, Ken."

"Am I? I happen to know that your sweet little prince got busted for Mummering along with his butt-kissers here, and all six of them got their butts beat!" he taunted. "I heard they all bawled like babies, including your brave prince! In fact, I heard he blubbered the loudest!" At this, Mac snorted and both boys laughed loudly.

Xavier was embarrassed beyond words. He couldn't see anything but Ken and Mac's sneering faces. The girls were staring at him, and he could hear their thoughts, wondering if what Ken had said was true.

To Xavier, what happened next occurred very slowly. An overwhelming, tingling energy ballooned inside him as goose bumps rippled across his body. It gathered in his hands like a warm breath. Jeremiah's chair screeched and clattered to the floor as Xavier flung the swirling energy toward the horrified boys. In the next instant, Ken and Mac were standing before the entire hall completely naked from head to toe. The crowd around them gasped, and Xavier's friends burst into loud, uncontrollable laughter. Garrett fell to the floor howling, and Court doubled over his chair, desperately clutching the table for support.

"Oh, Ken, I didn't realize you were so scrawny!" Erica blurted before succumbing to uncontrolled laughter.

Suddenly, Ken and Mac's clothes reappeared, and the boys sprinted from the hall.

"Xavier?" Jeremiah called loudly, and the buzz-filled room instantly fell silent.

He turned toward his father past the sea of smirks and hidden smiles. However, the king wasn't amused at all, and he beckoned Xavier to him with a finger.

Xavier turned to Maggie who, along with the entire

hall, had watched the exchange between father and son.

"Talk to you later. I hope," he muttered apprehensively.

Then, he meandered his way through the staring, whispering crowd to the front table and a very displeased king. Jeremiah whispered something to Catherine, kissed her on the cheek, and left the hall with his son's arm grasped firmly in his large hand.

Jeremiah didn't speak during the short trek from the banquet hall to the palace. They continued up the staircase and into the residence where Jeremiah led him to the sofa in front of the hearth. Xavier sank into the cushions and waited for the reign of anger to begin.

His father sat in an armchair across from him and stared stonily down at him. Finally he asked very quietly, "Do you mind explaining yourself?"

"Explaining what?" he grumbled.

Jeremiah glared at him. "Don't play games with me, boy. Why did you strip those boys of their clothes?"

"I didn't mean to do it. It just...happened," he retorted.

"Nothing just happens, Xavier. You had to have wanted it to happen," his father told him. "Can you tell me why you'd want to publicly embarrass the boys?"

"I don't know," he muttered, not at all sure he wanted to repeat what Ken had said. "Can't we just skip the talk and go straight to the punishment? I really don't want to talk about it!"

Jeremiah didn't respond.

"Father!" he spat. "I don't want to talk about it, and your silent treatment is not going to make me crack!"

There was another long pause before the king answered. "No, I need to understand why you did what you did in order to choose the appropriate punishment because, right now, boy, I have a good mind to ground you from the Old Christmas Dance and spank the hide off your bottom."

Okay, Xavier cracked, and he sat up rigidly.

"Do you still want to skip the talk and go straight to the punishment?" he asked.

Xavier shook his head and glanced submissively at his father. "They get a kick out of pushing my buttons and humiliating me! So I gave them a taste of their own medicine. That's all."

Jeremiah nodded understandingly. "What did they say to you?"

He sighed. "Ken told Maggie that she'd have to be desperate to go out with me, and then he licked her face." He made a disgusted face. "Seriously, if I were Maggie, I'd wash my face in scalding bleach water after that! Then, he teased me and the guys about getting in trouble for Mummering. He embarrassed us in front of all the girls telling them that we cried like babies when we received our punishments." He hesitated, still unsure if he should continue, but finally he did. "Then... he made a comment about you and Catherine. He said..." Xavier blushed and looked up at his father. "He made it sound like you and Catherine..." But he couldn't finish.

"I see," Jeremiah whispered as he stood and stoked the fire. Finally, he turned. "Xavier, I'm proud that you didn't resort to violence, but this wasn't the best way either. Though your attempts to embarrass Kenneth and Mackenzie were successful, you did so at your own peril. First of all, using empowerments in the heat of anger is a dangerous feat, son. It's hard enough to control a new empowerment in the calmest of situations. In your anger, you could have seriously injured those boys! Secondly, it's illegal to use empowerments against others with undue cause or reason."

Xavier looked up at his father horrified and muttered, "I'm sorry! I di...I didn't know!"

Jeremiah nodded. "I realize that, and I'll smooth things over with the High Council. But, son, how do you think your citizens, those dinner guests, felt about your little practical joke? How do you think it made you look in their eyes?"

Xavier grimaced as he realized that to the casual observer who hadn't heard their conversation he probably looked like a cruel jokester. And, now that it was clearly public knowledge that he was part of the Mummering shenanigans, he probably came across as an uncontrollable, spoiled prince. He looked at his father. "I looked pretty bad, didn't I? What should I do, Dad?"

"I know this is not what you want to hear, but you need to publicly apologize to Kenneth and Mackenzie. I can arrange for a microphone at the final rugby match and..."

"Whoa, whoa, wait a minute! A microphone? How public are you talking?" Xavier moaned.

"Xavier, how public do you think it should be? Everyone at the Old Christmas Dinner saw those boys in their birthday suits and all those people will most likely be at the match. Don't you think the boys have a right to an apology in front of those who witnessed your indiscretion?" he asked firmly.

"No," Xavier muttered, grimacing, "but I'll do it anyway."

"It's the right thing to do, son," Jeremiah insisted. "But let me make this absolutely clear to you. If you ever use your empowerments against someone again, I will give you a spanking that will make all the others seem like a patty cake game. Got it?"

Xavier nodded and squeaked, "Yes, sir."

Chapter 12

The Dance

Xavier's heart was lodged in his throat as he stood in the center of the rugby pitch with Jeremiah dressed in his royal rugby uniform beside him. Ephraim had gone into the stands to retrieve Ken and Mac for their apology, and they were now strutting cockily across the field toward him. He bit back the intense desire to punch the smirk from Ken's mouth.

"Ladies and gentlemen! May I have your attention, please?" his father called over the sound system, and almost immediately, the crowd became quiet. "Thank you. I apologize for the delay in the final rugby match, but your prince has something he wishes to say publicly."

Jeremiah held out the microphone to Xavier, who simply stared at it as though it carried the plague.

"Son, take the microphone," his father hissed.

Reluctantly, Xavier took it and cleared his throat. He looked at Mac and Ken and then toward the silent crowd. He cleared his throat again and spoke. "Ah, thanks for giving me this opportunity. You see I've done something today that I'm not very proud of. As many of you know, I used one of my abilities to humiliate two fellow citizens. At the time, I felt I was justified because they were dishonoring my father, and they..."

The king nudged him with his elbow and shook his head as the crowd in the stands mumbled.

With a sigh, Xavier continued, "Sorry. I guess it doesn't matter why I did what I did. I was completely out of line, and I'm ashamed of my actions. That's not the kind of king I want to be. So I offer my apologies to Kenneth Calhoun and Mackenzie Timmins for inflicting any pain or embarrassment on them. I hope they can accept my apology with the promise that I will never do it again."

Ken and Mac leered back at him, apparently enjoying his public penance. Jeremiah took the microphone and muttered, "You can go now, boys."

As Xavier walked across the pitch, Ken and Mac followed him, laughing and whispering. Once Xavier reached the staircase leading to the stands, he sprinted up them two at a time, trying to put as much distance between himself and the other boys. He didn't slow his pace until he reached the bench where his friends sat waiting.

"Oh, man!" Garrett moaned. "That was absolutely the most degrading spectacle I've ever had the misfortune to watch!"

"Imagine how I felt!" Xavier hissed.

"No doubt your old man made you do it," Beck remarked with sympathy.

"Well, yeah, sort of. It was either that or...I'd be grounded to the palace for the rest of the night." Xavier's eyes met Maggie's and he shrugged.

"Well," she replied softly once he had sunk onto the bench next to her, "it was the right thing to do, even though they totally deserved what you did to them."

"Thanks," Xavier whispered.

The rugby match was absolutely brutal. The

Wellington team members were nothing more than a bunch of cheaters. They committed foul after foul that went unnoticed by the officials. One particular foul was so gruesome and so blatantly intentional that the entire stadium erupted in fury. Ephraim, positioned as a halfback which a similar position to that of quarterback in American football, received the ball after a vicious scrum. He backpedaled and tossed the ball to Jeremiah, who was playing a wing position. Jeremiah maneuvered easily around several advancing players, but three Wellington players were in position to box him in if he kept the ball so he tossed it to Loren. This fact didn't change the course for the three opponents, and they continued to advance on the king as he retreated to another position on the field. He never saw it coming. King Wells was struck from behind, lifted off his feet, and drove into the icy turf.

The stands thundered angrily, and the players erupted in an outright brawl. Loren threw the first punch, striking one offender across the jaw, before lunging at another. Several more Royal players joined in the fight as Jeremiah got to his feet and charged toward the scuffle. He grabbed one of his teammates and threw him off the poor guy he was beating into a pulp. It took several minutes for the fight to be broken up, and as a result, Loren and the three Wellington players were red-carded. When the grisly match finally ended, the Royals won 10 to 7.

Following the match, the kingdom's citizens eagerly returned to their homes to get ready for the dance. Xavier was nervous, excited, and scared out of his mind all at the same time as he showered and dressed for the dance. Unable to tie the bow tie to his tuxedo, he went in search of his father.

"Dad?" he called, knocking on the king's bedroom

door.

"Yeah, come on in, son," he beckoned.

Xavier walked into the room and found his father standing in front of his bureau mirror, pulling on his tuxedo jacket and fitting it over his broad shoulders. Xavier stood beside his father, watching his father's reflection as he ran his hand through his hair in one smooth gesture. Jeremiah was a very big man, just as tall as Loren, but not quite as bulky; his father's muscles were more chiseled and sleek. Xavier's gaze fell to his own reflection, and he wondered if he'd ever grow to be as big and strong as his father. Finally, Jeremiah turned to him.

"What'cha need, son?" he asked with a broad smile.

"Ah, I don't know how to tie a bow tie," he muttered, placing the tie in his father's outstretched hand.

Jeremiah had the tie neatly knotted at his neck in a matter of seconds. "There you are! You look dashing!"

Xavier looked at his own reflection uncertainly and shrugged. "I guess. Dad? Could I borrow some of your cologne again?"

"Sure, but let's not shower in it this time," he replied, entering his bathroom and returning with two bottles of cologne. He handed Xavier one bottle and kept the other for himself. "Watch," he instructed softly. Xavier watched his father dab his cologne-coated fingertip to the pulse points on his neck and wrists and then along his jaw.

Xavier mimicked his father's actions and smiled up at him. "Is that good?" he asked.

Jeremiah leaned in toward the boy, sniffed, and straightened with a smile. "Ah, very good. At least now your cologne won't cause your date to pass out from its strength when you dance with her." Xavier glared up at his father as he laughed heartily. "Okay, Casanova! Let's get a move on! Grab the blankets on the corner of bed there," he told him, pointing to a pair of plaid blankets folded neatly at the foot of the bed.

"Blankets? Why do we need blankets?" Xavier asked.

"The girls will need them on the sleigh ride to the lake. Women tend to get cold easily, son. Which means we have a duty to keep them warm!" he answered with a wink and a mischievous smile.

"Dad!" Xavier groaned, rolling his eyes.

"Come on." Jeremiah chuckled. "Let's get going."

When they exited the palace, they found a magnificent sleigh drawn by two stunning, white stallions waiting in the drive.

"Where's the driver?" Xavier asked.

"You're looking at him," Jeremiah answered, as they clambered onto the sleigh. "Catherine and I will sit up front and you and Maggie can have the back to yourselves."

As they pulled up in front of Maggie's house, Xavier jumped from the sleigh before it came to a complete stop and raced to her door. Maggie opened the door before he could knock.

"Hi." She smiled bashfully. Xavier's gaze took in her beautiful hair spilling over her shoulders, her bright expectant eyes, and her lush pink lips. Without a word, Xavier's gaze fell down her body before floating back up to her eyes.

She gave him a fretful look. "Do I look all right?" she asked quietly.

"Ah...ah, y...you look great!" he stuttered.

She beamed at him, and Xavier's stomach did somersaults. Finally, he recovered enough to offer her his arm. She took it without hesitation, and he led her to the sleigh where his father waited, grinning. Jeremiah gave Xavier a wink as he helped Maggie into the sleigh and then climbed in beside her. The sleigh began to move again, and moments later, they stopped next to Catherine's house in the Wellington District. After helping Catherine into the sleigh, Jeremiah climbed onto the buckboard and snapped the reins. As icy air rushed past them, Maggie snuggled closer to Xavier under the blanket and nestled her head on his shoulder. Xavier's breath caught in his lungs and suddenly he was no longer cold. Heat coursed through his veins, and he had to force himself to exhale slowly.

Finally, the sleigh pulled up to the edge of the Wood and glided to a stop. "Well, this is where we walk," Jeremiah announced, motioning to the long stone walkway lit by large torches planted in the ground.

Xavier quickly got to his feet both relieved and, strangely, a bit sad that the bittersweet ride had come to an end. He climbed out of the sleigh and turned to help Maggie down. As Jeremiah and Catherine led the way along the path, Xavier brushed his hand against Maggie's and timidly held it. She turned and smiled at him, making his heart dance against his chest. Soon, they entered a breathtaking clearing. Icicles hung like ornaments from the tree limbs that canopied over most of the area and just above their heads, thousands of tiny lights the size of fireflies sparkled in vibrant colors. The ground was covered in iridescent snow, and enormous ice sculptures encircled the lake that was frozen into a solid transparent sheet. Embedded in the ice were orchards and lilies of every imaginable color, giving the dancers the impression they were dancing on a bed of flowers. Although the lake had been transformed into a winter wonderland, oddly, it wasn't cold. In fact, it was quite comfortable. It was, in a word, magical!

"Xavier!" Court called from the dance floor with Erica.

"Come on!"

Xavier looked to Maggie. "You ready to dance?"

She grinned. "You bet!"

The music for the evening was an eclectic mix of different genres. The current selection was jazzy and upbeat. Xavier watched the footwork of the others for a moment before joining in the dance. Several songs later, he looked at Maggie.

"Would you like to sit down and rest a bit?" he asked.

"Sure," she answered breathlessly.

Xavier took her hand and led her to a small table off to the side of the icy dance floor. He pulled out the chair for her and sat across from her. "Are you having a good time?" he asked.

"A great time! I could use a drink, though," she told him.

"Oh, okay. I'll get you one," he replied, grinning devilishly at her. But instead of walking to the punch and tidbits table, he couldn't help but show off a bit. He flicked his fingers at the refreshments and two glasses of punch floated into his awaiting hands. He turned and handed one to Maggie, who laughed.

"Thank you," she murmured, still grinning, and took a sip.

The music on the dance floor changed to a love ballad. Xavier watched his friends on the dance floor dancing awkwardly with their dates and snickered.

"What are you laughing about?" Maggie asked.

"Well, look at them! It's like watching porcupines dance with each other!" he laughed.

Maggie turned to watch the group, and soon she was laughing along with him. But, Xavier's laughter caught in his throat the moment his eyes settled on his father and Catherine Stokes. Unlike, his friends, his father was clearly very comfortable with dancing with a woman. They were close, very close, and those who weren't already on the dance floor dancing watched and smiled as the king spun Catherine in a circle before extravagantly dipping her and pulling her against him again. The group applauded and cheered on their king as Xavier's face flashed with heated embarrassment. But, what his father did next broke the last of Xavier's self-control. After another spin and dip, the king pulled his date back into his arms and kissed her in the middle of the dance floor for everybody to see!

Anger pounded in Xavier's ears and propelled him into action. Cursing under his breath, Xavier stormed across the dance floor and plowed between his father and Catherine, knocking them apart. Catherine staggered and if Jeremiah hadn't been quick on his feet, she most certainly would have fallen.

"Xavier! What the..." Jeremiah growled after him as he ran off the dance floor and down the path, putting as much distance as he could between himself and the lovebirds. He slowed once the lights behind him had faded from view.

"Xavier! Xavier, wait up!" Maggie called, running after him.

Xavier stopped and waited for her to reach him before continuing down the path, fuming.

"Are you okay?" she asked quietly.

"How can I be? Didn't you see them? Snogging in front of everyone! God! Now, Ken will have even more ammunition to torture me with!"

"What do you want to do?" she asked.

"I don't know," he muttered miserably.

Maggie took his hand as they continued to walk down the path and out of the woods to the parked sleighs.

"Why don't we sit in the sleigh for a while?" Maggie suggested.

Still working to squelch his dark emotions, he nodded and helped her into the sleigh before climbing in behind her.

Without a surrounding forest to shelter them, an icy breeze fell over them, and they had to pull the blanket over themselves. The night sky was clear and beautiful. The stars overhead winked down at them, and the moon gleamed like a single, magnificent pearl. As they sat in silence staring at the night sky, Maggie shivered before cuddling up against him. All his anger evaporated instantaneously and was replaced with a very hot, electrifying emotion he couldn't name. He only knew he wanted to kiss her. He wanted to kiss her so bad he hurt.

Finally, he whispered, "Maggie? I'd like...to...can I kiss you?"

Maggie smiled, which only strengthened his resolve to kiss her all the more. "Yes," she answered simply.

His heart soared from the sound of that simple word, and he grinned. Maggie gasped softly as his fingertips brushed over her lips. He leaned in and pressed his lips to hers. Electric! Real electricity erupted from him sending sparks above their heads. Stunned, they looked up at the dissolving glittery display. They stared at one another in silent amazement before bursting into a nervous, manic laughter.

Finally, after their laughter died away, Xavier stroked her cheek, the smile disappearing from his face, and he kissed her again. Her lips were sweet as he knew they would be. All he wanted to do was to spend the rest of the night kissing this girl. She made him feel as if everything in his life would work out brilliantly. She was quickly becoming his foundation, his sanity.

"Ah, Xavier," she muttered, and he pulled away. "We really should get back to the dance."

Xavier smiled. "Okay, come on," he replied, taking her by the hand and helping her out of the sleigh. He led her back down the path and onto the dance floor, grinning madly the entire time.

Beck noticed them returning and gave Xavier a thumbs up and mouthed the words, "Go, Prince Wells! Get to third base?"

Xavier smiled uncomfortably back as he searched the area for his father and Catherine. They stood just a few feet away on the side of the dance floor. Jeremiah was speaking to Catherine in low tones and from the looks of it, the conversation was serious. Then Jeremiah's sober eyes met Xavier's and his thoughts punched into Xavier's head. *"Son, don't go far. We need to talk."*

"Later," Xavier mouthed back as he led Maggie to the opposite end of the dance floor and began dancing. He loved being this close to her. She smelled so good and he loved the way she looked at him just now. But, seconds later, Jeremiah was at Xavier's side, grasping his elbow.

"Son? We need to talk, now," he insisted quietly, and then he looked at Maggie. "Please excuse us, Maggie."

"Yes, sire," she whispered, stepping out of Xavier's embrace and leaving father and son.

Jeremiah pulled Xavier off the dance floor and down the path. He didn't release him until they were well out of earshot.

Xavier spun to face him. "What?"

"What's with this attitude?" he asked irritably. When Xavier didn't answer, Jeremiah continued, "What's going on, Xavier?"

"Nothing!" he snapped.

"Nothing? You nearly knocked Catherine over with

your little temper tantrum!" Jeremiah barked.

"Temper tantrum! I'm not three!" Xavier spat.

"Then stop acting like you are and start acting your age!" his father barked.

"I am! You're the one not acting your age!" Xavier bellowed. "You and Catherine making out on the dance floor like a couple of teenagers! How am I supposed to live that down at school come Monday?"

"Please lower your voice, boy," Jeremiah hissed dangerously.

"Oh, forget it!" Xavier spat back. "You never think about me where Catherine's concerned, and I don't care anymore!" Before Jeremiah could say another word, Xavier turned and stormed back to the dance.

Xavier found Maggie standing next to the refreshment table, swaying to the music and watching the other dancers. Xavier approached her determined not to let his father and Catherine ruin his good time.

"Is everything okay?" she asked.

Xavier nodded curtly and asked, "Wanna dance some more?"

She gave him a hesitant look but nodded, and suddenly nothing else mattered. He took her hand and turned to lead her to the dance floor, but collided with a solid, unforgiving barrier. He stumbled backwards and peered up at his father's formidable, uncompromising face.

"Son? We didn't finish our discussion," he remarked forcibly, causing several bystanders to stop and watch.

Xavier didn't care; all he wanted to do was dance with Maggie and let all his problems vanish in her beautiful eyes. He glared up at his father challengingly and muttered under his breath, "Not now, Dad. I'm going to dance with Maggie." He tried to step around his father, but Jeremiah grabbed his arm.

"Xavier, don't compel me to take actions that will prove embarrassing for you," he growled.

Xavier hesitated. He looked at Maggie, who stood silently watching the tense confrontation with wide, alarmed eyes. He turned back to his father's stony expression.

"We're going home, aren't we?" he whispered.

Jeremiah nodded, his face unfaltering. "Yes."

Xavier sighed dejectedly. "Dad, please! One last dance and then I'll go without an argument or creating a scene. Please?" he pleaded.

Jeremiah's expression wavered and he nodded. "Okay, one dance."

Releasing a tense breath, Xavier squeezed Maggie's hand and took her to the dance floor just as an up-beat song ended. Xavier was pleased that the following tune was a slow rhythm; he wanted nothing more than to be as close as possible to Maggie for their last dance. They swayed across the floor, looking only at one another. When Maggie gave him a small smile, Xavier couldn't resist the urge to enter her thoughts. Even as he pulled her close and concentrated on connecting with her, he knew it was wrong, but he couldn't help himself.

"Please, kiss me, please, kiss me, please, kiss me!" her thoughts echoed into his mind.

Xavier grinned down at her, and she unsuspectingly batted her eyelashes at him and smiled back. As he brushed his lips against hers, he heard her inhale sharply. He withdrew and looked down at her questioningly. She looked up at him shyly, and he heard her pleading thoughts, *"Oh, don't stop, my sweet prince. Lord! He's so cute! Please, kiss me again."*

Of course, she didn't know he was invading her thoughts and he had no intention of telling her. When he kissed her again, he nearly burst into laughter at her next thoughts.

"Oh, this has to be what heaven's like! I could die now and be happy."

Xavier continued dancing with Maggie and listening to her thoughts about him. She wondered if Xavier found her pretty. She wondered if he liked her as much as she liked him. Although it was nice to know that she worried about that too, Xavier didn't understand why! Surely, she knew he liked her! After all, she could transform him into a stumbling, bumbling idiot with the smallest of smiles. Then when Maggie's thoughts turned bold, Xavier was stunned and he blushed. But then he guessed that even girls had the same kinds of thoughts as boys at times, and he smiled at the thought.

The dance ended much too soon, and they walked off the dance floor. Without a word, Xavier and Maggie followed Jeremiah and Catherine down the path. Xavier took Maggie by the hand and slowed their pace so they lagged a few yards behind the adults.

"I'm sorry, Maggie. If I had kept my cool, we wouldn't be leaving early," he whispered.

"That's okay. I was getting tired anyway," she told him. He knew it was a lie, but he was thankful for it all the same. "Xavier," Maggie began hesitantly, "maybe you should try telling your father about Madam Stokes. Maybe if you told him what she does that's suspicious..."

"He wouldn't believe me!" Xavier interrupted.

"Well, I think you should still try."

The children continued down the pathway in silence. When they reached the sleigh, Jeremiah turned to Maggie. "Maggie, Madam Stokes will take you home in the sleigh."

"Thank you, sire," she replied and turned back to Xavier. "Goodnight, Xavier," she whispered, kissing him quickly on the cheek.

"Goodnight," he muttered, and stood back as Jeremiah lifted her into the sleigh next to Catherine. Father and son watched the sleigh glide away into the darkness.

"Let's go, son," Jeremiah instructed squeezing his shoulder.

Father and son walked away from the Wood and passed the coliseum without a word to one another. After such an intoxicating dance with Maggie, Xavier was quite certain nothing could upset him now. He beamed into the cold night air.

Jeremiah caught the blissful smile on his son's face and shook his head, chuckling. "You really like that girl, don't you?"

"Yeah," he responded wistfully. "I really do."

"Son, I'm sorry that my dating Catherine bothers you. I know you might not understand this completely, but she makes me feel alive again. When your mom died, a piece of me died. Catherine makes me laugh; she makes me feel like a man. Do you understand what I'm trying to tell you?"

"No, not really," he mumbled. "Dad, I really don't want to talk about this now. Please!"

"We need to talk about this some time, Xavier," his father told him. "But, we'll save it for another day."

"Thanks, Dad." Xavier breathed a sigh of relief.

"There is something else I think we ought to discuss. Do you...has anyone...I mean..." Jeremiah gave a frustrated groan that made Xavier peer up at him puzzled. Jeremiah rubbed his jaw nervously.

"What?" Xavier asked, stopping.

Jeremiah turned and faced him. "Well, what do you know about sex?" Jeremiah asked.

Xavier nearly choked. "Oh, no!" he laughed nervously.

"Dad!" he whined and started to walk away, but Jeremiah stopped him.

"I'm serious, Xavier. Did your mother talk to you about it? Your grandfather?"

"Are you kidding? Does Grandfather look the type to have a sex talk with his freaky grandson?" he blurted, still laughing nervously.

Jeremiah gave him a reproving look. "Xavier, did anyone talk to you about sex?"

"Well, no, but I've heard things from friends," Xavier answered anxiously. He really didn't want to discuss this right now. "I know enough about it. Really! You don't need to do this. Please, don't do this."

"Your friends? Well, that's like the blind leading the blind!" his father muttered. "Yes, son, I need to do this."

Xavier realized there was no way he would be able to worm out of it so he just gave in. By the time they reached the palace, Jeremiah had covered all the bases from gentlemen's etiquette, to how to treat women, to safe sex and especially abstinence, and then to marriage. As embarrassing as it was to listen to this frank lecture, Xavier actually learned something and found that some of the things his friends had told him were completely wrong.

An uncomfortable silence fell between father and son as they climbed the steps and entered the royal residence. Jeremiah led Xavier up to his room, closing the door behind them. Pulling at his tie, Jeremiah finally asked, "Do you have any questions?"

Xavier sat on his bed and looked up at him shyly. "Ah, yeah, just one for now. What's third base?"

Chapter 13

Lover's Quarrel

Jeremiah didn't bring up Xavier's behavior at the dance again. He was quite certain he knew why Xavier had acted the way he did. For some reason, the boy felt threatened by Catherine. So Jeremiah took the day following Old Christmas off and spent it with Xavier playing games, talking, and simply goofing off.

"You can't move a bishop like that!" Xavier laughed after his father tried to move the black chess piece horizontally instead of diagonally.

"What do you mean?" Jeremiah asked angelically.

"Dad! Stop it!" he yelled, moving his father's bishop back. "You know, it's a very sad day in the kingdom when the king has to resort to cheating to beat his twelve-year-old son!"

"Sad day, huh? I'll show you a sad day, you pompous little prince," his father roared, lunging at him and scattering the game from the coffee table as they tumbled onto the floor. "How dare you question your father!" He laughed, pinning Xavier to the floor and tickling him relentlessly.

He tried to push his father off, but his massive body was too heavy and his grip too strong. In the end, Xavier was helpless and couldn't do anything but endure the giggling torture.

At lunchtime, Xavier sat on a stool in the kitchen as his father prepared two grilled salmon filets and wild grain rice. Jeremiah wasn't a bad cook if you didn't mind over-cooked, dried-out fish, and undercooked crunchy rice. Throughout dinner, Xavier stifled the aching need to rib him about it, until finally he couldn't contain himself any longer.

"Mmm, this is really good, Dad," he noted sarcastically, barely able to contain his laughter.

Jeremiah eyed him mirthfully and replied slowly, "Thank you, son."

"You're welcome." Xavier snickered. After a moment of them both eating quietly, Xavier blurted out, "I had always thought that rice was supposed to be soft and tender, but raw, crunchy rice is *sooo* much better."

"Well, that just goes to show you, you don't know anything about cooking. If you overcook rice, it cooks away all the nutrients," he retorted smugly, ignoring Xavier's sarcasm.

Xavier burst into laughter, and Jeremiah fought back a smile as he gave him a stern glare. Finally, with his stomach aching and tears running down his cheeks, he coughed out, "Dad? Could I have more water? Maybe Milton could drag in the water hose. I'm gonna need a ton of water to wash down this salmon. It's as dry as old shoe leather and about as tasty, too."

"All right! That's enough!" Jeremiah roared, jumping to his feet and lunging at the boy. Laughing, Xavier dove under the table and quickly crawled to the other side. Jeremiah chased him in circles around the table until Xavier finally bolted out of the room, but he was laughing too hard to run very fast. Jeremiah caught him easily and flung him over his shoulder like a sack.

"Put me down!" Xavier squealed, hardly able to breathe past his laughter.

"No, sir," Jeremiah scolded as he crossed the room toward the sofa. "You have a major beating coming followed by relentless tickling!"

"NOOOO!" Xavier yelled as Jeremiah tumbled onto the sofa with him. Suddenly the door burst open and Loren stood poised and very serious in the doorway. His expression only increased the hysteria of Xavier's laughter.

Loren relaxed considerably at the sight of father and son. "What are you doing to that poor boy, sire?" he teased.

"I'm preparing to beat him. Can you believe he had the audacity to ridicule my cooking?" Jeremiah demanded, mocking an injured ego.

Loren crossed the room and looked down at Xavier, who was fighting to breathe past his laughter. "I can't imagine anyone NOT ridiculing your cooking; it's usually a biohazard. In fact, I'm surprised the health department hasn't arrested you yet!"

Loren's comment sent Xavier howling with laughter again. Jeremiah jumped to his feet and lunged at his friend, tackling him to the floor with a loud thud. Xavier jumped to his feet, bellowed a primitive Tarzan-type yell, and jumped on top of the romping men. The shouts and banter as well as the thumps and thuds drew the remaining Royal Guard into the room looking tense; even Ephraim, who was off duty, came running into the residence. Once they found the rolling tangle of Loren, Jeremiah, and Xavier, the group chuckled dismissively.

Ephraim approached them, shaking his head. "You know, it's all fun and games until someone gets hurt. Now, Loren, Xavier, you two stop messing about before you hurt poor little *Jeremy*."

"Jeremy?" Jeremiah growled as he reached out, grabbed Ephraim by the ankle, and hauled him into the brawl. In the end, half a dozen guards were dragged into the ruckus.

That night, Xavier didn't want the day to end, and he tried coaxing his father into letting him stay up late.

"Come on, Dad! There's no school until Monday. Can't I stay up until you go to bed?" he begged.

"No, son, but if you'd like, you can sleep in my bed tonight."

Xavier, nodded sulkily and moments later, he was tucked into his father's massive king-sized bed.

"Goodnight, son," Jeremiah said, kissing his forehead.

"Dad? Today was really fun. Thanks..." Xavier mumbled, already feeling himself slipping into sleep.

"Thanks? Thanks for what?" Jeremiah whispered.

"Thanks for taking the day off and spending it with me. Thanks...thanks for being my dad." His eyes were already flickering shut.

"Oh, you're welcome, son. Thanks for being my son," he replied, stroking Xavier's head.

Xavier was asleep before Jeremiah turned off the light and closed the door.

That night, Xavier dreamt of the Center Square again. The eerily silent crowd surrounded him. Jeremiah was on the ground, his hair drenched with sweat and his back bloody. His entire body shimmied with strain and exhaustion as he struggled to his feet, only to topple over again.

Father O'Brien leered down at the king as if he were something vile and disgusting. "You have fallen from God's Grace, Jeremiah. You have tainted the throne. You have fallen from grace in your subjects' eyes. You should be ashamed. Your father would be..."

"Do not presume to tell me what my father would have thought of this entire situation, O'Brien!" Jeremiah bellowed with surprising force that Xavier wouldn't have thought possible. Slowly, with every ounce of his strength and with his arms quivering violently under the strain, Jeremiah pulled himself to his feet and glowered up at the priest. "My father believed in the absolute power of the monarch. He would not have allowed this to happen to himself. If you think back, O'Brien, this addition to the Codes was my doing! I proposed and lobbied for this amendment to prevent the mistakes and dangers of the past from being repeated! Therefore, *Father*, you have no authority to preach to me on such matters. Now, Loren, Ephraim, continue!"

But, Ephraim and Loren shook their heads, their faces pale.

"Hardcastle, Jefferson!" Jeremiah growled. "I just gave you an order!"

Loren approached him in a stumbling daze. Then, with a strangled groan, he raised his arm and struck Jeremiah, who fell heavily to the ground. Xavier fought vainly against the hands holding him.

"Stop! Stop it!" he sobbed. "Please!" he bellowed. "Father O'Brien, stop it. Please let them stop! Please!" But the only response he received to his pleads was a sadistic grin from Catherine Stokes.

Xavier sat up in bed moaning. "No!"

Suddenly, there was a flash of light and a loud crack that sounded like a shotgun. Xavier screamed. A large pair of arms enveloped him, pulling him back into the warm bed, and his father's soothing voice whispered, "Sh! It's just a storm."

Xavier shuddered against the fear mounting inside him that had nothing to do with the storm outside. “Dad! I had the dream again, the one where you’re getting beaten bloody by Loren and Ephraim. I’m telling you I think it’s trying to warn me!”

“Xavier,” his father replied tersely. “It was just a dream. Ephraim and Loren...”

“Would never do that, yeah, I know. But, dad, listen to me!” He wiggled out of his father’s arms and sat up. “In the dream, or vision, or whatever it was, you ordered them to do it. They weren’t betraying you; they were following your orders!”

“What?” Jeremiah demanded, flicking on the bedside lamp and blinking down at his son. “Xavier, what are you talking about?”

“You ordered them to do it, Dad! Why would you do something like that? Why would you tell your closest friends to beat you?” he begged, on the verge of tears.

Jeremiah looked down at him with an unreadable expression. Finally he smiled, though the smile didn’t quite reach his eyes, and he patted Xavier on the head. “Don’t worry about it, son.”

“But, Dad!” he gasped.

“Xavier, just forget about it. It was just a dream,” Jeremiah insisted, his voice a bit edgy.

Xavier nodded, but he knew he wouldn’t be able to just forget about it.

School was back in session the following Monday and Xavier was anxious to see Maggie again. He pushed past his friends and hurried up the walkway to the main entrance of the academy until he finally saw her. She stood at the top of the steps, talking to her friends and smiling. Xavier’s mind drifted to her, and he eavesdropped on her conversation with her friends.

"So?" one of her friends prompted. *"Did you have a good time at the dance with Prince Xavier?"*

He saw Maggie's smile broaden before he heard her respond, *"I had a wonderful time."*

"I saw you two dancing. Man, that boy can move!" another girl commented with a giggle as she imitated a dance move.

"Well, didn't you watch his father at all?" the first girl responded. *"Obviously, it runs in the family. And speaking of his father, did you see him plant one on Madam Stokes!"*

The other girls made groans of longing. Maggie, however, didn't comment.

"Yeah, it was so romantic!" one of the girls cooed.

"So, Maggie, does Xavier kiss like that?" another girl asked.

"I've never kissed the king, so how would I know that?" she responded, but her friends weren't going to let her off the hook that easily.

"Oh, come on! You know what I mean! Is the prince a good kisser?"

Maggie grinned and shrugged.

Xavier didn't need his telepathy abilities to hear the girls' reactions. A loud collective, "Ooooo!" attracted the attention of everyone around them. Maggie scanned the staring crowd and found Xavier watching her.

"Xavier? Are you using your telepathic abilities again?" she chastised as she directed her thoughts toward him, smiling.

He beamed at her innocently and shook his head no.

She laughed and her friends looked at her questioningly. *"Then, dear prince, how is it that you knew to answer me?"* she asked.

Xavier laughed and shrugged. *"Okay, busted,"* he responded telepathically. *"But, won't Headmaster Spencer be so proud that I practiced over the holiday break?"*

She laughed again and her friends followed her gaze to Xavier. He smiled and waved innocently at them, and again, the group of girls squealed.

"You're such a ladies' man," Court announced, stepping up beside Xavier.

He turned to his friend, grinning, "If the shoe fits..."

"And modest too!" Court laughed as the boys climbed the stairs and entered the school. Xavier threw a wink at Maggie, who blushed. "I heard you left early, or rather, you were made to leave early from the dance. What happened, mate?" Court asked him.

"Oh, God." Xavier groaned, rolling his eyes. "Don't ask!"

The day went quickly, and Xavier found himself going out of his way to see Maggie between classes. Unfortunately, this made him late for telepathy class, the one class he never wanted to be late for, and Spencer was ticked.

"Where have you been?" he spat.

"I'm just a couple of minutes late. What's the big deal?" Xavier shrugged nonchalantly.

Wrong answer, and definitely wrong attitude. Before Xavier could blink, Spencer was in his face. "Don't get smug with me, young man! I don't believe your father would agree that being late for class isn't a big deal."

Xavier immediately cowered. "Yes, sir. You're right. I'm sorry, sir." Spencer relaxed, but his ill mood lingered throughout the lesson. As a result relentless, head-splitting mental exercises followed, and when the class period finally came to an end, Xavier made a vow to visit

Maggie only when their classes were on the same floor and to never ever be late for telepathy class again.

After school, Xavier found Maggie on the academy front steps waiting for him.

"Hi! Can I walk you home?" he asked with a grin.

"I'd love that," she responded, smiling shyly back.

When she looked up at him with those enormous gray eyes and pouty pink lips, Xavier couldn't help himself. He leaned in and kissed her, inhaling the sweet aroma of her shampoo.

"Prince Wells!" Sir Spencer snapped. "Unless Miss Applegate has stopped breathing and you're attempting to resuscitate her, I highly suggest the two of you separate your mouths and head on home." Several students around them giggled.

Blushing, Xavier looked up at Spencer's stern face, but noticed a twinkle in the headmaster's eyes. "Yes, sir," he muttered.

He took Maggie's bag and threw it over his shoulder along with his own, and taking her hand, he led her away from the school. As they walked, Xavier began plotting the best way to steal another kiss until Maggie broke their blissful silence.

"Xavier?" she began, and immediately he noted the slight edge to her voice. "Can I ask you something?"

"Sure. What is it?"

"Would you promise me not to use telepathy on me again without asking me first? It really bothers me when you do it. I mean, it should be a girl's right to decide which thoughts she wants to share and which thoughts she would like to keep private. It bothered me this morning to find you had been listening in on my thoughts and conversations. It's embarrassing!" She looked at him hesitantly. "Please, promise me you won't do it again."

He glanced down at her sheepishly and nodded. “Okay, I promise.”

She eyed him suspiciously and pulled him to a stop. “Wait a minute. Other than before the dance and today, you haven’t used telepathy on me any other time; have you?”

He gaped at her and replied, his answer unconvincing even to himself, “Ah, n...no. Of course not.”

Maggie’s eyes flared with fiery anger. “Xavier! When? When did you do it?” she spat out.

“I didn’t!” he protested.

“Don’t lie to me! When did you do it, Xavier? Tell me! And, I’ll know if it’s not the truth! I’m a polygrapher; I can tell when someone lies to me,” she declared, glaring at him, her hands on her hips.

Oh, God! There was no easy way out of this. He would have to tell her. Xavier tucked his head with guilt. “Okay, yes. I’ve done it another time without you knowing, but just once! It was during...our last...dance.”

Maggie turned as white as his hair and looked at him, horrified. “Oh, God! Xavier! How could you? How could you? You heard all my thoughts during the entire dance?”

He looked at her, nodded, and muttered, “Yeah, pretty much.”

Maggie turned crimson. Then, without a word, she jerked her bag from his shoulder and stomped away from him.

“Maggie! Maggie, wait!” he called, jogging to catch up with her retreating figure.

“NO!” she snapped, turning on him so quickly he just about ran into her. “I don’t want to hear it, *sire*! What you did was unforgivable! I hate you, Xavier Wells! I hate you!”

She turned to walk away, but he grabbed her. “Maggie,

let me explain!"

"Let go of me!" she shouted, tears dropping heavily over her eyelids and down her cheeks.

It was distressing to see Maggie so angry and to know he was the reason there were tears on her pretty face. He didn't know what to do. In all his talk of gentleman's etiquette, his father had failed to mention what to do if you royally messed up and ticked a girl off.

"Please, just listen to me! Don't be upset. It was nothing! Boys have those kinds of thoughts all the time. I know I have..."

Maggie slapped him across the face. "You're such a jerk! Is that supposed to make me feel better, Xavier Wells? Is it? Well, it doesn't. It doesn't change the fact that you betrayed my trust. You humiliated me! Just...just leave me alone!" she screeched and ran off toward home. Xavier could only watch her go, rubbing his cheek despondently.

Chapter 14

The Date

Xavier didn't go home immediately; instead he wandered into the coliseum and sat, trying to figure out how he could have handled his fight with Maggie differently. His cheek still stung where she had slapped him, and he rubbed it absent-mindedly. Okay, so he shouldn't have listened in on her during the dance. He had tried to apologize to her, but she just wouldn't listen. Still no closer to a solution, Xavier stood and headed home. Surely his dad would give him some good advice on how to patch things up with Maggie.

When he entered the residence, all thoughts of having a father-son heart-to-heart talk vanished. Catherine Stokes sat in the receiving room with a glass of wine in hand, laughing at a typically boisterous and entertaining Loren.

"Great! This day just gets better and better!" he grumbled sarcastically, slamming the door shut behind him.

"Hey, Xavier!" Loren bellowed with an enormous smile. "How did your day go?"

"Fine," Xavier mumbled. "Where's Father?"

"Hello, Xavier," Catherine greeted sweetly from the sofa.

Xavier ignored her. "Loren, where's my father?" he repeated testily.

"Upstairs. Xavier, don't you think you're being a bit rude? Madam Stokes..."

He didn't wait for Loren to finish as he barreled up the stairs and into his father's room. Jeremiah looked up, startled at his loud, sudden entrance.

"Hello, son. You're a bit late getting home today," Jeremiah stated conversationally as he pulled a tailored dress shirt over his massive shoulders and began buttoning it.

"What's *Catherine* doing here?" Xavier snapped quietly.

Jeremiah turned to face him, tucking the tails of the shirt into his pants. His brow arched as he peered down at him. "Don't you mean Madam Stokes?" he corrected, fastening his pants and buckling his belt.

"Whatever," Xavier hissed. "Why is she here, Dad?"

"We have a date," Jeremiah answered unevenly, turning and grabbing his jacket before facing Xavier again. "And, this is not going to happen, Xavier. You seem to be in the mood to have one of your little rows with me, but it's not going to happen right now. We'll discuss this when I get home."

Jeremiah left the room, leaving Xavier with his disheveled feelings. This only made him more disgruntled and determined. Muttering a string of curses under his breath, Xavier ran after him and blocked his descent down the steps.

"Father! She's not honest! She's up to something. Even Maggie sees that! Why can't you?" he growled.

"Xavier, I will not do this right now!" Jeremiah repeated firmly, anger flashing across his face as he stepped around him, but Xavier refused to relent.

"I'm telling you! She's evil! Why can't you see it?" he yelled, jumping into his path again.

"Xavier!" Jeremiah barked.

"She's a witch! In my dream, she smiles when they beat you! I'm telling you..."

"THAT'S ENOUGH!" Jeremiah boomed with such intensity, it hurt Xavier's ears.

Xavier felt tears burning in his eyes, and he bolted to his room, slamming the door behind him and screaming with frustration.

Jeremiah sighed weightily and looked down at Catherine, who stood at the foot of the steps.

"Catherine," he muttered. "I'm so sorry. I don't know what has gotten into him."

"Oh, Jeremy, it's not your fault! You do so much for him. I don't know why he hates me, but maybe if I talked to him it would help," she suggested.

Jeremiah hesitated.

"What could it hurt?" she asked in a sing-song voice, smiling.

"Okay," Jeremiah muttered wearily and gestured up the steps toward the boy's room. "Help yourself."

Xavier lay on his bed crying silently into his pillow. He wasn't sure how his day could get any worse! Then, of course, it did; Catherine came into his room.

"Xavier?" she cooed.

He jerked upright. "What right do you have coming into my room? I didn't invite you! Get out!" he growled.

"Xavier, I only want to talk," she continued sweetly, as she breezed across the room toward his night table, where she picked up his mother's picture.

"I don't care!" he spat. "Get out of my room!"

She looked at him calmly and laid down Julia's smiling face. "I just want to assure you that I have no intention of trying to take your mother's place. I just want to be..."

"You have no right to even mention her to me!" Xavier said viciously, advancing on her.

"Xavier, isn't there something we could do to end all this..."

"Haven't you heard me? I don't care! My hatred for you has nothing to do with my mother, and it won't end until you're out of my father's life! I know you're up to something, and when I find out what, I'm going to stop you."

Catherine stared down at him, her sweet face melting away into an ugly snarl. Suddenly her arm shot out and she grabbed him painfully by the hair, hauling him close to her. "Now, you listen to me," she hissed, inches from his face. "I don't care what you say or do, *little boy*. You won't be able to stop me! Your father doesn't believe you, and he won't until it's too late. The Son of the Dark will come! And when he does, if you're still alive, you and your father will be his prisoners to do with as he wishes. Most likely he will kill you both, but it will not be instantaneous. Oh, no! It will be slow and painful. Jeremiah will be the first to die. Master will torture him until he begs for mercy, but he won't receive it." She smirked down at him. "Master will drag it out in the most excruciating, humiliating way possible. Then he will take your father's life bit by bit, piece by piece, one body part at a time, and all you'll be able to do is watch and listen to his agonizing screams and know that your fate will be the same!"

"No!" Xavier screamed, heaving Catherine away from him. She stumbled across the room, slammed against the door, and fell onto her rump. Xavier raised his hand with an electro force spinning menacingly in his palm. "Get out, you evil witch! Stay away from my father! If you don't, I'll kill you! You hear me? I'll kill you!"

She staggered to her feet with a grin. "We'll see about that," she whispered. She opened the door and walked out. Xavier raced to the door to shut it behind her, but stopped at the sight of his father's worried face. Jeremiah had heard the commotion and had been on his way up the stairs. Catherine stopped him before he reached the top landing.

"I'm sorry, Jeremy," she began tearfully, her voice quavering, "I think I've only made matters worse. There's so much anger in that little body."

He had to hand it to the woman; she was very good at manipulating any situation to her benefit. His father was eating out of her hands!

"Are you okay?" Jeremiah questioned, noting her trembling body. She wavered, and he reached out to steady her.

"Oh, yes, yes. I'm fine," she answered, smiling unconvincingly and patting his arm.

"What did he do?" Jeremiah asked, his voice growing.

"Nothing..." she told him, looking up at Jeremiah apprehensively. "Oh, there's no sense lying to you, is there? You'll just use telepathy to learn the truth." She sighed and continued in a rush. "He gave me a little push. That's all. I shouldn't have provoked him ..."

Jeremiah stormed up the steps past Catherine and stampeded toward Xavier like a raging bull. Xavier stumbled backwards into his room.

"Jeremy! Please, don't," Catherine called, racing after him. "He's just a boy. He didn't hurt me!"

The king was nearly through the doorway when Catherine grabbed him. "Please! Let's just go to dinner and give the both of you some time to cool down before you do or say something you'll regret!"

"Oh, I can guarantee he'll have regrets when I'm

through with him," he growled predatorily, stepping toward Xavier, but again Catherine stopped him.

"Jeremy, please," she pleaded, giving Xavier a triumphant smile.

Jeremiah visibly fought to rein in his rage. Finally, his body relaxed slightly, and he turned to Catherine. "You're right. Let's go to dinner." Then, he whipped around to Xavier. "YOU! You are not to leave this room while I'm out. Your dinner will be brought up to you. There will be no friends, no television, no computer, and no music! Understood?"

Xavier muttered, "Yeah."

"Excuse me?" his father challenged.

"Yes, sir."

"I'll deal with you when I get home!" he promised before closing the door. Then he took Catherine's hand and led her down the steps to the front door where Loren waited.

"Loren, Timmins will be my security tonight. I need for you to stay with Xavier," he ordered, as he removed his and Catherine's coats from the cloak closet.

"Yes, sire," Loren responded.

"If he gives you any of his cheekiness tonight, you have my permission to blister his butt," Jeremiah added, helping Catherine with her coat and then pulling on his own.

"We'll be fine, Jer. Don't worry. You two have a good time," he responded, opening the door for them.

Moments after the residence door closed behind the king and Catherine, music blared from the boy's room. Loren shook his head and headed for the stairs. The angry lyrics swarmed out of the room as he opened the door. The boy was lying on the bed, staring at the ceiling, his face set and angry.

"Oi, Xavier! Could you turn that nonsense down?" Loren hollered.

When the boy didn't respond, Loren marched over to the stereo and punched the power button. "Your father's gone so this attention-seeking rebellion is futile," he noted calmly.

Xavier sat up. "Hey! I was listening to that!" he yelled, jumping to his feet.

"Wait a minute there, mini-might. There's no need to give me your attitude!" Loren corrected. "But, I believe your father said no friends, no television, no computer, and no music."

"So? What's he going to do? Spank me twice?" Xavier spat, stalking over to the stereo, jabbing the power button, and returning to his vegetative state on the bed.

Loren was taken aback by the boy's blatant defiance and felt his own temper teetering. He grabbed the power cord and yanked it out of the wall.

"What are you doing?" Xavier yelled, stomping over to him.

"You know, I understand how you must be feeling with your father dating," he began testily, "but you know Catherine..."

"Shut up, Loren! You don't know anything about it!" he blared. "You and Father are blind idiots!"

"Xavier, that's enough!" Loren growled. "Catherine is not a threat to you..."

"Bull!" he yelled. "You know what, Loren? You don't have a freaking clue what's going on here. So just, sod off!"

Loren grabbed him and hissed, "I'm only trying to talk to you, Xavier. Why do I get this attitude?" When Xavier rolled his eyes dismissively in response, Loren thought he would strangle the boy. "AND," he added forcibly, "if you don't cool your jets, your temper won't be the only thing that'll need cooling when I'm through with you."

"You wouldn't! You're not my father! You have no..."

Loren's actions interrupted Xavier's ranting as he spun the boy, walloped his bottom, and spun him back to face him. "Attitude adjusted?" he growled.

He looked up at the general smugly. "You've got to be kidding! That didn't even hurt! Beck was right, you hit like an eighty-year old lady! "

Definitely the wrong thing to say! Xavier didn't realize how wrong until he saw Loren's normally mischievous, glittering eyes turn into two icy orbs. He could almost feel the chill from them, and he gulped. Loren jerked him roughly around, pinned him against his left leg and hip, and struck his backside repeatedly. Oh no, it did hurt, and he quickly regretted uttering anything to the contrary.

Finally, Loren released the sobbing boy and looked down at him sadly. "Attitude adjusted now?" he asked softly.

Xavier glared up at the man accusingly. "I thought you were my friend!"

"Xavier, I am! What kind of friend would let you go off your rocker like that without reigning you in?" he asked, reaching for him.

Xavier jerked away from him, crying. "No! I don't care! I don't care. I hate you! I hate Father! I hate all of you!"

"Xavier?" Loren consoled, stepping toward him.

"NO! Please, just leave! Leave me alone. Please!" he pleaded, throwing himself onto his bed and howling into his pillow.

As much as he wanted to comfort him, Loren obeyed the boy's wishes and left the room.

Chapter 15

The Epidemic

When Jeremiah returned from his date, Loren sat with his feet propped up next to the fire and a stiff drink in hand. Jeremiah smirked drily at Loren's bereaved face.

"That bad an evening, eh?" Jeremiah stated, throwing himself onto the sofa next to his friend.

"I don't know how you do it! That boy can be so incorrigible and then, when he gets what he has coming to him, he makes you feel like crap for doing it!" Loren gulped down the remains of the amber liquid.

"What happened?" Jeremiah asked.

Loren groaned, rubbing his face in his hands. "He's got a heck of a lot of animosity toward Miss Stokes, I'll tell you that. He wouldn't settle down at all. I ended up busting his butt." Loren paused in thought and looked up at Jeremiah warily. "Jer, I'm beginning to think that maybe his feelings go beyond jealousy and fear that Catherine will try to replace his mother. I get the feeling he knows more than he's told us, or that we've been willing to hear. Do you think there's any justification to it?"

Jeremiah shook his head. "No, I don't. Catherine is a sweet woman. I'm not sure where all his anger comes from, but I can tell you this; it's going to end."

Loren wished he could share his friend's certainty, but he didn't. He hadn't thought much about the king's relationship, but after Xavier's outburst, he began questioning everything about Catherine. Thinking back to earlier that evening, she had seemed pleased when the boy riled up Jeremiah. Had she smirked? He hadn't thought so at the time, but now he wasn't so sure.

That night, Xavier had a nightmare. He found himself wandering through a dense fog as he made his way toward Maggie's house. The bitter, cold air captured his body and sank deeply into his bones. He shivered violently; something was wrong. He could feel it. Then, the fog shifted like a curtain, and Maggie's house appeared before him. Like an omen, the house was dark and seemed unoccupied. Xavier raced to the front door, his uneasiness growing.

"Maggie?" he called. No one answered, and his uneasiness quickly pivoted into terror. Shakily, Xavier turned the doorknob and entered the deserted house. It wasn't just empty of people; it was empty of everything! The house had been completely stripped of furniture, wall hangings, and even the carpet was missing. All that remained were white patchy walls and the plywood sub-flooring. A soft moan drew Xavier's attention to the splintery steps leading to the upper floor.

"Maggie?" he croaked. "Maggie, are you up there?"

"Xavier," a weak voice moaned. "Xavier."

Xavier sprinted up the steps two at a time and raced down the hall. "Maggie? Maggie, where are you?"

"Xavier," the voice called again.

Xavier finally found her in a room that was so cold his breath formed little white clouds. Maggie lay shivering on a bare mattress in the corner of the room wearing only a thin nightgown.

"Maggie!" he yelped, running to her. He yanked off his coat and covered her cold body. "Oh, God! You're freezing!"

"Xavier," she groaned. "I hurt! I hurt so..." Maggie's eyes fluttered shut, and she went limp in his arms.

"Maggie?" he whispered. "Maggie?" He stroked her cheek and discovered she wasn't breathing. "No," he cried. "Maggie, don't! Please, don't! Wake up! Please, God! Wake up!"

Xavier awoke from the dream, crying. He wanted desperately to call to his father but stopped himself. After their confrontation over Catherine, he didn't want his father's help or comfort with anything. Instead, he stumbled into the bathroom and splashed water on his face, but he was unable to wash away the darkness the dream left behind. It wasn't until he heard Ephraim's urgent voice calling outside his father's room that the dream finally slipped completely from his mind.

"Sire, you need to get up! Jer! There's an emergency."

Xavier tiptoed to his door and listened as two sets of footsteps hurried by his door and down the steps. He cracked his door and listened.

"King Wells," Father O'Brien's voice began shakily, "I have some sad, sad news. We seem to have an epidemic affecting the kingdom's children. Ten children thus far have fallen ill; eight are dead already."

"What!" Jeremiah yelped. "An epidemic? What kind of epidemic?"

"Some kind of super-flu, I don't know for sure. I don't think even the healers are sure," he answered.

"Lord Almighty!" the king muttered.

"What do we do, sire?" O'Brien questioned.

"First, Father, you need to return to the church. There

are bereaved families in need of counseling. Has Mike Spencer been told?" Jeremiah asked.

"No, sire," Ephraim answered.

"Well, go wake him up. Until we are sure what we're dealing with here, school must be cancelled. Plus, I want to speak to the healers and see what the autopsies revealed, if anything. But, gentlemen, the most important thing we can do is to spread reassurance. We don't need an outbreak of panic on our hands," he ordered.

"Yes, sire," several voices echoed at once.

The front door closed, leaving Ephraim and Jeremiah alone. Xavier army crawled out onto the landing and peered down at the men below.

"Okay, Ephraim. What do you know that you're not telling me?"

"I've already spoken to the healers, sire. They're still running tests, but they did find one common thread among the children infected. All ten children are of mixed lineage; each had a common parent," he told him.

"Are you sure?" King Wells whispered.

"Yes, Your Highness," Ephraim responded gravely.

Jeremiah hissed a string of curses and began pacing like a madman as he tried to think it all through. "Ephraim, aside from the kids, has there been anything unusual, a breach in security, a questionable citizen acting suspicious, anything?" Jeremiah questioned, stopping to look at him.

"No, nothing so far," he answered. "We haven't had a chance to question all the questionables to see if they have alibis. Lord! Jer, you don't think William has something to do with this, do you? You don't think he would attack children?"

"Yes, I not only think he would, I know he would. Do you realize what this means? He knows the Chosen is a child of mixed lineage. If he realizes the Chosen has been identified…" he sighed heavily. "We're in an uphill battle to get that boy to his full strength. If William figures out who he is, he will do everything in his power to kill him before he grows strong enough to be a formidable adversary."

"What now, Jer?" the general asked.

"I want to know the names of the children infected. Maybe there's a bigger picture to all this than what's come to light so far," he responded.

"Yes, sir. I'll bring the list straight over the moment they release it to me," Ephraim answered before leaving the palace.

Xavier crawled back into his room, softly closed the door, and returned to bed.

When Xavier woke again, he found he wasn't alone. Jeremiah was sitting on the bed next to him with his head against the headboard, his eyes closed. The moment Xavier stirred, Jeremiah opened his eyes.

"Morning, son. How are you feeling?" he greeted with a weak smile.

Xavier sat up, rubbing his eyes and yawning. "Okay, I guess," he greeted before muttering dreadfully, "Are you here to punish me for yesterday?"

"I should, you know," his father answered warily. "But no, I'm not here to spank you. I need to talk to you."

He not only saw the change in his father's face but felt it in his gut as well. Something was wrong. "What? What is it?" he asked fearfully.

"Son," Jeremiah began, reluctantly facing him. "There's an illness spreading rapidly around the kingdom. Ten children have been affected. Nine of those children are dead, and the healers don't expect the tenth to live through the day."

"God! That's horrible," he moaned, but of course, he already knew this. Well, except that now nine were dead instead of eight.

"Son, there's more," he added, rubbing his face. When he looked back at Xavier again, heavy tears lingered in his eyes, and he tried to blink them back.

Xavier's stomach twisted. "Dad? What? What is it?"

"One of the children who got sick and died last night was..." Tears fell onto his cheeks. "Son, it was Maggie," he gushed, his voice cracking.

"What?" Xavier cried in a small disbelieving voice. It felt like he'd been hit by a jet. His head was flying, spinning, and somersaulting, and he felt nauseous. "No, it's not true. It can't be! I just saw her yesterday! She was fine! She was fine!" he uttered, growing panicked.

"I'm sorry, son. I'm so very..."

Xavier didn't wait for his father to finish. The nausea overtook him, and he raced to the bathroom and threw up. Jeremiah was behind him in an instant rubbing his back. When Xavier was through, he fell to the bathroom floor, his eyes wide with shock. Slowly, his face twisted in despair as he looked up at his father.

"Maggie's dead?" he whispered. Jeremiah nodded, and Xavier howled.

"Oh, God! Noooooo!" he choked out as a sob racked through his body. "Maggie. Oh, God, Dad. Why Maggie?"

The illnesses had baffled the healers until investigators discovered a strange red capsule among some of the children's belongings. After extensive testing, it was determined the capsules had served as vessels for the rare strain of flu. The children had been deliberately infected. Of course, this news wasn't widely known or shared for fear of a vigilante backlash on questionables. Questionables were citizens who had supported William LeMasters during his first uprising. However, many had claimed they hadn't known of LeMasters' plans to assassinate the king and queen and begged to be allowed to remain in the kingdom. Jeremiah had granted their request with two conditions: there would be weekly interrogations for the next five years, and they would face public retribution. Most loyalists, however, found it difficult to forgive and forget, and many questionables were subjected to discrimination and ridicule.

The next day, a public forum was held to discuss the illness and to console parents. Parents were warned that if their child appeared feverish or acted peculiar in any way, they were to report it immediately. Once the parents' concerns and questions were addressed, it was agreed that the school should reopen the next day.

Three days after Maggie's death, Xavier still refused to get out of bed and had stopped eating. He lay on his bed staring at the ceiling, waiting for the next agonizing blow to come. He couldn't sleep. He couldn't even close his eyes for each time he did, the image of Maggie's strained, pain-filled face would torment him. He tried not to think of her, but it was useless. Memories continued to spring out at him as though they were playing a cruel game of peek-a-boo. In the end, he simply gave up and began dwelling on every memory of her: her pretty face, her hypnotic eyes, and her infectious grin. The bittersweet memory of their last dance haunted him. These images would bring a brief smile to his face just before it all came crumbling down, and he would weep again. The grief came at him in waves, and each time it did, it felt as if an invisible force tore inside his chest, ripped his heart out, and stomped on it.

"Xavier?" a strange, slurred voice whispered from the

door. Xavier looked up into the gnarled face of the prophet, Abraham Vincent. "Now, do you believe? I tried to warn you, boy. You didn't want to take me seriously."

"Get out!" Xavier groaned, turning back to his mindless stare.

"I can't," he whispered. "I can't until you know all of it! This is just the beginning!"

Xavier stood and glared resentfully up at the strange man. Anger overpowered his grief, and he simply unleashed.

"I. Don't. Care! Get out! I don't want to know any more!" His voice broke as he fought back tears. "You hear me? I'm done! I don't want to know! It's...it's...too much." Finally, he crumpled to his knees and began sobbing. "I'm tired! I'm so, so tired!"

Abraham moved stealthily to him and knelt beside him. "I know you don't believe this, but I do understand what you're going through," he whispered softly, rubbing Xavier's back. "I know, but, Xavier, it doesn't change anything! You've got to know what I have foreseen."

Xavier's sobbing stopped, and he looked up at the horribly scarred face and into a pair of curiously gentle eyes.

"Xavier, the fact is your father will try to sacrifice his own life to save yours. You must stop him from doing it!"

"What?" he whispered.

"Listen to me, boy. There will be a mutiny within the kingdom. There's nothing you or your father can do to stop that, but he will try to run a diversion so that you can escape safely. He will fail miserably, and it will cost him his life! You must stop him!"

Xavier took in the news slowly, and even though he didn't want to believe the prophet, he did. After Maggie's death, he would believe anything this man told him.

"Xavier, there's more. Even though you must stop your father from sacrificing himself for you, your actions in doing so will sentence another to die in his place. This cannot be prevented, I'm afraid," Abraham added quietly.

"Who? Who will die in his place?" he asked.

"I won't tell you that. You must save the king; his role in your future is monumental. Without him, your future will be dark and painful. Knowing the identity of the man who will die in his place is irrelevant."

"Irrelevant? Irrelevant? I will cause a man's death simply by saving my father and you say it's irrelevant!" he growled.

"Yes, it is irrelevant in the scheme of things, young sire," Abraham told him sadly. "I know it's hard for you to see right now, but you'll understand one day."

"No," he spat. "I will never understand how a man's death can be irrelevant." He glared spitefully at the old man. "If you've told me all you needed to tell me, please leave. Just go and leave me alone." Xavier buried his head in his arms, trying to control the roller coaster of emotions sweeping through him.

"Sire? There's one more thing," the prophet whispered from the door. "When the mutiny erupts, you must get the King's Key from the vault! It's imperative that it remains with you, always!"

When Xavier looked up, the prophet was gone, and he was alone.

He lifted himself from the floor and went to his bed. He picked up his mother's picture, feeling another wave of despair wrenching at his heart like a vice.

"Mom," he choked out between sobs, "please, look after Maggie for me, and tell her I'm sorry that I messed things up between us the last time I saw her. Tell her I know it was wrong to invade her privacy like I did, and I'm so, so sorry!"

He fell back into the bed, sobbing with his mother's smiling face in his arms. He never saw the small capsule roll out from behind his mother's picture. Nor did he notice it as it rolled off his bedside table and hit the floor. He didn't see it burst open and begin emitting a nearly transparent yellow gas. He didn't notice any of this as he cried into his pillow.

Chapter 16

Infected

Jeremiah crept into Xavier's room shortly before midnight and found the boy asleep and peaceful. He sighed with relief as he sat on the edge of the bed and smoothed a curl from the boy's brow. Clutched tightly in the boy's arms, Julia's image smiled up at him. Carefully, he slipped the picture frame from his grasp and replaced it on the bedside stand. Then he kissed his son's temple and quietly left the room.

The next morning, Xavier awoke feeling oddly energized and antsy. He didn't even feel sad any more. Without putting much thought to his sudden change of emotional state, he set about getting ready for school. He showered, brushed his teeth, dressed, and was in the middle of pulling on his socks and shoes when Mrs. Sommers entered the room. She froze at the sight of him.

"Master Wells? What are you doing up?" she asked.

"What does it look like?" he snapped. "I'm going to school."

"Did you sleep well?" she asked.

He looked up at her irritably. "Does it matter? Stop hovering over me like my mother. You're not my mother!"

Mrs. Sommers took in his flushed face and bloodshot eyes. The boy didn't look well, but she imagined that

Maggie Applegate's death was to blame for it. "I know that, young sire, but I am your governess. I'm just looking out for you," she rebuked, stepping toward him and attempting to check his forehead with her hand.

Xavier jumped to his feet like a threatened, wild animal and pushed her away from him. "Stop it!" he yelled.

Mrs. Sommers stumbled and fell into his bookshelf and onto the floor. As Mrs. Sommers struggled to her feet, Jeremiah entered the room.

"Dear God, Emma. What happened?" he gasped, running over and helping her to her feet.

"I just lost my balance, sire. That's all," she lied, watching Xavier closely. Shock had flickered briefly across the boy's face, but now all that remained was a cool, cocky expression. "But, Xavier says that he plans to go to school today," she explained, nodding at the boy.

Jeremiah turned and looked at his with astonishment. "Really?"

"Yeah, really," Xavier answered haughtily.

"Son, you don't have to go today. If it's too soon..."

"It's not too soon, *Father*. Now, if you two don't mind, I need to get going or I'll be late." Then, without another word or a backwards glance, Xavier walked from the room, leaving a very baffled father and governess in his wake.

Xavier was met with numerous stares and whispers as he walked up the stairway to the front entrance of Wells Academy. Headmaster Spencer, drawn by the murmurs, looked down at him with surprise. "Xavier, I didn't expect you back so soon."

"Does that mean I can skip telepathy class then?" he joked.

Spencer narrowed his eyes on the pompous boy in front of him and tried to determine whether or not to take his comment seriously. "Ah, no. If you're at school, then you must come to telepathy."

Xavier nodded, walked past him, and entered the school.

In math class, Sir Underwood droned on and on about a lesson they had learned last week, and Xavier quickly grew bored. Why was Underwood teaching order of operations again?

"Good God! We've already learned this!" he blurted, stunning the professor.

Unsure of what to make of the prince's outburst, he ignored it and continued, "Many of you are still struggling with this concept. So, today we will review it and complete the practice problems on page 177. Now, let's discuss the examples on the board..."

Xavier didn't see why he had to sit through the lesson again! He already knew how to do this crap! It was stupid! He groaned and slumped in his chair. Idly, his attention drifted from the professor and settled on Maggie's empty seat. Sorrow slammed into him unexpectedly, leaving him on the verge of sobbing. His eyes ached with unshed tears, and his Adam's apple suddenly felt ten times too big. He tried to swallow away the tightness and pain lodged there, but the knot only grew. Soon, he was hyperventilating and couldn't catch his breath. He gasped desperately for air and bit back the sob that was fighting to escape. He needed to get out of there! He jumped to his feet with such force, his desk tipped and slammed to the floor as he raced from the room. He sprinted down the hall and out into the frigid air of the courtyard. Clumps of icy snow crackled under his feet as he staggered over to the large oak and leaned against it. Gasping for breath, he tried to blink back the tears filling his eyes but ended up wiping his cheeks as they slid down over his face.

When he woke up this morning, he thought he was together enough to come to school. He was sick of feeling depressed and sad; he was sick of hiding away in his room. He just wanted to get on with his life and feel happy again.

The grief continued to swell and fill his every thought until the tears fell in streams over his cheeks. Slowly he sank to the cold, wet earth and buried his face in his arms, giving into the tears that wrestled loose. For several long minutes, his body racked with sob after sob that he was powerless to stop. Then, as suddenly as the depression and sobbing had begun, it was gone, and he mopped his face with his sleeve. He looked around the frozen courtyard and took several deep breaths as he glanced skyward. A small seed of euphoria ignited in his chest and began to grow until his depression was replaced by giddiness and jubilation so intense that he began to giggle.

"Xavier?" a voice called calmly from courtyard doors.

He turned and found Spencer standing a few feet from him, looking worried. The euphoria ballooned inside him, and his giggle became laughter that soon developed into outright hysterics.

"Xavier? Are you all right?" Spencer asked, stepping tentatively toward him.

Finally, he managed to stifle his glee enough to answer, "Hey, Headmaster." But, then he burst into frenzied laughter once more.

Spencer crossed the icy ground and sat on a bench next to boy.

"Maybe I should call Jeremiah to come get you?" he suggested quietly.

Xavier only laughed harder and shook his head. "NO,"

he blurted through his giggles, "I'll... be okay. Just... give me... a... minute."

He looked down at him uncertainly but nodded.

After great effort, Xavier was able to contain the mania bubbling inside him. Panting, he swiped at his eyes with the back of his arm and looked up at the patiently waiting headmaster. "Sir, I'm okay. Really!"

"I don't think you're ready to be back at school. I really think I should call your dad."

"No!" he blurted as a wave of pain stabbed into him once again. "Please, don't do that; I can't spend another minute in that place thinking of..." His voice broke away as the pain quickly twisted into despair. Tears of a different origin filled his eyes, and he quickly looked away.

"Okay, you may stay," Spencer whispered, stroking his back. "When you're ready, you need to head back to class."

The headmaster stood and walked toward the building but stopped just short of reaching the door and turned.

"And, Xavier?" He waited until the boy's eyes met his. "If you need to talk about...anything, I'm here for you. Okay?"

He nodded. "Thanks," he whispered softly.

Then, Spencer turned and slipped through door, leaving him alone again in the courtyard. Michael Spencer was beginning to feel more and more like an uncle and less like just a headmaster. Another wave of delirium dominated his emotions, and he began to giggle again. It couldn't be good for a person to move from one emotional extreme to another. Surely, he would have a mental breakdown if it continued.

Xavier fought to control the changing emotions careening through him throughout the day, but found, like a runaway roller coaster, he had no means of controlling it. And, by Latin class, his self-control completely unraveled.

He sat next to Beck joking and whispering lightly, feeling almost normal when Catherine entered the room just before the bell and smirked at him.

"I see Xavier Wells has returned to school!" she announced smugly. "Glad you could make it today, sire."

"Yeah, right. You're as glad to see me as I am to see you!" he snorted before cracking up completely.

Oddly, Catherine's smirk widened into an enormous grin as if she alone understood the joke. "And I'm surprised to see that the young prince is in such good spirits. I would have expected that after the death of his little friend, he wouldn't be so jovial."

Anguish and despair sunk into him like a knife plunging deep into his chest while Catherine twisted it. The bell rang, and with a twisted smile, she turned back to the rest of the class and began the new lesson. Xavier was left fighting the overwhelming, dark mood once again and wishing he could die.

"All right, class. On the board is this week's new vocabulary list. Copy each word with its English translation and then, use the word in a complete Latin sentence."

Xavier watched as the class sprang into action, but he felt detached and empty. He simply sat and stared at his desk, sulking and hating Madam Stokes all the more. Slowly, a mischievous grin slid across his face, and he sneered at Catherine, who was busily adding words to the vocabulary list. Discreetly, he twirled a finger at her desk before sitting back to watch the mayhem unfold. At first, only a faint scratching came from one of the desk's drawers. But soon, it intensified so much so that the students in the front row stopped working and searched for the source of the sound. As the power in the desk grew the drawers began to rattle and drew more attention from the class. Even Madam Stokes became aware that something wasn't right. The rattling quickly intensified into a loud banging that shook the entire desk. Catherine flattened herself against the chalkboard and stared at the desk just a few feet from her as every student in the room watched. The desk rocked and shook until finally, its drawers exploded open and millions upon millions of wriggling, clicking cockroaches scurried out in a wave of black. Students burst into screams, storming to the rear of the room, many climbing on top of the desks.

However, Xavier didn't move. He simply sat in his seat laughing violently as he watched a terrified Madam Stokes. She squealed and tried to dance away from the infested desk, but with a slight flick of Xavier's finger, the insects rushed toward her and covered her like a second skin. He fell out of his chair in hysterics.

Suddenly the door flew open, and Sir Blaire burst into the room. Xavier stopped laughing almost instantly at the sight of his anima-linguist teacher's furious face.

"Help me," Catherine managed to gurgle through the thick blanket of cockroaches covering every inch of her.

Xavier was lost again to an uproar of laughter and tears fell from his eyes. As Sir Blaire rushed to Catherine's aid, Courtney grabbed the prince and pulled him to his feet.

"Come on, mate!" Court hissed, tugging him out of the room, down the hall, and into the boys' bathroom.

"Are you all right?" Court asked, looking at him shakily. When his friend nodded meekly, he groaned. "Holy cricket! Did you do all that?"

He nodded.

"Not that she didn't deserve it after that bit she said about Maggie, but X, you're going to get expelled for sure!"

Following these words, Xavier began laughing again, and Court looked down at him, bewildered. "Are you sure you're all right? You look flushed," he asked, touching the prince's forehead.

"Get off!" he bellowed, knocking Court's hand away.

"Bloody hell, X! You're really hot. Maybe you should go to Headmaster Spencer and tell him you're sick. You..."

"No! I'm not telling *Uncle Mikey* anything! He'll only send me home, and I'm not going!" he growled but then began giggling again.

"Xavier..." he began.

"*Courtney*," Xavier mocked and then giggled. "Come on, let's get out of here. It stinks!"

As the boys left the restroom, they found Courtney's oldest brother standing by the water fountain talking to a girl. From the looks of it, Drew Hardcastle was working hard to impress her, and he kept patting down his hair and straightening his uniform. Xavier grabbed Court and hauled him back inside the bathroom doorway.

Giggling still, Xavier whispered, "Watch this!"

With a slight swirling motion of his finger, he pointed at the fountain and then at Drew. Suddenly, water squirted at a perverse angle from the fountain, spraying the front of Drew's pants. He jumped back, cussing. Xavier burst into laughter and, reluctantly, Courtney joined in.

"Excuse me, Sire Wells? What do you think you're doing?"

Xavier turned and found Spencer leaning against the bathroom door behind them.

Xavier rolled his eyes despondently and growled, "Jeez, Spencer! What are you doing? Spying on me?"

Court tensed beside him, his eyes growing wide.

A flash of anger swept across the headmaster's face

before he could mask it, but as he studied the feverish boy before him, his face went pale, very pale. He pulled Xavier toward him and pressed the back of his hand to his forehead. Lord! The boy was on fire!

"Stop it! Get off!" Xavier hissed, wiggling in his uncle's grasp.

Spencer tightened his hold on the prince before turning to Court.

"Courtney, I think you better return to Latin class. I believe Sir Blaire has the infestation problem under control now."

Xavier burst into laughter again, slouching in Spencer's arms.

Court gave Xavier a fretful looked before whispering, "Is he going to be all right?"

"I'll take care of Xavier, Courtney. Please, go back to class," the headmaster insisted softly.

"Yes, sir," he answered and hurried away from them.

Spencer turned toward an infuriated Drew. "Andrew, go to the office. Jeanette should have an extra pair of pants for you, and then I suggest that I not find you or Miss Lowe in the halls again when you should be in class. Understood?"

"Yes, sir," he mumbled, and the two teenagers went their separate ways.

Michael Spencer turned his attention back to the prince still laughing uncontrollably in his arms. "Let's go, Xavier. We need to call your father," he said softly.

"NO!" he spat and twisted his way out of Spencer's grasp. "I'm not going home! You can't make me!"

"Sire, you're not well! You need to go home so you can get better," he pleaded.

"Forget it!" he growled, backing away from him.

"Well, I'm afraid you don't have a choice here. You will

be leaving!"

"No!" he retorted, but Spencer grabbed him, lifted him over his shoulder, and carried him to the office.

"Mike! Mike! Put me down! I swear to God! If you don't put me down, I'll blast you!" he screamed, squirming and punching at his uncle any place he could reach.

Spencer kicked the office door open, stormed past a stunned secretary and Drew Hardcastle, and marched into his office, slamming the door shut with his foot before sliding Xavier down from his shoulder.

"You jerk! You had no right! No right!" Xavier screamed, thrashing at the infuriatingly calm man barring his escape.

"You're sick, Xavier. I have every right to get you home and get you the care you need!" he told him evenly. "Now sit down while I call your dad."

"No! I'm going to lunch!"

"I'm afraid not, sire."

"Yes! I am!" Xavier yelled, raising the electro force spinning in his hands.

Spencer didn't see it coming and wasn't prepared for it. So when the force hit him, he was knocked clean off his feet and slammed against his desk. He struggled to stand but found his legs were numb and wouldn't obey the simplest of commands. All he could do was watch as Xavier opened the door and ran from the room.

Chapter 17

Delirium

By the time Xavier arrived at lunch, nearly every student was seated and eating. He quickly got a tray and hurried toward the back table where his friends sat solemnly, but he never made it. Someone tripped him, and he slammed hard to the floor, hitting his head. The room spun dizzily as he sat up and rubbed his brow. Laughter erupted around him, and he slowly got to his feet, brushing the macaroni and cheese from his arms and chest.

"Did you have a nice trip, Your Highness?" Ken leered, bursting into laughter with his friends.

Xavier's face twisted with fury as he glared at the laughing faces. He was sick and tired of people like Ken bullying him! He didn't have to put up with it anymore. He was the Prince of Warwood for God's sake! Without a word, he tackled the boy, slamming him to the floor. Then, as he held Ken down with his body, he began punching him. Mackenzie rushed to help his friend, but Xavier thrust his hand at the other boy, and with a loud whoosh, sent him soaring across the room and slamming against the wall, where he slid to the floor unconscious. As screams filled the cafeteria, he resumed pummeling Ken's face into minced meat.

"Xavier! Stop it! Stop it!" Robbie screamed, grabbing him and pulling him off the unconscious boy. Xavier turned quickly in her grasp and knocked her to the floor. He stood poised with a fist drawn back, but when he realized it was Robbie, he froze. Horror slipped across his face, and he went pale.

"Robbie? Robbie, what's happening?" he asked shakily, but in the next instant, the fear in his face was replaced by uncontrollable giggles.

"Here let me help you up," he called past the giggles and held out his hand to her.

Uncertainly, she took his hand and could feel the heat oozing from him. As he pulled her to her feet, she studied his flushed face and glassy eyes. Impulsively, she stroked his brow and cheek. He couldn't have been any hotter than if he were standing on the sun! She felt panic rise inside her. Xavier was sick; he had the super flu. Tears flooded her eyes.

"Oh, Xavier," she moaned.

However, Xavier, misinterpreting her actions, pulled her close and kissed her. Boy, how he had wanted to do this for months. He wasn't sure exactly when he had begun to think about Robbie in this way. Heck! Maybe, he never had seen her as just a friend. But as he kissed her, his heart soared, and he felt like he was flying.

"Xavier!" Robbie muttered. "Xavier! Stop it!"

When he drew away, he found they were hovering about a foot in the air. They dropped to the floor and stared at one another in shock. Xavier's manic laughter returned, and he hugged her.

"See? I can sweep you off your feet! Come on, Robbie! You like me! I know you do! It made you so jealous when I asked Maggie to the dance; didn't it? Admit it, Robbie! You've always liked me, just as I've always liked you! So why are you fighting it?"

Robbie squirmed in his grasp. "Xavier, please don't! You're not well!" she cried.

He chuckled loudly. "Let the jury note, the defendant didn't deny the charges made against her!"

"Xavier! Please, you're hurting me!" Robbie squealed, shifting and wiggling against his firm hold.

"X, mate, let her go!" Beck muttered, trying to sound composed and light-hearted but failing.

"Stay out of it, Beckley. You shouldn't interfere with true love! You might get hurt," he spat, glaring at him. "Robbie's mine. Hear me? She's mine! So stay away from her."

"Come on, Xavier!" Court called from behind Beck. "You're hurting her! You don't want to hurt your girl, do you?"

He looked down at Robbie with a very strange expression. "No. I would never hurt her," he whispered, hugging her again.

Robbie squealed and tried to twist away.

"Xavier!" Every head snapped toward the door and King Wells. Spencer stood next to him, both men looking apprehensive. "Let Robbie go, son," Jeremiah continued softly.

"No," Xavier replied weakly. "I love her, Dad. I can't let...I won't let anything happen to her."

"I know, son. I know, but right now, all you're doing is scaring her. Look at her, Xavier. Really look at her! Don't you see how you're frightening her?" Jeremiah prompted as he slowly approached him.

Xavier looked at Robbie's alarmed, wide eyes. Her face was flushed and moist with tears. He watched as a new tear formed, trickled down an eyelash, and fell heavily onto her cheek. Suddenly, he felt sick to his stomach knowing he was the reason she was crying.

"Oh," he whispered. "Oh, Robbie. Don't cry! I'm sorry! I'm sorry! I'm sorry! I'm sorry!"

Suddenly, Jeremiah's arms were around him and lifting him away from the girl. Spencer grabbed Robbie and pulled her into the safety of his arms.

"No!" Xavier blurted, struggling against his father's massive arms.

"Get the other children out of here, Mike!" he bellowed as he fell to the floor, trying desperately to keep a hold of the violently struggling boy. He could feel the fever radiating from his son's body. A lump wedged in his throat as he thought with horror of the implications.

"Let go of me! Get off, Dad!" the boy snarled.

"I can't, son. You're not well. We need to go to the hospital," Jeremiah soothed, looking desperately at Spencer and the watching children. "God, Mike," he yelled, his voice cracking. "Get them out!"

Spencer immediately began evacuating the room, and Xavier fought harder to free himself from his father's arms. He threw his head back and cracked the king on the chin, before twisting his body violently and jabbing his elbow into the tender flesh of his father's abdomen. The tight grip loosened marginally, but it was enough that Xavier was able to tear himself free. He rushed toward Robbie.

"Robbie! Robbie, please don't leave me! Please!"

Jeremiah lurched to his feet and managed to grabbed ahold of the boy's school blazer before he could reach the girl. "No, son. She needs to go home, and you need to come with me!"

"What about *Catherine*?" he hissed, twisting out of his jacket and freeing himself from his father's hold. "Where does she go, Dad? She's all you care about now-a-days. Do you realize that Mom hasn't been dead and buried for six months, and you're already shacking up with that floozy?"

His father's hand came so quickly that he didn't see it coming. He felt it though, and it nearly sent him to the floor. Jeremiah looked stunned.

"Oh, God! Xavier...Xavier," he muttered, reaching for him, but Xavier knocked his hand away.

"Thanks a lot, *Dad*!" he bellowed, rubbing his stinging cheek. "Well, at least I know where I stand now! Catherine is obviously first, and I'm not!"

He turned and sprinted toward the door.

"Xavier!" Jeremiah yelled. Xavier stopped but didn't face him. "I am so, so sorry for hitting you like that! I was completely out of line, and you didn't deserve it! I never wanted to treat you like my father treated me. But, son, I cannot let you leave here!"

He spoke without turning. "Then you're going to have to stop me, Father, because I'm not staying here another second!" He stomped toward the door.

"I'm sorry, son," the king muttered, raising his hands and sending a force pelting toward the retreating boy.

But, Xavier had anticipated the assault and instinctively conjured up an electro shield. His father's force struck the barrier, ricocheted back, and struck him. He fell into an unconscious heap, as Xavier fled the cafeteria.

"Jer! Jer! Are you all right?" Loren questioned, kneeling next to him.

The king slowly sat up and rubbed his head. "Yeah. I think so. Where did he go?"

"We got word from the gatehouse that Xavier forced his way out of the kingdom, but no one is sure where he went from there," Loren told him.

"What?" Jeremiah jumped to his feet. "Their own prince leaves the kingdom, but no one cares enough to try to stop him or even to find out where he's heading?" he barked as he stomped out of the cafeteria and down the hall.

"Jer! They were afraid. The boy has the fever! It's hard to say what he would have done to them if they had tried to stop him. There's no telling what he's capable of!" he reasoned, stepping in stride with the king.

"Loren, he's no more capable of what he was before. This illness doesn't change who he is. The fever intoxicates him for the lack of a better description. He loses his ability to control his impulses and therefore acts without thought or reason. But he's not dangerous," he told the general.

Wisely, Loren chose not to point out that the boy had knocked him unconscious.

The instant they exited the building, the king stopped on the steps and closed his eyes. Loren was accustomed to seeing his friend do this so he didn't question it. He simply stepped back and gave him some space and silence to concentrate.

Jeremiah tried to reach out to the boy but only found emptiness and silence. Baffled, he opened his eyes and looked at Loren.

"I can't. I can't reach him. God, the illness must be full-blown. If I can't connect with him telepathically, then I won't be able to teleport to him either. Loren, we've got to find him!" he choked.

"I hate him! I hate him! I'm never going back! He doesn't care about me! He only cares about Catherine! He doesn't love me! I hope he rots away with guilt for hitting me! God! I miss Mom! I really miss her!" Xavier sobbed as he continued to stagger along a rocky beach. The frigid

Atlantic wind blasted through his thin shirt and vest, and he wrapped his arms around himself, trying to keep his body from chattering apart. Off shore, a cluster of ominous black clouds peered down at him like a predator.

But, then suddenly, the cold no longer mattered as a fiery pain assaulted his body, sending him tumbling to the shore. He cried out as the seizure of pain rocked and slammed his body against the razor-edged stones covering the ground. His chest felt as if his life was being crushed from him, and he desperately gasped for air. He wasn't sure how long the spasm of agony coursed through him, but when it finally lessen, his entire body was burning and aching. Exhausted, he lay on the ground whimpering, too weak to move. He was barely aware of the lulling sound of the icy ocean as it stroked his burning legs and chest. The last image he saw before passing out into a black abyss was a snowy dove perched like a sentry on a nearby rock, watching him.

There was nothing Jeremiah could do but hope he would be able to break through the fever and reach his son. He knew it wasn't much to go on, but he refused to stop his telepathic attempts. He and Loren searched nearby marshes and moorlands while Ephraim and Spencer searched the nearest common villages for the boy, but the men failed to find him. It had been nearly three hours since Xavier had left the kingdom, and Jeremiah couldn't help but worry that with every passing moment that Xavier was lost to him, the greater the chance that he would die.

After a brief stop at the palace to pack hot tea and snacks for the long night ahead, the king was anxious to continue the search. He knew if he stood still even for a minute, he would lose it, which certainly wouldn't help

Xavier.

"Loren! Ephraim! Let's get going again!" he ordered, marching into the receiving room, but his generals were not alone. Father O'Brien stood just inside the door, and judging by Ephraim's scarlet face and Loren's clenched jaw, the men had been having a heated discussion.

"What is it?" he questioned immediately. "Did someone find my boy?"

"No, sire," Father O'Brien answered. The three exchanged looks of apprehension and animosity.

"Then what?" Jeremiah hissed impatiently.

"Sire, I think it's time you faced the facts," O'Brien began, stepping toward the king.

"Which are?" he asked icily.

"Your son has been infected by the super flu. Even if you're able to find him, he will not liv..."

"DON'T!" Jeremiah roared.

"I'm just saying..." Father continued quietly.

"DON'T!" he shouted again, lunging at the man, grabbing him by the neck, and slamming him against the door. "DON'T!" he repeated, his face contorting in anguish. "He's alive, and I will find him! Don't you ever come into my home again with this nonsense of me facing the facts! Do... you... understand... me?" Jeremiah yelled, slamming the priest against the door with each word. He panted, trying to reign in his terror and apprehension.

Slowly he released the priest and walked several paces before dropping to the floor in a heap.

"Oh dear God!" Jeremiah crumbled into tears. "God, he's only a boy! Loren! Ephraim! We've got to find him."

Loren immediately went to the fallen king.

Ephraim paused long enough to hiss at Father O'Brien, "Now, leave!" Then he hurried to help Loren tend to the king, and when he looked up again, Father O'Brien was gone.

When Xavier regain consciousness, it wasn't to a warm bed and the feeling of safety and security; it was to another bone-rattling, agonizing convulsion. His eyes snapped open from the intensity of it, and he screamed. But this time, the seizure didn't stop as quickly as the previous one had. The pain continued to rack and slam his body for several minutes. He clamped his eyes shut and sobbed helplessly against the pain. Pinpricks of white light exploded in the dark realms of his mind and he prayed, not for his survival, but for his death. As pain went, Xavier would have to rank it as the worst he had ever endured. Finally, mercifully, the seizure subsided, and he lay on the threshold of passing out again when terror grabbed him just as violently as the seizures. He was going to die! He was going to die, and he was going to die alone! Lord! He wanted his father!

He began to sob uncontrollably. "D...dad?" he sputtered out hoarsely. "Dad, w...where are you? Daddy, please! I'm sorry; I didn't mean what I said. I didn't mean any of it! Please!"

Chapter 18

The Cure

Xavier passed out. He didn't see or hear the loud whirlwind of blue light as his father appeared within a few feet from him. Blinking and confused, the king peered around at the rocky, ominous shore line. A moment ago, he had been with Ephraim, searching a marsh west of the kingdom. How had he ended up here? Then, his eyes settled on the small figure sprawled on the beach, partially submerged in the icy sea water.

"Xavier!" he choked, racing to his side. The boy's entire body was as pale as his hair, and there was a frightening blue tinge to his complexion. "Xavier?" he repeated, touching his cold face. "Oh, God," he cried. "Come on, son! Wake up! Wake up!"

Jeremiah lifted the boy out of the water and took him to gentler ground. He laid the boy on the snow-covered marsh grass and quickly peeled off his own fleece cloak and scarf. He wrapped the scarf around the boy's head and neck and bundled him in the cloak like an infant wrapped in a baby blanket. Then he lifted him into his arms and tried something he had never done before: teleporting with another person. Thankfully, it worked perfectly, and in the next instant, he found himself standing outside the infirmary building.

The moment the hospital staff saw the king carrying the unconscious prince into the triage, they immediately went to work grabbing IVs, oxygen tanks and masks, an EKG machine, and various common medical instruments. Empowered doctors not only possessed strong healing capabilities, but they were also licensed in common medicine. This flu was one of the few times their healing powers proved useless in treating an illness. None of the infected children had responded to healing empowerments, so common technology had to be used. But in the end, nothing seemed to work. All ten children had died. Now, they were faced with the quandary of their prince falling ill to the same deadly disease and most likely dying from it. Although the healers managed to stabilize the prince, he wasn't expected to live out the night.

A couple of hours later, Xavier slowly opened his eyes and was surprised to find himself in a warm, dry bed. Jeremiah sat in a chair beside him with his head resting next to Xavier's right hand.

"Dad?" he rasped out weakly.

His father's head whipped up. He looked horrible! His eyes were red and puffy, as though he had been crying a lot. There were dark circles under his eyes and his face was drained of color. He made a feeble attempt to smile reassuringly, but Xavier knew he was going to die.

"Hey!" he whispered. "It's about time you woke up."

"Yeah, well, I've been a little busy," Xavier joked weakly. "Dad, I really hurt! It's like every bone in my body is broken. I feel..."

But, Xavier couldn't finish for a new seizure of pain ripped through his body. His already sore muscles felt as if they were being torn apart, and his bones felt like they were being snapped into pieces. He screamed himself hoarse. He could feel his father's hands on him, and he could hear his voice, though he couldn't make out the words. Finally, the spasm ended, and Xavier fell back into the soft mattress sobbing.

"Dad, please," he pleaded. "Please, kill me! Please! If you love me at all, you'll not let me suffer like this! God! Dad, please!"

"I can't! I love you, son, more than you'll ever know, but I can't do what you ask. Though, I promise you this, I will find a way to cure you. If it's the last thing I do, you will get well!" Jeremiah choked on a sob and pulled the boy into his arms.

Xavier fell unconscious and didn't wake up again. The healers weren't surprised. All the children who had been infected by the virus had slipped into comas hours before their death. Upon hearing this, Jeremiah bolted from the hospital with Ephraim and Loren at his heels.

"I want Abraham Vincent! Now!" He barked, looking at Loren. "How do I get him?"

Loren glanced at him surreptitiously.

"Come on, Loren! Don't give me that look; I know that you know how to get a hold of him!" he blared, confronting his friend. "I want him in my residence within the hour! Understood?"

Loren nodded. "Yes, sire."

Jeremiah paced around the room like a convicted felon in his last hours before his execution. It had been nearly an hour since Xavier had fallen into a coma, and time was not a luxury he had to waste. Damn it! Where was Loren with the prophet? Xavier's torment-filled face as he begged him to kill him continued to haunt him. His throat constricted into a tight painful knot whenever he thought about everything that the boy had endured the last several months. No child should ever have to endure torture and despair as his son had, and it would all be for nothing if he died.

A light knock drew his attention to the door just as it opened, and Ephraim walked in. "Loren and the prophet are on their way up. Look Jer, I've never said anything before because I know how you respect the man, but I don't trust Abe. He's hiding something. I'm not sure what, but there's something he's holding back. Just...just be careful."

The residence door opened without a knock and Loren entered followed by Abraham Vincent. Jeremiah didn't welcome the man nor did he give him time to speak. Time was short. It was time for answers and action, not for formalities and niceties.

"How do I save him?" he blurted, brushing past Ephraim and approaching the older man. "Can he be saved?"

"Yes, he can be saved, sire," Abraham replied gravely.

"What are you waiting for then?" he spat, stomping to the door and throwing it open. "Let's get over there!"

"Wait, Jer," Loren interrupted. "There's more to it than that!"

"I don't care! I'd murder the pope if it meant my son would live!"

"No, sire. You must hear what repercussions *you'll* face as a result of your actions," the prophet demanded. The king deflated and hastily shut the door to listen. "If you choose to do this, Jeremiah, you will be breaking the very law that *you* pushed into legislation."

"Which law?" Jeremiah asked.

"Code 20," he answered gravely.

"Bloody... you're off your head!" Ephraim hissed.

The prophet ignored him and continued, "You will

need to use the King's Key to endow yourself with powerful rejuvenation ability. Only an extremely powerful healing power will save him. But, if you do this, you will fall from grace in the eyes of your citizens. You could lose their trust. There are members on the High Council who will seek retribution," the prophet answered quietly.

The king stiffened as he realized what ramifications breaking such a law would bring. It could mean his dethronement! Abraham was right; many of his citizens would see such an act as hypocritical and never trust him again. He would definitely fall from grace.

"Jer," Ephraim called quietly, "maybe we could call for an emergency High Council meeting."

He looked at his general with regret. "Hardcastle, you know as well as I do that there are some on the High Council who would drag their feet to spite me. I can't risk Xavier's life like that."

"You've got to try, Jeremiah! If you do this without approval..." he started.

"I know perfectly well what consequences will result, Ephraim! It doesn't matter. You know he must live! His destiny is too important." Jeremiah looked at the prophet determinedly. "What do I do?"

"We'll need the King's Key," Abraham stated simply.

"Okay, then. Let's get going," Loren stated.

"No!" Jeremiah snapped. "Your involvement ends here, Loren."

"But..."

"That's an order, Jefferson. When this all goes down, I don't want you or Ephraim anywhere near the heat! I don't want you punished for my actions. Is that understood? If you're anywhere near this, I'll treat you like I would treat anyone who gets in my way," he warned his friends. "Understood?"

Loren glanced anxiously at Ephraim before answering, "Yes, sire."

"All right then, you're both off duty as of now. Go home."

After the men left, Jeremiah led Abraham Vincent from the residence and down the royal staircase. At the bottom step, he stopped and studied the bottom pillar. He twisted the knob on top of the post and quickly looped around to a hidden door sliding open underneath the staircase. They entered a long dark stairwell lit only by floodlights embedded in the stoned walls. When they reached the bottom of the steps, the king stepped up to a steel-enforced door and placed his hand on a crystal panel to the left of it. The panel lit up, and the door cracked and squealed as it slid to the side, revealing a small white marbled room. Three armed guards stood at attention the moment the king entered the bright room.

"Sire..." The first guard's words were cut short when Jeremiah sent two electro forces spiraling toward him and a second guard, striking them and slamming them into the wall. Both men lay motionless as a third guard spun and raised his sword, looking positively terrified.

"Sire! Don...don't come...come any closer," the young guard sputtered.

"I'm sorry, kid," Jeremiah muttered, sending another force toward the young man, rendering him unconscious.

After a sigh of regret, Jeremiah marched to the vault door and threw it open. Once inside, Jeremiah paused and looked around the elaborately decorated room. Along the entire length of the far wall, the kingdom's emblem made of jewels and gold sparkled at him. Reverently, he approached the long altar and the key's vessel and muttered, "What do I do?"

"Take the key in your hands and think about what you

want to accomplish. Think about healing your son. When the process is complete, the key will grow cold to the touch," Abraham told him.

He nodded. Slowly, he opened the wooden case and lifted the small staff into his hands. Immeasurable power surged through his body, and he dropped to his knees with a gasp. He had never experience anything like it before. The key's power was beyond imagining. Instinctively, he knew that the key held every power known to man in the most concentrated, purest form.

"Now, concentrate," the prophet whispered from behind him.

Feeling light-headed, Jeremiah closed his eyes and concentrated on his son. He only wished to have the power to save him. He pictured the sick boy begging for death, and he couldn't help but groan. He wanted to cure his son, to end his pain. Suddenly, the key grew cold in his hands, and he opened his eyes. Staring incredulously at the staff in his hands, Jeremiah stood and lowered the key back into its vessel.

"So that's it?" he questioned and turned.

But, Abraham was gone.

The king hurried out of the palace and started to jog across drive toward the infirmary, but he didn't get far when Timmins Clarke, accompanied by half a dozen guards, confronted him.

"King Wells," Timmins called. "One of the guards in the security vault tripped the distress alarm. What's going on?"

"Nothing, Timmins. All is well," Jeremiah told him.

"Well, sire, if you don't mind, I'd like to see that for myself. Smith, Williams, go and check it out," Timmins ordered, and two young guards entered the palace.

"Well, if you'll all excuse me, I was heading to the

hospital to visit my son," Jeremiah declared, stepping around them, but Timmins moved into his path.

"Sire, if you'll just wait a moment, my men should be back momentarily and we'll escort you over," he replied stiffly.

"That's not necessary, I really need..."

"Sire, please stay where you are," Timmins warned.

Jeremiah's temper flared. "Timmins, if you don't remove yourself from my path, you'll be written up for insubordination!" he growled.

"Lieutenant! Lieutenant!" The two guards had returned. "The men in the vault were attacked! They... say the k...king did it!"

"Seize him!" Timmins yelled, pointing at Jeremiah, but they didn't get the chance. Jeremiah twisted away and pelted several electro forces at the men. One force hit the lieutenant with such intensity that it sent him airborne for several yards. This gave Jeremiah enough time to escape. He sprinted toward the hospital with four guards lagging behind him.

When he arrived at the hospital, Xavier's room was buzzing with activity, and a high-pitched tone from the EKG sent Jeremiah's heart to the floor. He was too late. His son was dead!

"Clear!" a healer yelled as he used an electro force in attempts to revive the motionless boy. It didn't work.

"Get out," Jeremiah growled.

The healers turned, stunned. "But, sire..."

"I SAID, GET OUT! GET OUT! GET OUT!" Jeremiah roared with an electro force spinning menacingly in his palm. The healers bolted from the room, and Jeremiah locked the door behind them.

The squeal from the EKG sliced into him as he looked down at Xavier's lifeless body. With a sob, Jeremiah fell to his knees next to the bed and buried his face in the boy's chest.

"No," he muttered feebly. "No, Xavier. You can't die on me. I can't lose you too!" Jeremiah lifted his head and looked at the soft, babyish face. "I won't let you take the easy way out! I won't!" he growled with determination, tearing the hospital gown away from the small body and placing his hands on his son's chest. The force grew inside him like a soothing, warm breeze, and slowly, the boy's entire body began to glow in a brilliant golden light. When the light finally faded, Jeremiah opened his eyes and looked down at his son. He still wasn't breathing and his lips were a horrific shade of blue.

"Come on, son, breathe. Breathe! I know you can hear me. Now, breathe!" he growled as he sent an electro force surging through the boy's body. The child's body fluttered like a rag doll from the electric shock, but he still wasn't breathing.

"Breath, damn it!" he yelled, sending another electrical shock through Xavier, but still he didn't stir.

Sobbing, he prayed, "Please, Julia! Help me out here. Help me, my love. Please, send him back to me." Jeremiah stood and sent a more powerful electrical force through his small body.

Finally, with a small groan, Xavier took a raspy breath and coughed. "Dad?" he muttered and began bawling.

"Oh, thank God! I'm here!" Jeremiah gasped, pulling the boy into his arms. "Sweet Jesus, I thought I had lost you."

"Dad, I saw Mom." Xavier cried into his shoulder. "She looked beautiful, like she did on the beach when I was a baby." He began crying harder. "I wanted to stay with her, but she wouldn't let me. She said...she said that my place was with you...that you needed me more."

Father and son held each other as if their lives depended on it until the insistent pounding at the door demanded their attention. Jeremiah slowly lowered the boy back into the bed and tucked the covers around him. He gave Xavier a doleful look and smiled. "I guess I'd better let the healers back in to check you out."

"Why are they locked out?"

Jeremiah didn't answer as he opened the door. Several guardsmen flew into the room, knocking the king across the room, tackling him, and pinning him to the floor.

"This is not necessary!" Ephraim shouted, crowding into the room. "Get off him! He's still your king, for God's sake!"

"What's going on? Stop it!" Xavier yelled, feebly raising his hand and trying to muster up an electro force. But he couldn't. Spencer was at his side in an instant.

"No, Xavier," he whispered, grabbing the boy's hands and gently lowering them. "It's okay. Ephraim and Loren will deal with it."

"Back off!" Loren shouted, throwing one of the men off Jeremiah.

"Get off him now, or I'll have all four of you on charges of unnecessary force!" Ephraim bellowed.

The men finally stood, and Loren helped Jeremiah to his feet.

"The king just assaulted me and six of my men, General. He must be taken into custody! If you don't do it, I'll file obstruction of justice charges on you!" Timmins Clarke challenged, clutching his profusely deranged arm.

"How dare you! This is treason!" Loren yelled at him. "He's your king. His son was at death's door! You can't just arrest him like a common thug!"

There was a sudden uproar as the group of men began yelling and shoving one another. Spencer held Xavier protectively, watching the exchange.

"Silence!" Jeremiah yelled, stilling the men. "Ephraim, Loren, Timmins is right. I've committed a crime. You need to take me into custody, Ephraim."

Ephraim shook his head unwillingly.

"It's okay, mate. Do it."

With a sigh of trepidation, Ephraim approached his king. Then after a reassuring nod from Jeremiah, he recited shakily, "King Wells, you have the right to remain silent, you have the right to representation, you have the right to face and answer the charges made against you in a court of law. Do you understand your rights?"

"Yes," Jeremiah answered.

"Dad? What's going on?" Xavier asked hoarsely, tears still fresh on his face.

Jeremiah looked at him and smiled. "It's okay, son. Everything's going to be okay." He looked back at the two generals. "I need someone to look after my boy."

"Don't worry about it, Jer. I'll watch out for him. Sir Blaire can cover my duties at the academy," Spencer announced, surprising everyone. "Look, Jer, you need Loren and Ephraim to investigate the culprit behind these illnesses. You know they're of better use to you in ways other than looking after Xavier. Please, let me do this."

Jeremiah stared at his brother as if seeing him for the first time and nodded. "Thanks, Mike," he replied quietly. "I should have known I could trust you to help when I needed it."

"You can always trust me, brother," he whispered.

Chapter 19

Arrested

King Wells was taken into custody and placed in a holding cell on the judicial floor of the Governing Hall where he would remain until his trial. He was charged with the illegal use of the King's Key and the unprovoked use of force on subordinates.

Xavier was released from the hospital the next day into Michael Spencer's guardianship. He was extremely weak and was unable to walk or even stand. The seizures had put an unbelievable amount of stress on his body. It shattered nearly every bone and shredded many of his major muscle groups. His bones and muscles were still in the process of fusing back together.

"You may take him home, Michael. Physical therapists will be by sometime next week. Hopefully, the king will be home then," the supervising healer said.

"Yes, I have every confidence that he will be. So, is there anything I should make sure he does until the therapists come?" he asked.

"No, he needs to remain in bed for the next couple days until the rejuvenation power completes its cycle. He'll be quite lethargic during this process, and that's to be expected," the healer told him.

Mike nodded. "Ok. I'll see to it he gets the rest he

needs. Thank you, Healer Dorne."

Spencer took Xavier home and settled him in bed with a night table full of snacks, comic books, and a hand-held Game Boy.

"Have you got everything you need?" he asked.

Xavier nodded solemnly before whispering, "I want to see my dad."

"I know you do. Maybe in a few days when you're stronger, okay?" he reassured him softly, stroking the boy's hair. "But for now, you need to get some rest so that your body can replenish itself."

Xavier nodded as tears filled his eyes and rolled down his cheeks.

"Xavier," Spencer whispered, patting his leg. "Everything's going to be okay. I promise. Your dad will be home soon."

Again, the boy nodded, wiping the tears from his face.

Over the next few days, his uncle spent a lot of time in his room talking and playing with the boy to keep his mind from fretting over his father's fate. Finally, to Spencer's relief, reinforcements arrived a couple of days after Xavier's return home.

"Oi! All right there, mate?" Court questioned loudly, barging into Xavier's room followed by Erica and a very calm Robbie.

"Court! Robbie! Erica! God, it's good to see you guys. I've been bored out of mind!" He exhaled with relief. "How are the guys?"

"They're fine, X. They know it was just the fever talking; so it's all brilliant," Court replied, plopping onto the bed next to him.

"What are you talking about?" Xavier asked.

"What do you mean, what am I talking about? Xavier, you..."

"Court, Erica, Robbie, Could I speak to the three of you for a moment?" Spencer called from the doorway.

"Yes, sir," Court answered, still looking at his friend as if he were a stranger.

They followed Spencer out of the room and down to the end of the hall, where he turned to face them. "Court, Xavier doesn't remember a thing about that day at school. The fever wiped it from his memory."

"Blimey, he doesn't know?" Court blurted.

"No, he doesn't," he responded, looking at Robbie in particular. "And he shouldn't know, not just yet. Don't you think he has enough to deal with right now?"

This news came as an enormous relief to Robbie. It would be easier being there for Xavier without all the baggage of what had happened weighing down on her. So she put the events of that day behind her and laughed as Erica teased Court about getting caught after sneaking out in the middle of the night.

"It was embarrassing!" Court complained loudly! "Drew ratted me out, of course! So, Dad comes tearing into the woods and drags me home in front of everybody! I'm blubbering like a git trying to explain to Dad that we were just celebrating Xavier not dying. Of course, Beck was laughing his butt off at me! Now, I'm grounded for life!"

Erica rolled her eyes at his melodramatic response.

"No, really! Those were his exact words!" Court insisted, and he made a face as he tried to imitate his father's demeanor and tone, "Courtney Aaron, how thick can you get? With all that's going on, you sneak out to play with your mates? You are grounded for life, and if you even think of arguing with me, I'll beat your arse and then ground you into the afterlife as well!" Court shook his head as he continued, "The only reason I'm allowed to be here is because Dad thinks it would be good for Xavier, but then, it's back to solitary confinement. God! Drew is such a prat! I swear! I don't see how we're even related! But I have a plan to get even with him."

"Court, you'll only make things worse! You always do! Then Uncle Ephraim will do more than ground you and take your Game Boy away," Robbie warned.

"I'm not afraid of my dad," Court rebuked.

Erica coughed out laughing, and Robbie rolled her eyes.

"I'm not!" he insisted.

"Oh come on, Court! You are too! You were scared speechless when he threatened to smack you for sassing your mom," Robbie teased. "And what about the time he caught you stealing those flatulent pills at Patterson's Prank and Games Shop? You nearly wetted your pants!" Robbie giggled, falling back into the bed.

Court shrugged, blushing.

"What were you planning to do with the flatulent pills anyway?" Erica asked.

He grinned. "I was going to put them in Drew's orange juice at breakfast before school."

Erica erupted in laughter and joined Robbie, rolling on the bed in hysteria.

"What do they do?" Xavier asked.

He gave him a wide, rueful smile. "They give whoever takes them a bad case of gas."

Xavier laughed at his answer.

The children kept the young prince company most of the afternoon. Even though he was still very weak and couldn't sit up in bed without help, it didn't stop the children from enjoying themselves and just hanging out. Though their visit was uplifting and pleasant, it left Xavier exhausted as well, and not long after his friends left, he quickly collapsed into a deep sleep.

He slept for nearly three hours when something stirred him awake. His eyes snapped open. Slowly he skimmed the room, but it was empty. Still propped up in a seated position, Xavier picked up a comic book just as the door quietly opened. He looked up expecting Uncle Mike, but instead he stared straight into the disdainful, leering face of Catherine Stokes.

"What are *you* doing here? Get out!" he demanded, sounding stronger than he was.

"Your uncle let me in. I told him I'd keep an eye on you while he attended a meeting with Loren and Ephraim in the Hardcastle residence. Since I'm Daddy's girlfriend, he didn't even hesitate." She smiled mockingly down at him.

"I don't want you here! Get out!" he spat hoarsely.

"Now, now. No need to get upset. Why don't I help you take a bath," she cooed wickedly as she crossed his room toward the bathroom. "It will make you feel better and less irritable."

"You're not helping me with anything!" he blared, but Catherine wasn't listening. Xavier listened to her humming as she started the bath water before returning to the room.

"The bath will be ready in a couple of minutes, *deary*," she sang. Then with a wicked smile, she asked, "Why don't you undress and I'll help you to the tub?"

"Forget it! The only way you can help me is by dropping dead!" he shouted.

"Your Highness, come on now, it's just a bath. Don't be so rude!" she chastised. "Come on now, undress."

Xavier didn't move.

Catherine giggled like a little girl, an evil little girl. "Oh, dear! I forgot. After that little virus I set loose, you don't have the strength to swat a fly let alone undress yourself.

You poor baby," she taunted.

"What! Y...you did this? You infected all those kids? YOU killed Maggie!" he yelled.

She grinned heartlessly, "Yes, but it was you I needed to kill all along, Your Highness. *You* are the problem. So, how about that bath?" She scooped him from his bed and carried him to the bathroom.

"NO! Put me down. You won't get away with it! I'll tell!" he screamed, hitting at her feebly.

She chuckled. "Oh, but young prince, I will get away with it. You see, dead boys can't talk. I will tearfully tell your uncle how I had checked on you earlier and you said something about a bath," she teased lightly as she sat him on the commode. Then, she demonstrated her response to his death and cried theatrically, "Oh, Michael! I didn't think he'd try to bathe by himself in his weakened state. I feel so guilty for not keeping a closer eye on him. Boohoohoo!" Then she cackled.

Horridly, Xavier could do nothing as the witch tugged off his shirt.

"Stop! What are you doing?" he cried.

"What do you think, you silly boy? No one will believe you drowned taking a bath if you're fully clothed. Now, will they?" she asked impatiently.

With heat licking at his cheeks, Xavier could do nothing as Catherine removed his clothes, lifted him, and turned toward the full tub.

"Stop!" he bellowed. "Help! Help! Someone help!"

"Now, now, that's enough. There's no one that can hear you," Catherine chastised as she lowered him into the tub. "Destiny or not, your future is no more, *Your Highness*," she hissed. Without another word, she pushed him under the water.

She was right. He didn't even have the strength to

remain upright on his own let alone fight against her. Even so, he still fought, kicked, and struggled against her arms, but it was no use. The only thing he could see was her distorted sneering face through the water. Her refracted image made her appear even more evil and suddenly Xavier felt very afraid.

Sharp pains stabbed into his chest as his lungs begged for air. His vision was quickly going black, and just as he was about to pass out, Catherine's evil snarl disappeared and a pair of large hands lifted him. Coughing and spurting, he looked up into his father's eyes.

"Dad?" he choked.

"It's all right, Xavier. I've got you," Spencer's voice reassured.

Xavier realized it wasn't his father peering worriedly down at him; it was his uncle. Tired and fail, he began to sob.

Spencer hauled his limp body from the tub and grabbed a nearby towel. He wrapped him up and held him as Xavier fought to regain control of his emotions. Beyond them, Loren had Catherine pinned to the tiled floor as Ephraim tried to tie the bucking woman's hands behind her back. Catherine fought them like a feral animal: biting, clawing, hissing, and squirming.

"Ouch! Holy... She bit me! The witch bit me! Slap a muzzle on her, Ephraim!" Loren spat, glaring at the woman just as Ephraim finished binding her hands and feet.

Once the woman was secured, Spencer carried the prince past the commotion and laid him gently on his bed. He looked down at him with concern, stroked his hair, and dried his eyes. "Are you hurt anywhere?"

"N..n..no," he stuttered, finally regaining control over his emotions.

Just then, the door crashed open and several guardsmen thundered into the room.

"She's in the bathroom," Spencer told them, pointing.

"She told me that she was the one who set the virus loose, killing all those kids," he whispered to his uncle, not quite trusting his voice.

"What? She what?" he hissed, shocked. "She killed all those innocent children?"

Xavier felt the tears returning as he nodded.

"I'll be there in a few minutes to fill out the arresting papers," Loren called as the guards took Catherine out of the room and out of the palace.

"Are you all right there, laddy?" Ephraim asked, his voice quavering.

Nodding, he swallowed back the tears that fought to escape. "Y..yeah. Thanks."

"Don't thank me, thank Loren. He's the one who knew something was up. When Spencer told him Catherine was keeping an eye on you, he bolted out of my flat! He's the one who knocked that madwoman off you," Ephriam responded.

"I hope to God I broke a rib," Loren muttered. "She deserves at least that much!" He looked down at the prince. "Oh, man. I'm really sorry, kid. I'm sorry I didn't believe you when you said she wasn't right. You owe me a good payback beating."

Xavier's laughter drove away his tears. "Yeah, I can see *that* happening. Don't worry about it! It's okay, really! I kind of deserved what I got. I shouldn't have talked to you the way I did. It wasn't your fault." Xavier grinned sheepishly. "Believe me! I'll never make the mistake by saying 'that didn't hurt' ever again!"

Loren had to laugh at that. "Probably an excellent lesson to learn, Your Highness."

But, smiling playfully, Xavier added, "But you still don't hit as hard as Dad."

Loren glared down at him and then grinned. "I'll remember that the next time I wallop your butt." Xavier snickered as Loren winked down at him. "Well, if you'll excuse me, I'd like to help process and interrogate that...*witch*! Ephraim, can you pull guard duty while I'm gone?" Loren asked.

"Sure, mate," he replied, and the two turned to leave.

"Wait! What about my dad? Have you heard anything? Will they let me see him?" Xavier blurted.

"Xavier, you're in no shape to even get out of bed. How can you visit your father?" Ephraim asked.

"Well, what about his trial? Has it been set yet?" the boy pressed on.

Ephraim hesitated a moment and then answered quietly, "Yes. It's been set for Thursday." Loren and Ephraim left the room.

"Let's get some warm, dry clothes on you, boy," his uncle announced, crossing the room and searching through Xavier's drawers for pajamas.

"Uncle Mike?" Xavier whispered in a small voice. The title took Spencer by surprise and he paused. Xavier must have realized it for he added quickly, "Is it okay if I call you Uncle Mike? I've never had an uncle before, and...well, you are my uncle."

"Yes, Xavier. You can call me Uncle Mike," he answered with a smile.

Xavier grinned up at him.

"What was your question, boy?" he asked.

"What's going to happen to him, my dad I mean," he muttered.

"It's hard to say for sure, Xavier," he told him, helping him into clean underclothes and pajama bottoms.

"What's the worst that could happen?" he asked.

Spencer glanced up at the boy solemnly. "The worst? Well..." He paused to consider the question. "He could be dethroned and banished from the kingdom forever."

"Seriously? Who would rule the kingdom then?"

Mike gave him a knowing look before saying, "Who do you think, sire?"

"But I'm just a kid. Who'd want me as king?"

"The citizens of Warwood would."

"You don't think that will happen, do you?"

"No, of course not," he answered dismissively as he pulled the pajama top over the boy's head and pulled his arms through the sleeves. "There are circumstances here that wouldn't warrant such harsh consequences. But with the kingdom dividing like it is, it's hard to say for sure what will happen."

"It's all my fault!" Xavier began, his voice breaking as fresh tears dropped onto his face. "He wouldn't be in prison if he hadn't been trying to save me! Maybe he would have been better off if he had just let me die!"

"Don't think that!" Spencer hissed, grabbing him. "If you think that's true, then you must not know your dad very well. He eats, sleeps, and breathes you, boy! You're everything to him. If something were to happen to you, Jer would never recover from it. Do you understand me?"

Xavier sobbed harder and nodded. Spencer slid on the bed beside him, pulled him into his arms, and held him. "Don't worry, Xavier. Everything will work out; you'll see."

A few days later, Xavier was strong enough to visit his father with the aid of a wheelchair. Spencer and Xavier were led into a holding block with three small cells. Jeremiah was in the first cell. At first, Xavier almost didn't recognize him. His father's long hair had been cropped short and his face was cleanly shaven. He looked young, almost like a teenager. Jeremiah looked up as they entered and his eyes widened at the sight of Xavier.

"Son, what are you doing here?" he questioned, jumping to his feet and glaring at Spencer. "You shouldn't be out of bed!"

"I needed to see you, Dad!" he responded as the guard opened the cell door. He struggled out of the wheelchair and stumbled into the cell. Jeremiah scooped him into his arms and hugged him close.

"I miss you, Dad. Why can't you come home? Why won't they let you stay at the palace until the trial? I need you, Dad," he cried into his father's shoulder.

"I know, son. I wish I could be with you," Jeremiah murmured, holding him close for several minutes. Finally, he drew back and settled the boy on his knee. "Now, I want you to listen to me very carefully." He stroked the tears from Xavier's cheeks as he spoke. "It's not your fault I've been arrested. I mean it, son. It's not your fault I'm here. I knew before I did what I did that this would happen. It was my decision to make. So I don't ever want to hear from Mike that you're blaming yourself for any of this again. Understood?"

"Yes, sir," he mumbled.

"Good. Now, I know that I owe you...Lord, an apology just doesn't seem to be enough," he hissed, rubbing his bare jaw and chin. "I'm so sorry I didn't believe you or listen to you about Catherine. You were right about her. It really gets to me that I didn't see it and that I didn't trust you enough to believe you. God, son, I'm so very, very sorry. What can I do to make it up to you?"

"Get out of here as soon as you can," he responded.

His father smiled. "I don't deserve a son like you."

Xavier laughed, wiping the remnants of tears from his

cheeks. "I'll remind you of that the next time I get into a spot of trouble with that overbearing, annoying headmaster."

"Hey! I heard that!" Spencer called from the doorway, grinning. "He's definitely your boy, Jer. He's stubborn, arrogant, and has the same cheeky sense of humor."

The king chuckled and ruffled the long curls on top of Xavier's head. "Yep, he's definitely his father's son."

Once the smiles faded, Jeremiah's demeanor grew quite serious and solemn. "Xavier, you know that the trial is tomorrow."

Xavier nodded.

"Well, I don't want you there."

"What? No, Dad. Please, let me come!" he whined.

"Son, you will stay at the palace with Mike..."

"NO! I won't! You can't make me!" he yelled, close to tears.

"Mike can and I expect him to," his father responded.

"I'll sneak out! I...I..." He looked up at his father's set face and felt his own face crumple. "Please, Dad! I have to be there. I have to, please."

"Jer," Spencer interrupted quietly, "it may not be a bad idea for the boy to be seen there. It may remind the High Council of what you were fighting for; it may work out to your benefit for them to see Xavier in his weakened state."

Jeremiah considered the idea, staring thoughtfully at Xavier.

"Please, Dad! Let me come!" he begged with renewed hope.

After a moment, he nodded. "Okay." Then, he looked up at Spencer. "But, Mike, if there's any trouble, any at all, you're to get him out of there!"

"I give you my word that I will, Jer," he vowed.

Chapter 20

The Trial

The day of the trial, Xavier refused to allow Spencer to cart him into the courtroom in a wheelchair. He walked on his own. The sudden hush from the crowd drew the High Council's attention, and five pairs of eyes watched with apprehension as the prince struggled and staggered down the aisle of the packed room toward his father sitting in the front. King Wells followed the Council's gaze and jumped to his feet, nearly toppling his chair. Xavier was sweating and out of breath from the physical exertion it took just to make his legs work. Then, halfway up the aisle, he stumbled and fell to the floor. Without hesitation, Jeremiah jumped the small wall separating the galley from the witness area and ran to him.

"I've got him," he muttered to Michael who had reached down to help the boy.

"Dad," Xavier gasped as his father lifted him from the floor.

"Why aren't you in a wheelchair?" he asked.

"I didn't want to be rolled in here like some kind of weakling. I wanted to walk in," he muttered.

"Yeah, and I can see how well you've accomplished that," His father commented and smiled down at him.

"Well, I walked this far, didn't I?" Xavier remarked sheepishly.

He chuckled. "Yes, son. You sure did."

The king carried the boy the remaining distance and settled him on the bench directly behind the defendant's chair.

"Are you okay?" he asked, stroking Xavier's cheek with his forefinger.

"Yes, sir," he answered with a small grin.

With a nod to Mike, Jeremiah returned to the defendant's chair next to Dublin Minnows.

"Is Mr. Minnows defending Father?" Xavier asked Spencer quietly.

"Your father wouldn't trust anyone else to do it," he responded.

"Hear Ye! Hear Ye!" Father O'Brien called, silencing the crowded courtroom.

As O'Brien rattled on about proper courtroom etiquette, Xavier studied the members of the High Council and tried to determine who would most likely vote against his father. Governor Yaman would definitely be a problem, especially now that his niece had been arrested for attempt of murder. The governor didn't even attempt to mask his contempt and kept throwing troubled looks toward Xavier. Father O'Brien was presiding as chairman of the High Council and seemed to be thoroughly enjoying the power he held over the king. He was, without question, a problem. Governor Bracus seemed very solemn and business-like, but when he made eye contact and winked, Xavier knew he had an ally on the council. Definitely not a problem. The next council member was a pinch-faced, middle-aged man with rectangular glasses. He watched Father O'Brien studiously and seemed enamored by his every word. Xavier wished he had the strength to use his telepathy powers. Telepathy would make this process easier and definitely more accurate. The healers had told him he would eventually regain the use of his powers; just as in time, he would regain the use of his body, but that didn't help his current dilemma much. He frowned as he studied the man a moment longer. He obviously respected Father O'Brien greatly, and it was highly probable the priest could easily sway him. Okay, he was questionable.

Xavier moved on to the last member of the Council and felt his stomach drop to the floor when he saw Lana Applegate. That's right! Maggie had told him once that her mother was a member of the High Council. A surge of guilt and despair clawed at him. He had survived the same virus that had taken her daughter's life. Was she resentful? Did she blame his father for not finding the cure soon enough? Would she use it against him now? However, all Xavier's insecurities diminished the moment Lana Applegate looked at him; he knew he had another ally. So, the possible vote was two to two with one questionable member as a tiebreaker. Xavier didn't like the odds, and it didn't make him feel any less nervous.

O'Brien had finished his opening statement and swore in all the witnesses.

"The Council asks for King Wells to rise," he stated, and his father stood, looking proud and tall. "Sire Wells," he continued smugly, "you have been charged with the use of empowerments against a subordinate with the intent to kill or maim as well as the illegal use of the Clavis de Rex for your personal gain; therefore violating Codes 1B and 20 of the Codes of Warwood. How do you plea, sire?"

"Guilty, Mister Chairman. I knowingly broke the Codes in order to save my son's life," Jeremiah stated simply and sat back down.

"Mister Chairman, with the permission of the Council, I'd like to submit written testimony from the healers regarding King Wells' reasons for the use of the Clavis de Rex," Dublin announced, standing and holding out a file of papers.

"So be it," O'Brien stated indifferently, waving Dublin over to him.

It took the Council several minutes to sort through and read the remarks. At one point, Ms. Applegate gasped and clamped a hand over her mouth, stifling a cry. Governor Bracus shakily rubbed his jaw and peered up at Xavier, tears flooding the large eyes behind his glasses. Every council member seemed shaken by the healers' testimony; every member except Governor Yaman, who sat staring at Xavier with narrowed, cold eyes.

"Let the record show that the boy was indeed clinically dead when King Wells arrived at the hospital," O'Brien noted hoarsely.

The crowd in the gallery gasped at the declaration and several quiet, anxious conversations broke out around him.

"Silence in the gallery, please!" the priest ordered. "Defense, call your first witness."

Dublin stood. "The king calls Ephraim Hardcastle to the stand." As Ephraim approached the witness chair and sat down, Father O'Brien reminded him of his oath.

"Now, Mr. Hardcastle. Did King Wells, fully aware of the repercussions, knowingly and willingly disregard Code 20 and empower himself with additional powers?" O'Brien asked.

"Yes, Mr. Chairman, but..."

"Is it also true that he used his empowerments against his subordinates without due cause or provocation?" Father O'Brien interrupted.

"Yes, but there's more to it than that!"

"Thank you. That will be all!" O'Brien ordered, cutting Ephraim off.

"Now, wait a bloody minute!" Ephraim bellowed.

"You're out of order, Mr. Hardcastle. You've been dismissed. Please step away, quietly," O'Brien warned.

"Out of order! Out of order? I'm out of order for trying to give you all the bloody facts? This is barmy!" Ephraim shouted, his Yorkshire accent growing thick. Xavier usually found it humorous when Ephraim got so excited that his British accent became highly pronounced, but today he didn't find anything about this situation funny.

"Not another word, sir, or I will hold you in contempt of these proceedings!" O'Brien growled.

"Ephraim," Jeremiah spoke softly. "Let it go, friend. Just let it go."

Ephraim looked at him and opened his mouth to protest but then closed it, looking baffled and angry. He slowly stood to leave, but Ms. Applegate's next words stopped him.

"Mister Chairman, I would like to hear Mr. Hardcastle out. I would like to know all the facts in this case. After all, this isn't an ordinary man we're passing judgment on. Therefore, it is imperative we give leniency and allow the witnesses to elaborate on their testimonies."

Father O'Brien's face erupted in fury. "Are you saying, Madam Applegate, that Jeremiah should be given special privileges because he's king?"

"That should be King Wells to you, O'Brien! He's *your* king as well!" Loren shouted from Xavier's left.

The uproar from the gallery drowned out the priest's response. "Order! Order!" he tried to shout over the ruckus, but it was obvious he had lost control of the proceedings.

Finally, it was Jeremiah who ended it. He stood and faced the angry crowd. "Please," he called over their grievances and insults. "My friends, please settle down. Father O'Brien is right. I do not wish to be treated any differently than if it were one of you in my place. No one should be above the law, most of all, the king." The crowd grew silent almost instantly. "However," he continued, turning to face the High Council, "I believe all members of the High Council are permitted to question each witness." He glanced briefly at Lana Applegate and Simon Bracus.

Lana gave him a small smile as he sat back down. "You're quite right, Your Highness." She looked back to Father O'Brien's reddening face. "I choose to question this witness further, Mister Chairman."

Father O'Brien was caught, and he knew he would have to allow it. He grimaced at her and after a moment, gave her a curt nod.

With a grin, Ephraim sat back down in the witness chair.

"Mr. Hardcastle, were there any special circumstances surrounding King Wells' choice in committing these crimes?" she asked.

"Yes, ma'am. The prophet, Abraham Vincent, told him that the only way he could save his son was to obtain a more potent supplement to his existing rejuvenation powers. The healers' powers as well as his own were not powerful enough to cure such a violent virus," he told her.

"So he sought only to strengthen an empowerment he already possessed in order to save the prince's life?" she asked.

"Yes, ma'am." He grinned.

"Why wasn't this explained to the guards on duty in the vault that night?" the pinch-face man asked.

"There wasn't time, sir!" he exclaimed.

"So, instead, he just chose to use his empowerments on his trusting and loyal Guard," O'Brien spat.

"There wasn't time for anything else! The boy was already comatose, and King Wells barely made it in time to save him as it was!" he elaborated fiercely.

"Yes, I realize that from the healers' reports, but are you sure about that? Couldn't he have implored the guards to trust him and follow his command without question? Wouldn't this have been a better course of action and possibly even more time-efficient?" O'Brien questioned.

Xavier saw his father's shoulders slump, and he realized that Father O'Brien and the pinch-faced man had broached upon an issue futile to argue against. Ephraim realized it as well for he looked to Jeremiah for guidance, but receiving none he remained silent.

"Are there any further questions?" O'Brien asked confidently, and when there weren't any, Ephraim was excused from the witness stand.

The rest of the trial didn't go any better. Timmins Clarke gave a very angry and biased testimony that made Jeremiah appear to be some kind of warmonger. He obviously had some kind of vendetta against the king, and Xavier chalked him up with the list of people who couldn't be trusted.

Finally, after all the testimonies were heard, Father O'Brien looked down at Jeremiah in something just short of delight. "King Wells, is there anything you have to say on your behalf before we close all discussion and retire into an executive session?"

His father slowly stood, looking humble, which bothered Xavier for some reason. "Yes, Mister Chairman. I admit that with thoughts to recourse, I willingly and knowingly broke the Codes. My only defense is that my son was dying, and when I was presented with a means of saving him, I did what any father would have done; I proceeded with a vengeance. I accept, willingly, and without threat of retribution, any verdict and penalty the High Council decides to render." Jeremiah sat down and Dublin immediately began whispering in his ear.

For the next thirty minutes, the Council, red faced and short-tempered, discussed the facts and testimony as the gallery and Jeremiah looked on.

"Okay, Okay!" Yaman snapped. "There's no sense in rehashing through all of this again. Call for a vote, O'Brien."

Father O'Brien glared at Yaman, but finally he called for the vote. "All who find King Jeremiah Xavier Wells IV guilty of infracting Code 1B, the use of empowerments with undue cause against a subordinate by a person of political power, indicate by raising your right hand."

Xavier watched with trepidation as slowly all five hands rose. Jeremiah didn't even look up.

"Let the record show the High Council finds King Wells guilty by a vote of five to zero. Now, as for the next charge, all who find King Jeremiah Xavier Wells IV guilty of infracting Code 20, the unlawful use of the Clavis de Rex for personal gain, please indicate by raising your right hand."

Xavier wasn't surprised to see Governor Yaman's and Father O'Brien's hands go up first. The pinch-faced man looked apprehensively at Father O'Brien before looking at Xavier. Then he smiled, and Xavier no longer felt distrustful of him. The man turned back to O'Brien and shook his head ever so slightly. O'Brien didn't look happy.

"L...Let the record show the High Council finds King Wells n...not guilty with a vote of three to two." The gallery erupted in cheers and yells.

"Order! Order!" O'Brien boomed above the crowd. Slowly, the people grew quiet again. "May I remind the gallery that this is an executive session and comments from the crowd are forbidden? If you cannot contain yourselves, I will clear this courtroom! Now," O'Brien began, returning his attention back to the Council. "Marcus, according to the statute, what possible sentences can be enforced here?"

The pinch-faced man opened a large maroon, leather-bound book in front of him. After a moment of regarding the book in silence, he looked back to the Council. "According to the judicial guides, we have several choices of recourse in this situation: suspension of duties up to a year, banishment, royal caning, imprisonment from a month to ten years, house arrest up to a year, and/or probation," Marcus stated.

Xavier felt the blood drain from his face and leaned toward Spencer. "He still might have to go to jail?" he squeaked.

Spencer patted his hand reassuringly. "I don't think it will come to that. Those are just all the possible choices of punishment for his crime. Your father didn't severely or permanently injure anyone. So I'm sure he'll get a lesser penalty."

"I think we can immediately rule out imprisonment and banishment," Governor Bracus declared. "No one was permanently harmed."

"I agree," Lana Applegate replied.

"I move that we rule out imprisonment and banishment as possible recourses," Governor Bracus announced formally.

"I second that motion," Lana blurted.

"Okay, any discussion?" O'Brien stated, and there wasn't any. "All right then, all in favor of the motion on the floor signify by raising your right hand." The vote was nearly unanimous. Everyone but Governor Yaman raised their hands in agreement. "Let the record show the motion passed four to one."

"I move that the sentence for King Wells for the said crime be a royal caning," Governor Yaman called out.

Instantly there was another loud outburst from the crowd, and Xavier looked around puzzled.

"Order! Order!" O'Brien shouted. "Guards, clear the courtroom! No one is to remain unless they are somehow directly connected to this case."

The guards swept the crowd from the courtroom, leaving only a dozen or so people.

"Now," O'Brien continued, "we have a motion on the floor. Do we have a second?" There was no response. "Okay, I'll second the motion. Is there any discussion?"

"It's preposterous!" Bracus called out. "A royal caning? Isn't that a bit barbaric?"

"Would you rather call for a suspension from duties? I don't think the kingdom could tolerate Sire Wells away from his duties at a time such as this! And you can't possibly expect him to get off with just probation?" Yaman barked.

"Yes, I had expected probation!" Bracus bellowed, standing. "Jeremiah Wells has always been and still is a superb king, who simply made an error in judgment while attempting to save his son's life! Tell me, which of us might not have made the same mistake if we had been in his shoes!"

"He still used his powers against his subordinates, Bracus!" Yaman yelled back.

"Gentlemen," Father O'Brien interrupted, "a shouting match will not solve a difference of opinions. Let's call for the vote. All in favor of the motion signify by raising your right hand."

Yaman's hand shot up, of course. O'Brien raised his hand as well, staring at Jeremiah with vindication. Both Applegate and Bracus sat back in their seats with their arms folded across their chests and muttered, "Nay."

So, it all came down to the pinch-faced man, Marcus. He seemed to be wavering from Xavier's good guy list. He looked at the ugly red scar on Timmins' arm and then to Henrick, whose leg had been fractured in several places during the altercation and still wore a brace while the bones finished the healing process. Slowly, Marcus' hand joined Yaman's and O'Brien's.

"Oh, Jesus," Spencer muttered.

"What? What does it mean?" Xavier hissed, but Spencer didn't answer.

"The motion passes three to two. King Wells, please rise," the priest ordered, and Jeremiah stood with his shoulders straight and proud. "You have been charged and convicted of a Code 1B infraction and are hereby sentenced to a royal caning to be administered two weeks from this day at noon in the Center Square. Until then, you are released under your own recognizance. This hearing is adjourned."

Jeremiah turned and shook Dublin's hand. "We'll appeal, Jer," Dublin said quietly.

"No. I said I'd accept their ruling and I will," he told Dublin.

"But, Jer, a royal caning?" he hissed.

Jeremiah gave him a feeble smile. "Well, at least my critics can't say I got off lightly, can they? Now, if you don't mind, I'd like to take my boy home and spend some much-needed quality time with him." He didn't give Dublin another chance to argue as he turned and went to Xavier. "Come on, boy. Let's go home." He grinned, lifting him into his arms and carrying him home.

Chapter 21

Fallen

The afternoon following the trial, physical therapists came to the palace to begin Xavier's therapy.

"Now, sire, we'll come every afternoon to work with the boy, but his recovery will be more successful if you'll help him with these exercises each morning and once again in the evening," the male therapist told him, handing him a pamphlet.

"Not a problem. I'll see to it that he does the extra sessions," Jeremiah responded as he flipped through the booklet.

"Good. Now, let me show you how the exercises are to be done," the therapist continued, leading the king over to where his female partner had already begun working with Xavier on leg stretches.

"Now, it's very important that he stretches before he engages in any physical therapy exercise. Jane is doing that now."

He watched and listened as the therapists demonstrated and explained each exercise thoroughly. The boy wasn't able to do more than four or five repetitions of each exercise, and when the therapists left an hour later, Xavier fell back into his bed exhausted.

"Rest up. We'll go through the routine again this

evening," Jeremiah told him as he strode toward the door.

"What? You've got to be kidding!" he blurted at his father's retreating back.

He turned and smiled. "No, I'm not. You will do the extra sessions religiously and without fail, son."

It wasn't long before Xavier discovered just how devoted his father was to overseeing the additional therapy sessions. In fact, he was quite relentless and overbearing.

On one such morning, Jeremiah charged into Xavier's room full of energy and enthusiasm. "Okay, sleepy head. Wake up! It's time for your morning exercises!" he announced, sweeping the curtains aside and flooding the room with light.

Xavier sat up blinking viciously at the sudden brightness. "Now?" he grumbled.

"Yes, son, now," his father answered as he crossed the room and pulled away the covers. Xavier groaned a protest. "Now, we'll have none of that, boy. You'll recover faster if you do your exercises as the therapists suggested."

Ten minutes later, the king was stretched out on the floor next to the prince coaching him through the grueling exercises. "Come on, son! Last leg lift!" he urged.

"I'm trying," he growled as he strained to lift his right leg. Shakily it rose a few inches before dropping back to the floor.

"Good! Now, five more!" he ordered.

"Stop it!" Xavier bellowed, bursting into tears from frustration. "Stop it, Dad! I can't do anymore. I can't! It's too hard."

"I know it's hard, son. It's not supposed to be easy, but you have to push yourself to do more each time so your legs will regain their strength. You want to play rugby this spring, don't you?" his father challenged.

"I'd settle for being able to walk without collapsing," he mumbled grumpily but continued with the leg lifts.

As much as Xavier resented his father's pushing, the extra therapy sessions paid off. In a week, he could go on short walks without stumbling and staggering. By the middle of the second week, although he tired easily and became dizzy if he exerted himself, he was able to maneuver up and down steps. As the therapy exercises continued, he grew stronger and stronger. Father and son were so focused on his recovery that it was easy to forget about the sentencing that would be administered the next day. However, by dinnertime, the pending punishment came into focus.

"Son, we need to discuss tomorrow," Jeremiah started, leaning back in his chair. He had hardly touched his food, Xavier noticed.

"Yeah," he whispered, losing his appetite.

"I'm not sure you should be there," he told him.

"What? Why? We're family! We should be there for each other no matter what, Dad. No matter what!" he countered.

"Son," Jeremiah hissed softly, looking away. "Do you understand what my punishment will be?"

"It doesn't matter! I want to be there for you. You'd do the same for me," he responded.

"Xavier, do you understand what a royal caning is?" he repeated stoutly.

"No."

His father's gaze dropped before he answered, "A royal caning is a public whipping."

His eyes widened, and he asked quietly, "They'll hit you?"

"Yes, son. But it's more than that. It can be quite brutal; it will be difficult to watch. Are you sure? Are you sure you still want to go? I won't forbid you, but you've got to understand it won't be a pleasant sight."

No, Xavier wasn't sure, but he nodded all the same. "Positive, Father."

The next day, Loren and Ephraim entered the residence wearing the Royal Guard dress uniforms. Both men looked at their king with strained, somber expressions.

"Sire? You need to change," Ephraim noted softly, handing him a white linen robe.

Without a word, Jeremiah stood and took the garment from his general.

"Jer..." Loren began.

"No, Loren," Jeremiah interrupted simply. "I know what you and Ephraim are planning, and I forbid you to go through with it. There can't be any favoritism. The High Council will be watching for it, especially from the two of you."

"But, Jer," Ephraim started.

"General Hardcastle, that's an order! The Council will replace you, and I want... no, I need my friends there. I can bear anything so long as it's you doing it!"

"What?" Xavier hissed. "You mean, they're the ones who will beat you?"

"Yes, son. The caning of a king is always administered by selected members of the Premier Royal Guard."

"But...but, you're Dad's friends! How could you? How could you be a part of all this?" he yelled, and the men tucked their heads.

"No, Xavier. Stop it," his father corrected him, grabbing his shoulders and turning him. "Look at me, son. It's their duty, and I wouldn't have it any other way. If it were you, would you rather have strangers punishing you or people who care about you, your friends?"

Xavier paused before answering miserably, "My friends."

Jeremiah gave him a weak smile. "That's how I feel, son, and I don't want you to be angry with Loren or Ephraim. They are only doing what I've ordered them to do."

Xavier nodded slowly, on the verge of bawling. "It's just like the dream, Dad. This is what my dream was trying to tell me, that this would happen."

Jeremiah knelt, pulling his son into his arms. "I know, son. But, I promise everything's going to be all right."

Xavier began to cry then. He was afraid, afraid for his dad, afraid to witness the brutality toward his father at the hands of his best friends, afraid to see his father anything but strong and right.

"You know," his father whispered as he stroked his back. "I'm still not sure this is a good idea. It's okay if you don't want to go. You could stay with Rebecca and the other children."

"No!" Xavier responded, wiping his eyes and looking at his father with conviction. "I will go with you, Father. I want to be there for you."

Jeremiah nodded, patted the boy's cheek, and stood. "Gentlemen, do we all understand what is to happen today?" he questioned.

"Yes, sire," the men responded.

The late winter air was barely above freezing, but the king showed no signs of being cold as he sauntered down the cobble streets toward the Center Square in the thin linen robe. When Xavier had questioned why they weren't taking the car, Loren had quietly explained that it was customary for a condemned king to walk to the Center

Square as part of his redemption.

The crowded sidewalks were strangely quiet, but an occasional shout of encouragement would propel from the crowd to offer support to the king. Then the positive air around them changed when a man from the back of the group shouted, "Neo-lover!"

The king and his generals came to an abrupt halt, whipping their heads in the direction of the insult. At least, Xavier guessed it to be an insult, and judging by Loren and Ephraim's expressions, his guess wasn't wrong. The crowd around them erupted into shouts and reprimands, and Ephraim moved aggressively toward the man, but Jeremiah stopped him.

"No, Ephraim. I need you with me today, not locked up in jail for assault," Jeremiah whispered. Fuming, the general nodded and simply glared at the man who had hurled the insult.

"What's a neo?" Xavier asked.

His father hesitated before answering. "Neo is slang for neophyte, a religious term that means beginner or novice. For many years, the empowered society called common, average humans neophytes. It's a universal view in our world that common humans are the beginnings of our race. However, a group of empowered citizens began to view all neophytes, or commons, as lesser beings. They believed that because of our abilities, we were meant to conquer and enslave them. So the word developed into the racial slur neo."

"Oh. Well, why would he call you..." Xavier began before he realized the truth in what the man had said. He winced. "Because of Mom, right?"

His father didn't answer, but he didn't need him to. His expression was answer enough, and suddenly Xavier shared Ephraim's desire to pound the man into the ground.

"Hop on, kiddo. Save your energy for the Square," Loren remarked, stooping to give Xavier a piggy-back ride.

Xavier clambered onto the general's back, and they continued the walk to the Center Square in silence. When they finally reached the market area, Xavier found that all the peddlers and merchants' stands had been removed, and a marble pedestal stood alone in the center of the tiled groundwork, just like in his dreams. Across the courtyard, on an elevated platform, the High Council sat watching their approach. The moment Jeremiah stopped next to the forsaken pedestal, the Royal Guard, standing at attention to their right, suddenly knelt. The people they had passed on their way to the Square began filling in behind them, and oddly, for a large group of close to six hundred, it was silent, not even a cough could be heard.

Xavier slid off Loren's back and moved to stand next to his father, glaring defiantly up at Father O'Brien's pudgy face. However, as O'Brien stood to begin the proceedings, an insistent, dark voice pounded into Xavier's thoughts. Instantly, his eyes drifted to Governor Yaman. A cold, sneering smile slithered across the governor's pale, round face, and he heard his greasy voice brag, *"Yes, boy! Watch! Watch the beginning of the end."*

Xavier reached for his father's hand, fearful of what was to come, and the king gave his hand a reassuring squeeze.

"Jeremiah Xavier Wells IV, king and rightful heir of Warwood, you have been charged and convicted of infringing Code 1B, the unlawful use of empowerments on subordinates with intent to do harm. For the said crime, you've been sentenced to a royal caning," Father O'Brien announced. Aside from a woman sobbing, the crowd remained silent as Father O'Brien regarded them. "As citizens of Warwood, it is your duty and obligation to bear witness to this punishment. However, if you have children in your presence, you are dismissed from these duties. Are you prepared to fulfill your duties?"

"We are," the crowd chanted together, sending a cold chill down Xavier's spine.

"The Royal Guard may rise," the priest ordered, and like a well-maintained machine, the guards did so in unison. "Premier Guardsmen, please step forward and face the High Council." Three dozen men moved to stand before the Council. "It is your duty to administer this punishment. If for any reason you feel incapable of meeting this obligation, please speak now so a replacement can be selected." No one responded. So, eying Loren and Ephraim closely, O'Brien continued, "If the Council finds there is any tendency toward leniency, the guard member doing so will be replaced. Now, General Jefferson, General Hardcastle, please prepare the king and select the caners."

Immediately, Ephraim stepped forward and selected two guardsmen while Loren turned to the king. Without a word, Jeremiah humbly knelt in front of Loren, and from the look on the general's face, it was the first time the king had ever done so. Daunted by this, Loren slowly removed the linen robe from the king's shoulders. Then Jeremiah stood, the muscles in his bare chest and legs contracting against the frigid February air.

"Dad?" Xavier whispered.

The king looked down at him and smiled. "It's all right, son. It's time. You need to go with Dublin," he announced, motioning to Dublin Minnows, who was waiting among the crowd of citizens.

"No. I want to stay with you, Father!" he cried as

plump tears rolled down his cheeks.

"Xavier," his father began softly while stroking his head. "You can't stay with me. You need to go with Mr. Minnows." He turned to Dublin. "If this gets to be too much for him, I want you to take him back to the palace."

"Yes, sire," Dublin responded hoarsely.

Xavier felt a pair of warm, gentle hands on his shoulders, turning him and leading him to where Mrs. Minnows and Lucy Jefferson stood on the fringe of the watching crowd.

From his new vantage point, he watched as his father knelt next to the pedestal to pray. His stomach twisted into a knot as he watched Loren, Ephraim, and the two selected guards pull long whips from a wooden sheath. Finally, his father completed his prayer with the sign of the cross and stood.

"How many?" Xavier squeaked to Dublin Minnows.

Dublin frowned down at him. "How many what, sire?"

"How many times do they," he cleared his throat and peered up at him, "hit him?"

"You mean you don't know? Your father didn't tell you?" he asked, horrified.

"Tell me what?" he questioned, his voice raising an octave.

Mr. Minnows shared fretful looks with his wife and Mrs. Jefferson before crouching in front of the boy and taking his hand. "Xavier, the caners will strike your father until he can no longer stand."

"What?" Xavier hissed. "No! No, they can't! They can't do that! I won't let them!" Xavier tore out of Dublin's grasp and raced to his father and the men circling him. "NO!" he shouted, plowing into Ephraim and sending him stumbling backwards. "You can't do this, Ephraim! You can't!"

"Xavier," Jeremiah called, reaching for him, but Xavier turned and attacked Loren, pelting him vainly with his fists.

"No, please don't. Don't hurt him, Loren. Please!" he sobbed, tears streaming down his cheeks. "You're his friend. You're his friend!" Loren looked down at the boy hurling punches at him and felt his resolve melting away.

"No, Xavier!" his father called firmly as he lifted the boy away from Loren. Xavier clung to him, crying. The crowd was no longer silent. Many were shouting and echoing Xavier's words and some were simply crying along with the prince. "Xavier?" Jeremiah whispered. He looked at Dublin, silently questioning him. As the reality of what had happened sunk in, he sighed and caressed his son's back. "Son? Go with Dub. Go on."

"Nooooo," Xavier sobbed.

"Yes, boy. Go with Dublin," he insisted, kissing Xavier's forehead as he handed him over to Mr. Minnows. "Take him back to the palace," he whispered to Dublin.

"NO!" Xavier shrieked. "No, I want to stay with you! Please! I promise, I won't interfere again, just...just...let me stay," he wailed.

His father hesitated but then, muttered, "All right, son. All right." He nodded to Dublin, who carried the boy back to the side of the Square. Tamarah and Lucy engulfed Xavier into their arms trying to soothe him.

Jeremiah turned to Loren and Ephraim. Loren looked as if a good stiff wind would knock him over. "Loren!" he barked. "You have your orders! Both of you!" He gave each general a harsh glare. "Do not disobey me, or there'll be hell to pay!"

The men nodded as conviction returned to their eyes, and Jeremiah turned, grasped the pedestal, and readied himself as the Royal Guard assembled behind him. He looked at his son clinging to Lucy and gave him a playful wink.

"You may proceed," Father O'Brien called, and Xavier's stomach dropped like a crashing wave.

Loren struck the king first. He lifted the whip, stepped forward, and lashed it across the king's back with a loud crack. Jeremiah grimaced and wobbled slightly. Then, Ephraim's whip struck him, leaving a savage red mark snaking across his back. Jeremiah winced and his face contorted with pain. Again and again, the caners pelted him with blow after blow, as he clung white-knuckled to the pedestal with his eyes clamped shut. Slowly, the ugly welts on Jeremiah's legs and back began to be replaced with open wounds. It was at this point that Xavier stopped watching and simply buried his face in Lucy's shirt, sobbing loudly.

Nearly twenty minutes later, two replacement caners were chosen: Henrick Davies and Timmins Clarke. Loren and Ephraim, however, refused to relinquish their positions and chose to continue. After a brief intermission for the reappointments to select a whip, the beatings continued for another twenty horrible minutes until the king finally fell to the ground. Xavier wasn't sure which was more difficult to watch: the beating or his father's fall. The guards backed away and watched as the king dragged himself to his feet.

"Why doesn't he just stay down?" Xavier sobbed to Dublin.

"He can't appear too weak. He must endure the beatings as long as possible without so much as a groan. As barbaric as it seems, this is a test for your father, a test to prove his strength and endurance," he responded hollowly.

The whippings resumed, and Jeremiah's back and legs

glistened in blood. He had endured nearly an hour of caning, and his entire body shook from the strain. Tears, sweat, and agony covered his face, but he remained on his feet and didn't utter a sound.

Loren continued to throw his entire weight into each blow, determined not to give the Council any cause to replace him. Both generals looked nearly as exhausted as the king, but they refused to relinquish their positions as caners.

Then, for a second time, Jeremiah fell to the ground, and the crowd gasp. His entire body shimmied with strain and exhaustion as he struggled to his feet, only to topple over again. Father O'Brien looked down at Jeremiah as if he were something vile and disgusting.

"You have fallen from God's grace, Jeremiah. You have tainted the throne. You have fallen from grace in your subjects. You should be ashamed. Your father would be..."

"Do not presume to tell me what my father would have thought of this entire situation, O'Brien!" Jeremiah bellowed with surprising force that Xavier wouldn't have thought possible. Slowly, with every ounce of his strength and with his arms quivering violently under the strain, he pulled himself to his feet and glowered up at the priest. "My father believed in the absolute power of the monarch. He would not have allowed this to happen to himself. If you think back, O'Brien, this addition to the Codes was my doing! I proposed and lobbied for this amendment to prevent the mistakes and dangers of the past from being repeated! Therefore, *Father*, you have no authority to preach to me on such matters. Now, Loren, Ephraim, continue!"

But, Ephraim and Loren shook their heads, their faces pale.

"Hardcastle, Jefferson!" he bellowed. "I just gave you an order!"

Loren approached him in a stumbling daze. Then, with a strangled groan, he raised his arm and struck Jeremiah, who fell heavily to the ground. Xavier fought vainly against the hands holding him.

"Stop! Stop it!" he sobbed. "Please!" he bellowed. "Father O'Brien, stop it. Please let them stop! Please!" But the only response he received to his pleads was a sadistic grin from Catherine Stokes.

Chapter 22

Invasion

Shock and fear rocked through Xavier at the sight of the murderous temptress, but when he looked again, Catherine was gone. The whistling sound of a whip snapped his attention back to the caning. The king collapsed completely to the stone covered ground with a groan. Xavier struggled against Dublin's embrace. "Please," he begged, "Father O'Brien! Let them stop!"

O'Brien ignored Xavier's pleas and continued to watch Jeremiah.

Finally, Xavier tore free from Dublin's grasp and raced to his father. Loren was drawing back and preparing to strike again, but Xavier stepped between them. "Loren," he begged. "Loren, please don't."

Loren's face fell with anguish, and he dropped the whip. Slowly, he sank to his knees and buried his face in his hands. Only Timmins Clarke remained standing with a whip ready in his hand.

"No more, Mr. Clarke. Please, no more," Xavier groaned.

"Boy! You are interfering with a court process! Remove yourself, now!" O'Brien bellowed, standing.

"That's not just a boy, O'Brien!" Dublin shouted angrily. "That is your future king, and you should address him as such, Wesley!"

The crowd around him shouted in agreement to Dublin's words and began chanting, "Release our king! Release our king! Release our king!"

With great effort, Jeremiah staggered to his feet and waved his hand at the irate crowd, and instantly, they went silent. Then, he turned to Xavier.

"Son?" he said hoarsely. "You promised me that you wouldn't interfere again." He looked up severely at Dublin. "Dublin, get him out of here and take him back to the castle."

"No, Dad! I'm sorry, but I can't stand by and let you kill yourself because of me! I can't!" Xavier cried.

"I'm afraid I'd have to agree with him, sire. So, I guess you'll have to bring me up on insubordination charges because I will not take him back to the palace. I'm going to help him stop this brutality."

"Dublin, so help me..." the king growled.

"That's exactly what I plan to do, my friend, help you," he countered as he walked past him and approached the High Council. "Father O'Brien, King Wells has endured over an hour of punishment. You know he will not stay down unless he is an inch from death. Are you willing to kill your king in the name of your precious court process? Is death a just and deserving punishment for the crimes he committed in order to save his son's life?"

The crowd exploded in shouts and grievances. Father O'Brien raised his hand, trying to silence them, but it took several minutes for him to succeed in doing so.

"If he's had enough, he should stay down!" O'Brien shouted, nodding at Timmins who readily swung his whip, striking Jeremiah. The king fell to the ground and for the first time, cried out. Nonetheless, he struggled to his feet as Timmins prepared to strike again.

"No!" Xavier yelled and tackled his father to the ground with a loud grunt. "No, Dad! Please, stay down," Xavier cried, using his weight and all his strength to keep Jeremiah down.

A whooshing sound was the only warning Xavier received before Timmins' whip snapped against his backside. Xavier screamed. Timmins wasted no time in swinging the whip again, but it never made contact. Ephraim clobbered Timmins to the ground.

"You son of a ..." Ephraim growled, wrapping his hands around the man's neck. "You hit the prince! You hit the prince!"

Violence ignited all around them, and the crowd rushed forward to attack anyone they felt had it in for their king. However, the well-trained Royal Guard acted quickly and managed to barricade most of the crowd out of the square with an electro shield.

"Xavier? Are you all right?" his father asked, sliding Xavier off him.

"Yeah. I think so. Are you?" he asked.

Jeremiah nodded and surveyed the chaos around them.

"Help me up, son. I need to stop this," he insisted flatly. Xavier struggled to help him to his feet.

"Please! My loyal friends please, that's enough!" However, the chaos continued. Ephraim held Timmins to the ground and was pulverizing the man into a bloody mess.

"I said, that is enough!" his father's voice boomed with unquestionable dominance that sent goose bumps over Xavier's body. Every person in the vicinity froze and looked at the king, who was hanging onto his son and the pedestal, trying to remain upright. After a couple deep breaths, he released Xavier and the pedestal and slowly straightened to stand tall and proud. "Enough," he repeated. "I appreciate what you're trying to do here..."

A deep rumbling sound like a distant storm stole the rest of the king's words, and he looked toward the kingdom's gatehouse. The sound quickly grew, and in the next instant, Xavier found himself being hurled to the ground as the earth shifted and shook violently under his feet. Even in his weakened, injured state, his father hauled Xavier under his body to protect him.

'Oh, God! It's an earthquake!' were Xavier's first thoughts.

Suddenly, a loud, teeth-rattling, ear-splitting boom shook everything around them. Screams filled the dead air following the explosion as the crowd scattered for shelter. When Xavier looked beyond his father's bulk, he couldn't believe what he saw. The front gatehouse was simply gone! Stone, boards, and dust were all that remained of the kingdom's first line of defense against an outright invasion. Then just as he began to wonder what had happened, he saw the answer. The image filling the vast void where the gatehouse once stood turned his blood to ice. Row upon row of soldiers dressed in black carrying gleaming swords were swarming into the kingdom, and just beyond the invading army, upon a white stallion, was none other than William LeMasters.

The Royal Guard reacted quickly to the intrusion and met the dark soldiers just inside the gate, but suddenly, the guards halted and lowered their swords. What was going on? Why weren't they attacking the intruders? Then Xavier saw why. The dark soldiers leading the invasion were primarily children. The Guard had hesitated because they hadn't wanted to harm children. Of course, LeMasters had counted on that, and in the next instant, the child-soldiers attacked the Royal Guard with a fury of electro forces.

"Jer!" Loren yelled. "We've got to get to the palace!" He grabbed the king by the arm, pulled him to his feet, and threw the linen robe over his shoulders. Ephraim hoisted Xavier into his arms, and they sprinted toward the palace with Dublin, Lucy, and Tamarah following close behind. Xavier watched over Ephraim's shoulder as another squad of the Royal Guard fought to keep the dark soldiers from coming further into the kingdom. They were succeeding until a small band of Warwood citizens attacked them from behind.

"What are they doing?" Xavier cried. "Ephraim, our own people are attacking the Royal Guard!"

The group stopped and turned just as the last of the guards loyal to the throne was wiped out in a sudden fury of electro forces from the traitorous citizens and dark soldiers alike. LeMasters' army stormed into the kingdom like a stampede of termites, destroying anything and anyone in their path.

"Dear God! It's a mutiny!" Ephraim gasped and turned to Jeremiah. "Sire, we need to sound the evacuation alarm, and you and Xavier must flee the kingdom immediately!"

But, the king didn't respond. He was fixated on the invasion and the slaughter of nearly half of his Royal Guard that had taken place in a matter of minutes.

"Jeremiah!" Ephraim snapped. "Order the alarm!"

The king was jolted into action and looked at Dublin. "Dub, can you sound the alarm?"

"Yes, sire," Dublin responded and turned to his wife. "See ya soon, my love," he whispered, kissing her before sprinting toward the pandemonium at the gates. As he ran, Dublin transfigured into a dog.

"Whoa! I didn't know Mr. Minnows was a

transfigurer!" Xavier exclaimed in awe.

"Jer, we've got to keep going. Dub will be okay. You and Xavier cannot be caught! You know what LeMasters will do to you if he catches you," Ephraim insisted.

"Yes, you're right. Let's get going."

As the group moved forward, Xavier continued to watch the battles behind them. Another unit of the Royal Guard and a few loyal citizens had joined the fight against the intruders and the traitors. Dublin the dog weaved his way, unnoticed, through the fighting men toward the bell tower next to where the gatehouse used to stand.

When the group finally reached the palace gates, an additional three-dozen Royal Guards were organizing and scrambling nervously to counter a defense.

"King Wells! We understand that there's been an invasion. We are nearly ready to join the others to defend Warwood, sire," a young guard remarked unsteadily.

"No, corporal, you will not join the others. The evacuation alarm will sound at any moment. Your orders are to secure the palace, find your families, and evacuate the kingdom. Follow the refugee protocol, and I shall see you all soon," Jeremiah ordered.

This message seemed cryptic to Xavier, and he wasn't sure he understood any of it. However, the guards seemed to understand it perfectly for they immediately sprang into action barricading the palace gates. Then, a high-pitched alarm blared from the bell tower.

When the group entered the palace, Rebecca Hardcastle and the rest of the children stood in the foyer, with bags in their hands.

"How did they know?" Xavier questioned as Ephraim slid him to the floor.

"How do you think?" he asked, nodding toward Jeremiah.

"Oh, yeah," he muttered stupidly.

Seconds later, Milton and Mrs. Sommers rushed out of the royal residence carrying two backpacks, a black duffle, and a first aid kit.

"Here you are, Your Highness," Mrs. Sommers called, handing Jeremiah a change of clothes. Milton dropped a backpack and the duffle next to him and instantly set to work on cleaning and dressing the wounds on his back and legs. Jeremiah hissed a string of curses as Milton hurriedly doused an antibiotic astringent over the lacerations on his backside before Loren closed the wounds with his rejuvenation abilities. Then, shielded by Milton and Loren, Jeremiah stripped the blood-soaked linen from his body and pulled on the clean dry clothes.

"Xavier?" Mrs. Sommers called softly, handing him his own backpack. "There's a change in clothes and some necessary items in your pack. We'll see you soon." She kissed him lightly on the cheek, and Xavier wrapped his arms around her.

"Be careful," Xavier mumbled into her shoulder.

Once Jeremiah was dressed, he regarded the group in front of him. "Let's get out of here. Milton, Emma, get yourselves and your families to safety and follow refugee protocol. We'll see you soon."

"Yes, sire," they responded and hurried from the palace.

"Jer, we should use Loren's passage. It leads directly to the woods. Then we can make our way from there to the Northern emergency escape route," Ephraim suggested.

Jeremiah nodded. "That sounds like the best route. Has anyone seen Mike? I can't seem to connect with him."

"No, sir. He wasn't at the administration of the sentence either," Loren added.

"He told me he couldn't watch, Jer. So as far as I know,

he stayed home," Ephraim told him.

Just then, an explosion rocked the palace, and the children screamed.

"Sire, there's no time! Mike will have to look after himself! We've got to get you and the prince out of here!" Ephraim yelled, pulling Jeremiah into the Jefferson residence.

"Xavier, follow your father," Loren called, nudging him through the door behind Ephraim and Jeremiah.

They followed Ephraim through the residence and into Loren and Lucy's bedroom. Loren shoved the bed to the side just as another rumbling blast shook the palace. With a sense of urgency, Loren pulled a large D-ring fastened to a hatch on the floor, revealing the ladder and passageway below. Jeremiah was the first to clamber down.

"Give Xavier to me," he called from below.

Loren grabbed Xavier abruptly and lowered him down into the dark opening. Xavier felt his father's hands grab him and lower him to the floor of the tunnel.

The rest of the group followed quickly behind them, and they made their way down the passage using small, controlled electro forces for light. They walked in silence for several minutes, hearing and feeling the earth above them grumble. Finally, they came to an opening covered by a thick, ivy curtain. Xavier was just about to exit the passageway with his father when a thought stopped him dead in his tracks. Oh, God! He had to go back to the palace!

"Wait," Xavier muttered as the ramification of what had to be done sunk into him. "Dad, I have to go back."

"What? There's no way you're going back there," Jeremiah ordered.

"I have to! I have to get the King's Key! I can't leave without it! The prophet told me this would happen! He told me there would be a mutiny and that I wasn't to leave the kingdom without the key!"

Jeremiah's face grew white, and he gasped. "Dear Lord! But, son, LeMasters' army has already seized the palace. There's no..."

Xavier didn't wait for his father to finish. He shoved his way through the group and raced back toward the palace.

"Xavier, no!" his father yelled after him.

The passage was pitch-black, and just as Xavier thought of conjuring a light, he stumbled and banged his head on the side of the passage. He sat for a moment gasping for breath and rubbing the dizziness from his head. Slowly, he stood and continued down the passage using a small electro force for light. When he reached the Jefferson's residence, he extinguished the force and looked up. A thin strip of light outlined the trapdoor above him. Carefully, he climbed the ladder and listened for signs of movement. Hearing only silence, he slowly opened the door and peered out into the bedroom. Suddenly, a pair of large hands yanked him roughly back down into the passage, and the trapdoor smacked back into place above his head. An electro force spun above his father's fiery face.

"What do you think you're doing?" he hissed. "Xavier, you can't go back in there!"

"Haven't you been listening, Dad? I have to! It's not just what Abraham Vincent said; I have this gut feeling that the key must be with us! It's like our lives depend on it!" Xavier whispered fiercely.

Jeremiah studied him a moment, at a loss for words.

"Please, Dad. I'm telling you it's important!"

"Okay, but let me go up instead. If I don't make it, maybe I can distract them long enough for you to..."

"No!" Xavier yelped. "No, Dad. We do this together!" Xavier finished firmly and climbed the ladder again. Slowly, he opened the trapdoor and found that the room was still empty. They quickly clambered up and out of the passage. Jeremiah, resigned to the task at hand, grabbed Xavier's arm, pulled the boy behind him, and took the lead.

"Follow me," he told him telepathically. They crept across the bedroom to the door and hesitated a moment before slipping through the Jefferson residence. After checking the foyer for enemy soldiers, Jeremiah stealthily crept toward the royal staircase and twisted the end post before motioning his son to the sliding door hidden underneath the staircase. Xavier moved quickly and slipped through the hidden door with his father close behind him.

"This way," Jeremiah ordered, leading him down a narrow staircase.

They approached a large, steel-enforced door; Xavier watched as Jeremiah placed his hand on the crystal panel next to it. The panel lit up, and the door moaned softly as it opened. They stepped inside a very bright room; when suddenly, his father grabbed him and pulled him roughly behind his body. Someone else was in the room, but Xavier couldn't believe his eyes! The man standing in the room smiling at them was his father!

Chapter 23

The Sacrifice

"I figured you'd eventually turn up here," the imposter stated his voice identical to his father's. "You know, sire, if you were this slow on the rugby pitch, even I would be able to run circles around you."

Xavier felt the tension leave his father as he released him and smiled.

"The only way I'd ever be that slow is if I were unconscious. Hello, Dub! I figured you would have caught up with everyone in the woods by now."

The man leaning casually against the pale wall laughed as he straightened and approached the king and prince. As he drew closer, the king's image melted away and left a grinning Dublin Minnows in its place.

"I intend to do just that after I help you get the key safely out of the palace. You're going to need it to make your stand against LeMasters," Dublin announced, looking at Xavier.

"Yeah, I know," he muttered.

"Yes, and we need to get the damn thing and get going Dub. LeMasters has already infiltrated the palace," the king remarked, as he stepped past Dublin, opened the large, golden door, and entered the vault.

"Holy cow!" Xavier gasped as he looked around the

small room. The long cherry altar that held the vessels for the King's Key and the Chronicles was exactly how he had dreamt of it three months ago. Only the small black capsule was absent, but of course, it had been used during his divination. The wall behind the altar was even more magnificent than a dream could ever do justice. It seemed brighter, more radiant; it appeared as though the wall itself emitted the light for the entire vault.

"What is it, son?" Jeremiah asked.

"This room, I've been here," he whispered, unable to take his eyes off the kingdom's emblem and the dancing light it cast around the room. It was mesmerizing.

The king cast his son a bewildered look. "You've been here? How could you?"

"I've been here in my dreams, Dad," he answered, turning and looking at his father's paling face. "It's exactly how I dreamt of it ... only better."

"That's not possible. It's sealed in lead. You couldn't have had a monition of it," Jeremiah muttered, staring at him.

"Yes, sire. It is possible," Dublin whispered.

Father and son spun to look at Dublin, who stood just inside the doorway staring down at Xavier with reverence. It was the same look Xavier had received from the group who attended his divination, everyone except Dublin, who had separated himself from the group and wept. Suddenly, it occurred to Xavier to ask why. Why had Dublin removed himself from the group? Why had he sat in the last pew of the church by himself and cried? Had he learned of a different destiny, a different truth?

"He's telling you the truth, Jer. There are truths here that have not yet been revealed. You are only just now beginning to see the extent of the powers the boy will possess as a man." He smiled at Xavier, but there was sadness in the way he smiled. "The key must be with the boy, always. It's not just the King's Key, Jer. It's *this* king's key," he finished, nodding at the boy.

Suddenly, a loud boom shook the room and vibrated through their very souls. Jeremiah and Dublin looked back into the other room.

"Dear God! They're trying to breach the outer entrance!" Jeremiah gasped. "We're trapped."

Xavier raced to the old derelict box, grabbed the key, and tucked it in his waistband. "Well, let's get out of here, then! Dad, teleport us to the woods."

"I can't, son. This vault, the entire palace for that matter, is lined in lead. It wouldn't be a very secure place if people could easily teleport in and out of it," he noted, sounding defeated.

Another loud explosion rocked the room, and Xavier fell to the floor.

"Xavier, we need to get you to safety," his father declared, pulling him to his feet. "So, I... I'm going to turn myself in as a diversion. Maybe it will distract William's men long enough to give you and Dublin time to escape..."

"NO!" Xavier screamed, wrapping himself around his father's body. "No, Father. You can't! They'll kill you! They'll kill you!"

"Better me than you, son," he told him as he peeled him from his body.

"No! You don't understand! If you die, I might as well too! The prophet told me! He said you would try this, and you would die!" he yelled, panic creeping into his voice.

The king looked down at the frantic boy. "Son, I don't want to die, but if it means that you would be safe, then I'd die eagerly, willingly."

"NO! NO YOU CAN'T!" Xavier screeched hysterically. "He said that my life would be full of darkness and pain if you sacrificed yourself. Don't you see? If you die, the kingdom, my kingship will die with you! I *need* you, Dad!" Xavier sobbed uncontrollably, clutching desperately to his father's waist.

"Son," Jeremiah began shakily, his resolve melting away.

"No! NOOO," Xavier wailed, tightening his hold on his father.

"Jer," Dublin called softly, holding out a tattered envelope to the king, who took it and looked bewilderedly at his friend. Tears fell onto Dublin's cheeks as he looked determinedly back at him. "Give that to Tamarah, and promise me something. Promise me you'll watch out for h...her and... my girls."

"Dub..."

"Promise me, damn it!" he barked, his tears running freely now.

"Okay I will, but, Dub, I can't let..."

"There's nothing you can do about this, Jer," he hissed, embracing his friend. "It's destined to be this way, just as it is destined that you be there to take care of your boy. It's been an honor serving you, King Wells."

Slowly, Xavier began shaking his head as he realized who would die in his father's place, and he wasn't sure he could endure such an enormous penance.

"Mr. Minnows, n...no," he groaned.

Dublin looked down at him with a sad smile. "Xavier, it has to be this way. This is my destiny; I foresaw it at the divination. But to be honest, I hadn't expected it to occur this soon." Dublin gave a dry, feeble laugh.

Xavier began sobbing. "It's my fault. All of this is my fault. If it hadn't been for me, Dad wouldn't have been caned, and you wouldn't be doing this!"

"No!" Dublin barked, shaking Xavier. "This is not your

fault! It's not! It's not your fault." He looked meaningfully up at his unsteady friend. "And, it's not your dad's fault. This is my choice. Do you understand me? It's my choice."

Sobbing beyond words, Xavier could only nod.

With a deep sigh, Dublin stood and embraced Jeremiah. "You are twice the king your father ever thought about becoming. Don't doubt your instincts. They've always been uncannily accurate. Teach him well, sire. He is the hope, the future. I love you, my friend," he whispered and then stepped back.

With one last look at his kings, Dublin's face hardened with determination. He turned and transfigured back into Jeremiah's image before racing from the vault. Father and son stood a moment, shell-shocked. Then, Jeremiah pulled his son into a bone-crushing hug.

"Xavier, we've got to get moving or...Dublin's sacrifice...will have been for nothing," he whispered, his voice breaking, overwhelmed with emotion.

Xavier wiped at the tears on his face and nodded.

The king led the way out of the vault to the slightly ajar, charred outer door. The smell of melting metal filled the foyer, but other than the thinning smoke, it was empty. Quickly, he pulled the boy across the empty space and into the Jefferson's residence. They no sooner made it through the door when a group of dark soldiers stormed into the foyer with Dublin, who was no longer in a transfigured state. Jeremiah pulled Xavier into the shadows of the doorway and peered back out into the foyer. He looked desperately around, trying to find some way to save his friend. But before Jeremiah could formulate a plan, the lead soldier grabbed Dublin roughly by the throat and drove him to his knees at the foot of the royal stairs. The soldier turned, and he saw Danson LeMasters' elated face.

"Master! Master, my brother! I have something for you!" he called up the royal stairs.

A moment later, William LeMasters appeared from the royal residence, and when his eyes settled on Dublin, a wide sneer unfurled across his face.

"Well, well, well. What do we have here? Isn't it Dublin Minnows, the prince's keeper? If I'm remembering correctly, you didn't do a very good job of it at those filthy commons' home."

Dublin didn't respond, but his shoulders dropped marginally.

"So, tell me, did Jeremiah punish you for your negligence in allowing me to take the boy? If it had been me, you would have been executed."

Slowly, Dublin's shoulders straightened. His head lifted proudly as he met William LeMasters' leering eyes with calmness, and he smiled. "Well, you see, Billy, that's the difference between you and Jeremiah. He is a great and honorable king, whereas you, you're...nothing but a second-class king wannabe!"

"SHUT UP!" LeMasters yelled, storming down the steps.

"Ouch," Dublin taunted. "Did I touch on a sore spot, *Billy*?"

"I said, shut up!" he spat. "I don't think you appreciate the dire situation you've gotten yourself into, Minnows." LeMasters glared down at Dublin's ever-widening smile. "What are you grinning at, you fool? Don't you realize what I have in store for you?"

"Yes, I know exactly what your plans are for me, Billy. But, I also know what is in store for you." He laughed.

"SHUT UP!" William bellowed, scraping his sword from its metal sheath as he fought for control over his raging anger. Finally, he was able to continue more calmly, "If you tell me where Jeremiah and the boy are, I may be inclined to spare your life."

"You must think that I'm an idiot! You and I both know I will die here." Dublin laughed harshly. "I will not betray my kings. The boy's life is worth more than mine, and someday he will have more power than you could ever fathom! He will bring you to your knees begging for mercy."

William LeMasters' face erupted in fury as he stomped further down the steps, lifting his sword. Xavier hid his face in his father's side and wished desperately he could block out the sounds.

He heard LeMasters' chilling growl, "So be it. Let it be a comfort to your wife and children that you died for your kings."

Then to his horror, Xavier heard as LeMasters' sword whispered through the air and sliced through Dublin with a soft, moist thud. The utter silence that followed screamed death. He knew without looking that Mr. Minnows had been beheaded.

His father clamped a hand over his mouth just as he began sobbing, but not quickly enough. William had heard, and his cold, savage eyes darted in their direction. Jeremiah scooped the boy into his arms and raced through the residence to the trapdoor. He threw open the door and dropped into the dark hole, not bothering to use the ladder. Then, with a flick of his hand, the hatch slammed shut, and the bed overhead squealed back into place, hiding the trapdoor from obvious view. Jeremiah didn't wait to see if they were being followed, for he was certain that they were, and he raced down the dark tunnel. He didn't use a light for fear it would make their escape more dangerous. He traveled a hundred or so yards when he heard a loud slam echoing down the passage. Voices and footsteps reverberated from behind them; undoubtedly LeMasters and his men had found the passage and had begun following them. Jeremiah shifted a sobbing Xavier more firmly in his arms and increased his pace. He only needed to get out of the passage and into the woods. Then, he would be able to teleport them to safety.

"Oh, Jeremy," William's echoing voice taunted. "Come on! You know there's no sense in running. I will catch you sooner or later." Then he laughed, cooing wickedly. "Aw, what is Prince Xavier so upset about? Is it Dublin? Dublin didn't suffer, boy. Beheading a man is usually quiet painless. Though, I think I might taxidermy his head and mount it above the hearth in my new flat."

Squirming in his father's arms, Xavier screamed, "I'll kill you! I'll kill you! I swear to God I will!"

LeMasters cackled contemptuously.

Jeremiah couldn't keep a hold of the wiggling boy any longer and dropped him. Xavier landed on his feet and sprinted back toward LeMasters and his men.

"Xavier! No!" Jeremiah yelled, racing after the boy. Then, just as Jeremiah grabbed him, Xavier conjured his first electro force since his illness, and it was extraordinarily potent. The blinding force erupted from his hands with a loud thump, propelling father and son backwards several feet as it punched down the tunnel toward LeMasters and his men. A fraction of a second later, an explosion nearly shook the passageway apart and a large section collapsed a few feet away from them, cutting off LeMasters and his men.

Choking on the dust and debris, Jeremiah lifted the sobbing boy into his arms. "Come on, son. Let's get going."

As soon as Jeremiah stepped from the passageway and out into the dappled sunlight, he teleported himself and

Xavier to the rendezvous point for the northern escape route. The rest of the group had obviously gone ahead for the vehicle was missing from the shed. Jeremiah lowered the boy to the ground and staggered to the shed, where he sat, burying his face in his hands.

Xavier walked to his father and put his arms around him, crying harder at the sight of his father's anguish. Jeremiah reached up, pulled him into his arms, and held him like a small tot. They allowed the grief to come then, holding onto one another for support.

Finally, Jeremiah took hold of his grief and took several long, deep cleansing breaths. Then, he turned his attention to the boy in his lap and brushed the tears from his grime-smeared cheeks before hugging him tightly and kissing his forehead.

"Son? I'm going to teleport us to the evacuation airfield. Everyone is there waiting for us. So, as soon as you're ready, we'll go," he told him softly, and Xavier nodded.

After a moment, Xavier was able to contain his weeping. With a painful tightness in his throat and chest, he looked up at his father and croaked, "I'm ready."

"Okay then, let's go," he whispered hoarsely, tightening his hold on the boy. Then, he stood and teleported them to bare field. A small, private jet waited to their right, and Loren hopped down the steps to greet them.

"Thank God! We were starting to worry," he gasped, searching the empty field behind them. "Got any idea where Dub is? Tamarah is getting worried."

Jeremiah didn't answer as he lowered Xavier to the ground. "Son, give the key to Loren."

He obediently pulled the key out of his belt loop and handed it to Loren. Feeling very close to tears again, he blindly followed his father up the steps and into the aircraft. When they entered the cabin, the Jeffersons, the Hardcastles, and Tamarah and her daughters all gasped in relief.

"Good grief!" Tamarah sighed. "You boys had us worried to death." She looked beyond the king and prince to the empty space behind them just as Loren entered the cabin. "Where's Dubby? Didn't he come with you?" she asked, her smile still lingering on her lips.

With a heavy sigh, Jeremiah moved to her and grasped her shoulders. "Tamarah, Dub... didn't... make it," he muttered softly, his voice breaking.

Tamarah Minnows began shaking her head long before the king got the words out. "No," she whispered. "Oh, no, no! Jer! God, no!" The tormented, strangled cry that erupted from Mrs. Minnows made Xavier shudder. Jeremiah pulled her into his arms as she wailed uncontrollably. Rebecca Hardcastle comforted Brit, who was crying nearly as hard as her mother.

Whereas, Robbie simply sank to the floor and muttered, "No, no, no, no, no."

Xavier felt helpless. He didn't know what to do. He knew from first-hand experience that nothing anyone said would make Robbie, her sister, or her mom feel better.

"Jer," Ephraim whispered. "We've got to get going before we're discovered."

Jeremiah nodded and pulled Tamarah into a seat next to him, buckled her seatbelt, and looked at his son. "Xavier, get Robbie into a seat."

Nodding, he approached the despondent girl. "Robbie," he whispered. "Come sit with me."

Robbie stood and followed him without a word, without a sound. They settled into a pair of seats across from his father. Jeremiah continued to hold Mrs. Minnows, muttering, "I'm sorry, Tamarah. I'm so sorry.

Everything's going to be okay. I promise."

Xavier turned to Robbie. She had her head turned away from him, apparently watching out the window as the plane began taxiing to the end of the field to prepare for takeoff.

"Robbie?" he whispered.

She didn't respond or turn. Xavier reached for her hand and found she was trembling. "Robbie? Look at me," he called softly. When she did, he felt his stomach drop at the sight of her swollen, red eyes, and tear-soaked face.

"Xavier," she gasped and leaned into him, crying. Awkwardly, Xavier held her and patted her back as she sobbed against his shoulder.

Chapter 24

The Gathering

The flight to wherever they were going was long, and almost everyone fell asleep, except Xavier. He couldn't sleep, despite his raw, heavy eyes. Every time his eyes fell, he would hear Dublin's voice vowing never to betray his kings, and he would jolt awake again. Robbie slept fitfully against his shoulder, and his arm screamed in protest from the weight of her head. He desperately wanted to shift into a new position but feared waking her. So he wiggled in his seat trying to fight the tingling sensation prickling up and down his arm. Then, he glanced at his father and found him watching him. Xavier gave him a feeble smile, which his father returned.

It was nearly dark when the plane finally landed in an empty field surrounded by forests and mountains. Jeremiah relinquished Tamarah to her sister as he and the men removed the baggage and set up camp under a nearby canopy of trees. By the time the campsite was erected, it was dark, and Xavier didn't get much more than a glimpse of the landscape. As the men ushered them to the campsite, the plane took flight again.

"Dad? Where's the pilot going?" Xavier questioned.

"He's flying to Coasta to inform their king of our predicament. We're going to need their help in regaining our kingdom," he explained, turning to face the group. "Tomorrow, we will teleport to Mirror Lake and join up with other survivors and loyalists. For the next several days, we'll be roughing it, and you'll need to get as much rest as you can. It's going to be a tough week."

Everyone nodded and set about preparing for bed.

"Son, we'll be sharing a tent with Mrs. Minnows and her daughters. I want you ready for bed in ten minutes," he told him.

"Yes, sir," he answered, heading toward the woods to pee.

Although the tent was a bit crowded, the group remained comfortable and warm. The children cuddled around the adults like puppies. Tamarah continued to cry into the night, and it was nearly midnight when Jeremiah was finally able to lull her to sleep. Xavier lay next to his father, listening to the even breathing of the people around him and wishing he could sleep, but every time he closed his eyes, he heard the sickening thud of Dublin's decapitated head falling to the floor in the palace's antechamber. He shuddered and snuggled closer to his father's side, fighting off the chill sweeping through him. His father's warmth melted away his uneasy feelings, and he began to relax. Then, just as he began to drift off, Tamarah's voice snapped him from his blissful slumber.

"Dubby? Oh, Dubby." Tamarah moaned sleepily.

"Sh," Jeremiah murmured. "It's okay, Tamarah."

"Oh, Dublin," she cried softly, followed by a brief rustling.

"Tamarah?" his father hissed. "I'm not... Honey, it's Jeremiah!"

"What? Oh, God! I'm so sorry, Jeremy," Tamarah groaned miserably. "I thought you were...I thought it had all been a dream," she cried.

"I'm sorry, Tammie." he sighed. "I wish to God it were."

"Xavier?" His father's strong voice in his thoughts made him jolt. *"Go to sleep."*

"I can't, Dad. I keep hearing William LeMasters murdering Mr. Minnows," he answered telepathically. *"Is Mrs. Minnows okay?"*

"She'll be fine, son. Try to get some rest, would you? We have a long day tomorrow."

"Yes, sir," he responded, rolling over and nestling farther into his sleeping bag. After a long while, he finally fell asleep, listening to Tamarah's hiccups and his father's soothing words.

The next morning, Xavier got his first good look at his new surroundings and found himself at the base of an enormous white-capped mountain range. A luscious green forest ringed the base of the gray mountains, and cotton-candy clouds hung so low in the sky, they appeared touchable.

He sat next to the campfire poking at the still glowing coals with a stick. His father had sent him out of the tent earlier that morning without explanation, but he hadn't needed one. He had seen the tattered envelope in his hand and quickly slipped out of the tent without arguing. The rest of the group was still sleeping, except for the Hardcastles. He could hear Rebecca and Ephraim's voices whispering from behind their closed tent flaps.

A few moments later, his father joined him looking drained and tired. Xavier guessed that he probably didn't get much sleep last night. Father and son sat in silence for several minutes, listening to the light weeping from their tent.

"Are they okay?" Xavier finally asked.

"They will be. It's hard to lose someone you love...of course, we know all about that," Jeremiah concluded softly, draping an arm over his shoulders.

"Yeah," he agreed wistfully. Another long moment passed, and the sobbing from the tent lessened. He glanced over his shoulder, and as a light breeze fluttered the tent flap back, he saw Mrs. Minnows, Robbie, and Brittany clinging to one another. It wasn't a comforting sight. It only reminded him that Dublin was dead, and he had played a major role in it. He tore his eyes away from the tent and once again took in his surroundings.

"Where are we?" he asked his father for no other reason than to get his mind off the pain on Robbie's face, and the fact that he had helped put it there.

"Switzerland," he answered simply.

"Where are we going to go?"

"First, we're meeting all the survivors from the invasion at Mirror Lake. We'll camp there for a week or so, and then from there, we'll go into hiding while we prepare to make our stand against LeMasters."

"Where will we go to do that?" Xavier asked.

"A place called King's Mountain. My great, great-grandfather, Michael Abraham Wells, built it long ago after Warwood's fallout shelter had become so decrepit that it was no longer safe to use in the event of an emergency. The construction of the refuge in King's Mountain took years to complete. Those involved in the construction were brought to the site in blindfolds and were required to remain in the mountain until the project was completed. Its location has been safely guarded for four generations. So, to ensure the mountain's security and the safety of its residents, only I know of its location," he answered.

"Have you ever been there?" Xavier asked.

"Just once," his father replied in a puzzlingly brusque tone, and he showed no signs of explaining.

A couple of hours later, the group packed up the camping gear and tents and gathered around the extinguished campfire.

"Since Ephraim and I are the only experienced teleporters, we'll have to take turns teleporting everyone to Mirror Lake. Xavier, you and Loren will be teleported first. Grab your backpack, son."

Xavier threw the bag over his shoulders and stepped into his father's embrace. The instant he did so, he felt the familiar, but by no means relaxing, sensation of an unseen entity reaching inside him, grabbing his very soul, and lifting him up and out. He closed his eyes to this wheeling sensation, waiting for it to end. When it did, he opened his eyes and found himself standing next to a massive, clear lake. It was quite obvious how the lake obtained its name. Mirrored in its shimmering surface were the towering mountains to its north and west. But what took Xavier's breath away wasn't the natural beauty of the land; it was the hundreds upon hundreds of people who had set up camp all around the lake's edge.

"Xavier," his father whispered. "Stay with Loren. You are not to leave his side. Do you understand me?"

He looked up at his father and nodded. Jeremiah looked at Loren, exchanged silent words, and simply vanished again.

"Well, little sire, what do you say we head to our camping site and start a fire?" the large general suggested, clapping him on the back.

"Sure," he muttered.

"Oi, Wells!" Beck Wilcox's voice called from the crowd as he ran toward him and tackled him to the ground, laughing. "It's bloody good to see ya, Your Highness! I should've known LeMasters wouldn't get his slimy claws into you! Where are your sidekicks?"

"They're coming. Hey, look, Beck, I should tell you..."

A flash of blue light preceded the king's return. He had Tamarah Minnows in his arms, and Ephraim appeared beside him with his wife, Rebecca. The sisters clung to one another and made their way toward Loren as Ephraim and Jeremiah disappeared again.

"Xavier, let's go. We need to prepare the campsite for the others," Loren called.

"I've got to go, Beck. I'll catch up with you later, okay," he mumbled, climbing to his feet.

"Sure," Beck answered. "See ya."

Xavier followed Loren as he led them to an elevated portion of the lake's shore. It reminded him of a Greek acropolis that he had seen pictures of in his history book, only smaller. From its summit, he could see the large mass of people moving about as they set up camp around the lake. For a couple hundred people, it was eerily quiet.

"Come on, kid. I need help finding wood for the fire," Loren whispered from behind him.

They gathered wood and kindling, and within minutes, they had a small fire flickering lazily in the light wind. Rebecca led Tamarah to a fallen log next to the fire just as Brittany and Robbie joined them. Brittany ran to her mother and climbed into her lap, very close to tears. Robbie simply sank to the ground next to her mother, staring absent-mindedly into the flames.

Soon, the entire group had been teleported to the lake, and they began setting up camp. Xavier helped his father erect their tent and move their bags inside. Afterwards, he sat next to the camp fire watching his father prepare to tour the camp.

"Oi, Dad!" Drew called from the lake's basin. "We're going to take a look around."

"Okay, don't go far and keep an eye on your brothers!" Ephraim called.

Xavier scrambled to join the Hardcastle boys when his father's voice stopped him.

"Xavier, stay here with Ephraim. Don't wander off."

He nodded begrudgingly biting back his complaints as he watched Court and his brothers scatter into the crowd.

"We shouldn't be long. I need to scan the crowd, get an idea of who's here, and determine if there are any threats," Jeremiah told Ephraim.

Soon after Jeremiah and Loren left, Rebecca and Tamarah retreated into the Hardcastle tent, and Xavier flopped himself on the log next to Ephraim, sighing. Brittany had disappeared into the tent with her mother, but Robbie was nowhere in sight. Worried about her, he went looking for her. He found her sitting on a rock overlooking the lake. He crossed the short distance between them and stopped behind her. He studied her slumped shoulders in silence, trying to think of something to say.

"Leave me alone," she hissed with such ferociousness that Xavier stepped back.

He studied her a moment longer before stepping toward her again. "Robbie? Are you okay?"

"Am I okay? Am I okay? You've got to be kidding me!" she growled, turning to face him. "How would you expect me to be, Xavier Wells? My father is dead! If it hadn't been for you, he'd be here. He'd be with us. My mom wouldn't be crying herself to sleep at night! Brittany wouldn't be scared half to death to leave Mom for fear that the same will happen to her! How am I supposed to be okay with that?" she finished fiercely, attracting the attention of several nearby camps.

Xavier felt the suspicious, curious stares of the unwanted spectators pushing in on him. "Robbie, I'm sorry. If I could have done something to save him, I would..."

"But you could have done something! You could have saved him, *Your Highness*! You could have saved him and you didn't! You didn't!" she yelled, jumping to her feet.

"What are you talking about?" he asked, his own temper rising. "How could I have saved him? What did you expect me to do? Was I supposed to hand myself over in exchange for him? Well, let me tell you, Robbie, it wouldn't have worked! Or, have you forgotten? I was held captive and tortured for two months by that maniac! I know how his sick mind works! He would have still killed him, and I'd be dead too! Is that what you wish? That I was dead too?" he asked grabbing her arm when she tried to walk away.

"Let go of me, Xavier," she spat out loudly.

"Answer my question first! Is that what you wish?" he demanded.

"I said, Let. Go. Of. Me!" she screamed, jabbing her bony knee into his groin.

He crumpled to the ground like a rag. He couldn't breathe, and he felt dangerously close to throwing up.

"Robbie!" Ephraim snapped, racing to the prince. "Xavier, are you okay?"

He coughed and gagged unable to answer. No, he wasn't okay. He wasn't sure he could even feel his legs.

Ephraim turned to Robbie and snarled, "What's the matter with you?"

"You *know* what's the matter, Uncle Ephraim!" she sobbed. "Why is my dad dead when we all know Xavier had the power to stop it?"

"Robbie, that's not true..."

"What's she talking about?" Xavier croaked weakly, trying to take a full breath.

"Nothing, Xavier. She's hurting and lashing out in any means she can," Ephraim answered.

"Shut up, Ephraim!" she screamed. "You know perfectly well what I'm talking about, but no one wants to tell *Prince Wells* the truth. Well, fine!"

"Robbie..." Ephraim warned with quiet sternness.

But she ignored the warning and continued, "Let's start with the obvious, *sire*. Have you ever wondered why you have this morbid knack of getting the people you supposedly care about killed: my dad, Maggie, your own mom? Did you ever wonder why at the age of twelve, you have five abilities when everyone else just has one or two? It's not because you're royalty like everyone wants you to believe, either. Even your father only had two abilities when he was your age. You're different. You could have saved my dad. Heck, you probably could have saved everyone! You're..."

"Roberta? What's going on here?" King Wells questioned, looking down at the girl and then at his out-of-sorts son, but he didn't wait for Robbie to answer. "I think you better join your mother and sister in Ephraim's tent. You could use some rest. Don't you think?" he asked pointedly.

Robbie's momentum evaporated as she peered up at the king. "Yes, sire," she muttered.

"Good, go on then," he insisted unwaveringly. "I will speak to you about this later."

Robbie paled and started toward the tent, but she wasn't done with Xavier. She whirled around and glared at him. "Oh, and for the record, *Prince Wells*, I never *liked* you, and I was never jealous of Maggie Applegate.

And...and...you kiss like a goldfish!" she spat, turning and stomping into the tent as several on-lookers snickered.

Ephraim helped Xavier struggle to his feet.

"What in the world is she talking about? What does she mean, she never *liked* me? I never said she was jealous of Maggie. Did Maggie tell her I kissed like a goldfish? Dad? Dad, what's going on?"

"Come on, son. We need to have a long, overdue talk." Jeremiah sighed and waved the boy to him.

Chapter 25

Treason

Xavier closed his eyes in horror following his father's lengthy description of his behavior while he was infected with the super flu.

"Oh, God. Oh, man! I did that? Oh, jeez!"

"Son, you were sick! You weren't right in the head. Don't be so tough on yourself," Jeremiah told him.

"But Robbie thinks I kiss like a fish!" he muttered miserably.

Jeremiah had to laugh. Of all the things, the boy was worried that the girl thought he didn't kiss well.

"It's not funny, Dad!" he growled.

"I'm sorry," he replied with a grin. "Son, she doesn't think that. She was trying to hurt you, like she's hurting. Just give her some time. She'll be all right. She needs to come to terms with this in her own way."

Xavier groaned. "I hope you're right. I'm not sure how long I can stand Robbie hating me."

When father and son finally exited the tent, Ephraim and Loren were sitting next to the fire talking in low tones. They turned the moment Jeremiah emerged from the tent.

"Sire, we really need to finish scanning the crowd," Loren urged.

"Yes, we will, but first I should make an address. We

have a lot of frightened and hurting people out there in need of a leader. Ephraim, would you ask your boys to help gather wood for a commemorative bonfire and set it up in the northern clearing?" the king requested, pointing.

"Yes, sire. I'll round them up," he replied, leaving them.

As the Hardcastle boys trickled into the campsite and Ephraim organized them, Jeremiah prepared for his address. Henrick Davies stood by ready to perform the amplification so that everyone at Mirror Lake could hear their king.

"How does the amplification work?" Xavier asked Henrick.

"Well, young sire, I can manipulate my electro force into a kind of PA system. You see, speakers create sound through electromagnetism which generates vibrations that the human ear can interpret into understandable sound." Henrick laughed at the boy's blank look. "It's hard to explain and not any easier to do, but I'm one of few people who have mastered the ability. So, long as I am touching your father, anything he says will sound as though it's being broadcasted over a speaker," he explained.

"You're kidding?" Xavier gasped.

Henrick chuckled. "Just wait and see, sire."

"Henrick, it's time," Jeremiah announced, calling the man to him.

Once Henrick's electro force was spinning above the lake like an enormous glowing speaker, Jeremiah began his speech.

"Good afternoon, my loyal friends and brethren." He was unable to continue for the crowd immediately erupted into cheers and applause. Xavier grinned up at his father as he shrugged meekly down at him. Once the cheers subsided, the king continued, "Thank you. Though, I'm not so sure I deserved all that. I stand before you humbled and ashamed. I did not foresee this catastrophe, and I should have. And because of that, many loyal good men and women have died. I would gladly endure another caning if I could exchange a single life for it."

The crowd burst into boos and whistles. This brought a brief smile to Jeremiah's lips. "I appreciate your support and loyalty, my friends, but the fact remains that I swore an oath to protect Warwood and its people, and I've failed you. For that, I beg for your forgiveness, but I promise you, it will never happen again so long as I still draw breath." Applause interrupted his address again, and Jeremiah waited patiently for it to end.

"Tonight shall be a time of mourning for our lost loved ones. Take some time today to remember a fallen loyalist. A commemorative fire will be lit and, at midnight, your memorial letters can be sent to your loved ones in heaven. Until then, you can spend your time securing your campsites and writing your memorial letters. We shall camp here for the next week or so to ensure we have all surviving loyalists with us. I ask for everyone's help in sending all new arrivals to me. I cannot stress the importance of this enough. Every person must be inspected in order to ensure our safety. Then we will begin our pilgrimage to King's Mountain, and from there, we will prepare for our stand. We may have fallen, but we are not beaten!"

The crowd's cheers were deafening and again, Jeremiah had to wait for the noise to die down. "We will stand again, my friends, and when we do, we will be mightier than before. We will crush LeMasters and take back what is rightfully ours!" There was another intermission of cheers and screams. "And, we will have penance," Jeremiah told them, his voice quavering, "for our lost loved ones! William LeMasters will stand in judgment!"

The crowd burst into a turbulent roar that surrounded them and echoed off the mountains, multiplying the noise ten-fold. Xavier was overwhelmed by its intensity and simply stared. Jeremiah turned with an enormous grin and patted him on the shoulder. "Some days, being king is a burden, and then there are times when it knocks your socks off." Xavier could only nod, and his father chuckled. "Come on, son. The Royal Guardsmen are on their way here, and I need to prepare for the debriefing. You should be a part of it," he added, leading Xavier into their tent.

Jeremiah knelt next to the black duffle Milton had given him at the palace and opened it. Inside were a dozen scrolls tied with small ribbons of assorted colors, each secured with the kingdom's seal. Jeremiah quickly searched through the bag and pulled out a scroll with a black ribbon. Without a word, he zipped up the bag, stood, and exited the tent with Xavier lagging behind him. Outside the tent, nearly three dozen men, many in tattered Royal Guard uniforms, stood silently waiting for their king. The moment Jeremiah emerged from the tent, each man sank to one knee and bowed his head.

"Please, don't," Jeremiah muttered. "Stand. Today we are equals, my friends. We have important matters to discuss and plan."

"Before we do, sire," Timmins declared, stepping forward hesitantly, "I want to offer you my deepest apologies."

Timmins looked as though he had been trampled on by a herd of rhinoceroses. No doubt it had been Ephraim's doing, in retaliation for striking Xavier. From the looks of it, the general had managed to get in several punishing blows before Jeremiah could stop him.

"I fear that I am as guilty as you, sire, more so, in allowing my emotions to rule my head. After the prince attacked Mackenzie at school, I didn't care that the illness had caused his moment of indiscretion; I only cared to seek retribution for my boy. I apologize for being so single-minded and failing to see the big picture. It is more my fault than anyone's that all of this has happened. After all, it's my duty as defense captain to assess and be aware of any possible dangers to the kingdom's commonwealth. I failed you, sire, and for that I am truly sorry and offer you my resignation. I'm sure someone else could do a better job." Timmins knelt at Jeremiah's feet, holding out his Premier Royal Guard medallion.

Jeremiah looked down at the man. Xavier thought for a moment his father might thrash Timmins, and he wouldn't have blamed him if he had, but he didn't. Slowly, the anger washed away from the king's face and he answered quietly, "I refuse to accept your resignation, Clarke. Right now, I need my best men on this task. You and I will work this out later. Understood?"

Timmins stood and glanced timidly at the king. "Yes, sire," he muttered.

"Now," Jeremiah began, untying the ribbon from the scroll and breaking the wax seal. He quickly unrolled the paper, which turned out to be several copies of some kind of a map. "We'll need to depart from here in numerous groups to avoid drawing too much attention to ourselves. Premier Guardsmen, you will be responsible for organizing and safely guiding your group to King's Mountain. The regular Royal Guard will be at your disposal to assist you in whatever you need," he told them, distributing copies of the map. "This map is not to be shared with anyone. You and only you are to view it. Understood?"

"Yes, sire," the men answered in unison.

With a nod of satisfaction, the king continued, "There should be fifty to sixty people in each group. We will begin departures from Mirror Lake in one week. Make note of the highlighted areas on the maps. These marked areas are ideal locations for your group to rest and camp as you make your journey. Are there any questions?"

"Sire?" a guard interrupted, "judging by the map, we could easily complete this journey in less than two days. Why are there three camping sites?"

Jeremiah looked at the man patiently. "Yes, Peterson, *you* could cover the ground in a day and a half, but you will be leading women, children, and the elderly through the mountains, and they cannot. Stick with the more leisurely pace." The young man nodded and Jeremiah turned back to the group.

"Henrick, though you have a map, you have a different task altogether. I need you to gather up a group of fifteen to twenty strong men. Your group will be in charge of gathering supplies from a multipurpose warehouse in Bern. There's a common man who lives there and has trucks available for you to teleport the goods. Here are his name, address, and the supply list," Jeremiah stated, handing Henrick a very long list. "When you and your men have gathered the supplies, follow this route here," Jeremiah explained, pointing to an area on Henrick's copy of the map. "You won't be able to drive the entire way to the mountain, so I'll have teleporters meet you here," he continued, jabbing at the map, "to teleport you and the goods the rest of the way to King's Mountain. Are you with me so far?"

"Yes, sire," Henrick replied.

"Good. Now, I'll need a list of the men you intend to take with you by tomorrow evening, and then you may set out the next day. I expect it may take you a week or so to accomplish this task so take what supplies you'll need for that amount of time."

"Yes, sire."

"Okay, do any of you have any questions regarding your jobs?"

There were none so he dismissed the men to begin arranging their groups. However, Timmins lingered.

"Sire, Governor Yaman organized the uprising within the kingdom on LeMasters' behalf. When LeMasters stormed the front gates, I heard Yaman give the order for the mutinous citizens to attack the Royal Guard."

Jeremiah nodded solemnly. "I figured as much. It occurred to me that he orchestrated the caning to coincide with LeMasters' arrival. I imagine the virus was also a part of that plan. They will be dealt with in time, Timmins."

"Yes, sir. Sire? I would like to discuss my punishment with you now if we could. I don't feel worthy of the trust you've bestowed on me. Please, King Wells, for my own peace of mind, I'd like to take care of this now," Timmins pleaded anxiously.

Jeremiah sighed and crossed his arms over his chest. "Okay, Timmins. What do you feel would be a fitting penance for your behavior?" he challenged.

Timmins had obviously thought this through and had an answer ready. "A caning, sir."

Jeremiah looked at the other man with something close to shock. "A caning? That's a bit...extreme, don't you think?"

"I deserve it, sir!" he exclaimed defensively.

"I don't think you deserve to be beaten until you no longer have the strength to stand..."

"But, I do! Sire Wells, I...I helped...the mutiny!" he concluded miserably.

"What?" Jeremiah roared.

"You son of a..." Loren spat disgustedly.

Timmins fell to his knees and began to sob. "I don't know what came over me, sir. After my boy had a couple of run-ins with the prince, I thought you had lost sight of the kingdom's well-being for the boy's. I thought maybe your priorities had been misplaced and that it would be best if you were removed. I had no idea that Governor Yaman was organizing the mutiny for William LeMasters! I thought he intended to create a democratic government. I had no idea about William, sire. I swear!"

"And that's supposed to make everything okay? Good God! You're guilty of high treason! King Wells could order your death for this!" Loren yelled.

"I know," Timmins cried uncontrollably. "And Dublin is dead because of it. Many are dead because of my petty jealousies! You see, Your Highness, I do deserve it! I do!"

Swelling with anger, Jeremiah peered down at the man and grumbled, "All right, Timmins. You will be caned, twenty lashes. You will also be demoted from the rank of Captain in the Premier Royal Guard to a private in the regular guard."

"Yes, sire," he agreed eagerly.

"I am not finished!" Jeremiah barked, stepping toward Timmins threateningly. "And for the next two years, you will report to me once a week for a mind evaluation to ensure your loyalty remains with the crown. Understood?"

Timmins bowed his head submissively and muttered, "Yes, sire."

"Your caning will be tonight. Report to me before the commemoration," Jeremiah stated stonily.

Timmins nodded miserably, but he looked relieved when he left. Jeremiah watched him disappear into the dense crowd of camps and people.

"Father? Why would anyone *ask* to be caned?" Xavier questioned.

Jeremiah looked down at him thoughtfully before answering, "Sometimes when a person is in extreme distress, they seek physical pain to alleviate their mental pain."

"Was it that way for you? With your caning, I mean?" he asked, watching his father closely.

Jeremiah shot him a quick look before answering, "Yes."

"Why is that?" But Xavier never got his answer.

"Your Highness!" Henrick gasped urgently. "Come quickly. It's your brother! He's just arrived, but he's...he's seriously injured, sir!"

Chapter 26

Unknown Powers

The King and Henrick sprinted into the crowd with Xavier racing after them. As they zigzagged through the campsites, the sea of people parted from their path and knelt at the sight of their king, which made the sprint to wherever they were going all the easier. Even so, Xavier found it difficult keeping up with his father when he was in an outright sprint, and soon he lost sight of him. If it hadn't been for the wake of bowing citizens, he would have never known where to go. Then, the trail of curtsies vanished, and he found himself standing in front of three campsites.

"Xavier?" a sweet voice called from behind him.

He spun around. Even with disheveled hair and a smudged face, Lana Applegate was still beautiful.

"Ah...ah, Mrs. Applegate!" he gushed breathlessly.

"Are you looking for your father?" she asked.

"Yes, ma'am," he answered, suddenly feeling awkward.

"Well, he's in that tent with your uncle right now," she told him, nodding to the nearest tent.

Suddenly, Michael Spencer's voice bellowed out, "NO! Damn it! Jer, no! I won't let them take it! I'd sooner die! Do you hear me? I'd rather die!"

Xavier started toward the tent when Lana arms

encircled him and pulled him away. "I don't think it's a good idea for you to go in there right now. Why don't you come and sit with me for a spell?" she suggested, leading him away from Spencer's yells.

They sank on a log in front a small waving fire, but Xavier's eyes were fixated on the other tent. He listened miserably as Spencer's screams intensified.

"I have some hot tea and biscuits. Would you like some?" Lana asked, prying his attention from the agonizing yells bellowing from neighboring camp.

"No, ma'am," he muttered and looked into Mrs. Applegate's beautiful face. He didn't mean to stare at her, but he couldn't help himself. Maggie had looked so much like her mother. It was like staring at Maggie twenty years older. *"Maggie!"* he thought with despair and turn away.

"You know it's not your fault that Maggie's dead, don't you?" she whispered, stroking his cheek.

He nodded, but he didn't look at her and didn't speak.

"She really enjoyed your company, Xavier. She talked nonstop about you, especially after Old Christmas. It comforts me to know she was so happy in her last days," she finished with a sad smile.

"But," he muttered, tears building in his eyes, "she wasn't! We had a fight. I messed up."

Mrs. Applegate looked down at him and shook her head. "She told me about that. Now, I'm not saying that using telepathy on her wasn't wrong and that it didn't bother her, but she wasn't herself. She was sick with the super flu, and she overreacted. I'm certain that her feelings for you would have outweighed her irritation, and she would have worked it out with you. Besides," she smiled down at him, stroking his hair out of his eyes, "even your father struggled with this issue when he was young. But his indiscretions got him into some serious trouble when he was about fifteen. It led to a legal judgment, and it was months before Lucy spoke to him again."

"What do you mean?" he asked.

She looked at him in wonder. "You mean you haven't heard about this?" Xavier shook his head. "Well, I guess you wouldn't have," she muttered to herself before continuing. "Lucy was his first love. Everyone in the kingdom thought she would be the next queen, but following the incident, they never dated again."

"What did he do?" he asked, his interest sparked.

She gave him a coy smile. "Well, that's a question I think is best answered by your father."

Suddenly, a loud crash came from Spencer's tent.

"Sire!" a deep voice yelled. "You must hold him down! If we don't amputate now, he will die!"

"No!" Spencer screamed. "I swear before God, Jer, if you let them do this, I will cut yours off in your sleep! I mean it! I would rather die!"

Xavier listened to his father's voice drawl smoothly behind the tent, but he couldn't understand what was being said. Then, an older man with wild white hair pushed his way out of the crowd and slipped into the tent. Simultaneously, loud, argumentative voices burst from the tent, and within seconds, several men rushed out with indignant, flushed faces.

"Hmm, that's odd. I wonder why the healers are leaving," Lana remarked, standing.

A moment later, the elderly man reemerged from the tent with Jeremiah following close behind him. His father looked furious and was spouting a few selected words at the older man. But the man wasn't listening. Instead, he frantically scanned the area as though he was looking for something or someone.

"Where is he, sire?" the man spat impatiently at the king as he continued to scan the crowd. Then, the old man's eyes fastened on Xavier, and he grinned. "Xavier! Come, young sire," he called, waving the prince over to him.

Xavier approached the man with misgivings. He looked and sounded oddly familiar. When the old man bent down to eye level with him, he was sure he knew the man but just couldn't place him.

"Your uncle is gravely injured. He will die unless you help him. Will you do it, Xavier?" he whispered urgently.

"Abraham, he's been through too much; he can't do this!" Jeremiah growled, stepping protectively between the old man and Xavier.

Whoa! Did his father say Abraham? Was this man Abraham Vincent, the prophet? It couldn't be! He looked...well, normal! It was as if his scarred face had never existed. Though he had to be close to seventy, Abraham looked youthful and strong.

"He can, and he must," Abraham insisted firmly, his face rigid. The men stood in a staring dead lock until Abraham growled, "Lord, you're a stubborn man! Listen to me, sire. Xavier must do this because it is meant to be. This is his first taste, his first realization that he's meant for more!"

Jeremiah immediately softened and whispered, "But, Abe. He's only a boy."

Abraham nodded, frowning. "I know, but unfortunately his calling doesn't recognize that. Look, I appreciate your fatherly protectiveness, but Mike will die unless the boy does this! Only Xavier can save him, Jer."

There it was again! He was the only one who could save someone, first Robbie and now the prophet. Once more, Xavier had a distinct feeling that the people closest to him were keeping something from him. His father nodded and looked down at him with both awe and pity.

Abraham stooped to look at the boy again. "Do you recognize me, young sire?"

"You're Abraham Vincent, but what happened to your face? How come it's not...scarred?"

Abe laughed deeply and heartily. "I'll explain that some other time, boy, but right now, we have more pressing matters to take care of. Come," he instructed, taking him by the hand and leading him into the tent. His father followed, silently watchful.

Governor Bracus stood over a cot of blood-soaked linens. As Xavier moved farther into the tent, his stomach dropped at the sight of Spencer lying motionless with his dark hair plastered to his forehead with perspiration. His legs looked as though they had been caught in a meat grinder, and Xavier's stomach twisted at the sight of them. For a moment, he thought he might throw up and staggered away from his uncle's motionless body, but Abraham stopped his retreat. The instant Abraham grasped his shoulders, Xavier felt anchored and the feelings of nausea dissolved.

"Take it easy, boy," Abraham soothed, and Xavier stiffened with shock. It wasn't what Abraham said to him that stunned him as much as *how* he said it. He hadn't said the words aloud; he had used telepathy! Xavier turned and stared up at the old man in wonder. *"We don't have time for this, Xavier. Your uncle is dying,"* he continued nonverbally. Xavier's gaze snapped back to Michael Spencer, who began moaning fretfully. The prophet released his shoulders and moved to the other side of the cot, watching him intently.

"Put your hands on him, boy. Place one on his head and the other on his chest," Abraham instructed softly, and Xavier complied without hesitation.

"King Wells, Xavier will need your help to relax and reach into the depths of his rejuvenation powers."

"But I don't have rejuvenation p..." Xavier began.

"If I say you do, boy, then you do!" Abraham snapped. "Now, sire, stand behind the boy and place your hands on him," he continued. Jeremiah did as he was told without rebuttal or question.

With his father's hands on him, Xavier immediately felt more relaxed and confident. He listened to the prophet's low, smooth voice.

"Close your eyes and relax. Concentrate on your father's hands stroking away all your fears and constraints."

He did just that. He inhaled deeply and focused on his father's hands caressing his head, back, and shoulders. All his worries left him.

"Now, shift your concentration, boy. Envision your uncle; can you see his face? Can you see his agony and pain?" Abraham's voice penetrated into his peaceful, hypnotic state.

"Yes." he gulped.

"Good. Now think about what you wish to happen; concentrate on what you want to accomplish. Picture Spencer's legs. Can you see the wounds? Think about them healing and ending your uncle's suffering." Abraham paused only a moment as Xavier obediently focused on his uncle's legs. He could see the deep, bone-exposing wounds and cringed.

"Easy, boy. Now, you need to really focus; this is the hard part. Imagine the wounds closing. Concentrate. Can you see the bleeding stopping? Be diligent. Envision the bleeding stopping and the wounds healing back together. Concentrate, boy!" Abraham hissed.

Xavier's brow twisted and creased as he desperately tried to see the images Abraham was describing. Beads of sweat strung across his forehead as he watched with his mind's eye as the wounds on Spencer's legs first stopped bleeding and then slowly closed. He panted for breath as the vision drained him of all his strength, and he fell into his father's arms, exhausted.

Jeremiah slowly lowered him to the floor and stroked the moist hair away from his face.

"Are you okay?" he murmured.

Nodding, he finally opened his eyes. Abraham stood on the opposite side of the cot beaming down at him. With a quirked brow, he nodded toward the motionless man on the bed. Xavier struggled out of his father's arms, stood, and looked down at his sleeping uncle. Mike was pale, but the strained look of pain was gone, and he was resting peacefully.

"Look at his legs, Your Highness," the prophet called softly as he pulled back the blood-soaked sheet. All that remained of the grotesque wounds were angry red scars carved in Spencer's legs.

Xavier felt everything around him swirl as the ramifications of what had just occurred flooded over him. He looked at each man's face in turn. Aside from Abraham's elated face, the governor peered down at him with wide-eyed awe, and his father wore a guarded expression as if he was waiting on Xavier's reaction.

"I did that?" he whispered.

"Yes, son, you did," Jeremiah confirmed quietly.

"Yes!" Abraham agreed, still beaming down at the boy. "You accomplished what no healer could. You saved your uncle's life and his legs from amputation."

Xavier shook his head against this declaration, as Robbie's accusations pounded down on him like a jackhammer. "*You could have saved him and you didn't. You didn't!*"

"No," he croaked. "It isn't true."

The prophet's smile dropped as he watched the boy's face twist into torment. "Oh," he muttered almost too quietly for anyone to hear.

But, Jeremiah had heard and shot him a bewildered look before turning back to his son. "Xavier, it's okay. You've saved your uncle's life. I know..."

"What, Father?" Xavier demanded. "What do you know? You didn't seem surprised at all that I could do that!" He studied his father's forlorn expression. "That's...because...you already knew! Isn't it?"

"Xavier, I..." Jeremiah began.

"Isn't it?" he snapped.

His father's eyes flashed with anger. "Son, I don't appreciate this tone..."

"Well, I really don't care whether my tone offends your or not, *Dad*! Why didn't you tell me I had other abilities? Why didn't you...hang on!" Xavier paused, glaring up at his father as other thoughts occurred to him. "That's what Dublin meant when he said it was a glimpse of what was to come. Robbie was right! Wasn't she? I could have saved Mr. Minnows. I could have used some other unknown ability and saved him!" Xavier screamed as tears flooded his eyes and spilled over his cheeks.

Jeremiah stepped forward to comfort the boy, but he jumped out of his reach. "No! Don't touch me! Just...just leave me alone!" he moaned, pushing past the men and running out of the tent.

Xavier plunged into the crowd, trying to put as much distance between himself and the men, but there was no way he could outrun the guilt pounding at him. As he hurried past campsite after campsite, he noticed people were beginning to part and kneel, which could only mean one thing; his father was near. Xavier glanced over his shoulder and saw his father jogging after him. He tried to sprint away and lose him in the dense crowd, but it was futile. His father was too fast and had him in his grasp within seconds.

"Let me go!" he raged with strangled despair. "You should've told me!"

"Son, please calm down." Jeremiah's breath swept across his neck as he whispered, "Let's go back to the tent and discuss this."

"No! I'm not going anywhere with you! You lied to me! You lied! Do your *loyal* subjects know what a liar you are?" he spat loudly.

He was goading his father intentionally, but he didn't care. Xavier was beginning to understand his father's explanation of why sometimes people seek physical pain to ease an emotional pain, and at the moment, Xavier would welcome a spanking, a slap, anything to take his mind off the guilt punching away at his soul.

"Xavier," his father warned, his strong fingers digging into Xavier's arms.

"You're a liar! Liar! Liar! Liar!" he yelled, taunting his father like a schoolboy chastising another classmate.

Jeremiah hoisted the boy over his shoulder and began carrying him through the staring crowd.

Xavier pummeled Jeremiah with punches, kicks, and taunts. "Put me down, you jerk! Put me down! You're nothing but a big fat liar! I hate you! Liar, liar, li..."

Finally, the king's tolerance was spent, and abruptly, he dropped the boy to the ground, turned him roughly, and swatted his backside with two quick, sharp blows. He spun the boy to face him, pinning him with steely eyes.

"That's enough!" he growled and watched as the boy's

lower protruding lip quivered.

"Sire?" Abraham's voice called quietly. "Get him to your tent. I hadn't realized he'd react this way... We need to talk, the three of us."

He hoisted the now sobbing boy into his arms and made his way through the crowd and into their tent on the small plateau. He didn't lower him until they were inside his tent.

"Xavier, you need to stop crying," Abraham ordered firmly. The men waited patiently for the boy to calm before continuing. "Now, you asked your father a tough question back there, and I'd like to try to answer it. You see, as the prophet, I have seen and can foresee things your father cannot. He couldn't answer your question honestly because it's more complex than that, boy." He gave a ragged sigh as if contemplating how to continue. "Could you have saved Mr. Minnows? No, you couldn't. At the state you were in following the super flu, there was no way you could have done anything to prevent Dublin Minnows' death. Even if you had been fully recovered, you couldn't have done anything about it. Now, could you prevent it a few months from now? Maybe. In a year from now? Most likely. Five years from now? Most definitely. Your father didn't lie to you. He gave you the only answer he could." Abraham paused a moment, watching Xavier as his explanation soaked in. "Even if you had been able to save Dublin, I would have interfered."

"What?" he hissed unbelievingly. "Why? Why would you try to stop me from saving Mr. Minnows?"

Xavier wasn't sure he would answer, but after another long sigh and a sideways glance at Jeremiah, he answered quietly, "I'm not sure you're ready to hear this or that you'll even understand it." He sighed again. "But there are three types of destiny. There are destinies that are so volatile that they must be altered for the betterment of humankind. Saving your father and keeping possession of the King's Key is an example of this kind of destiny. If your father had died, or if the key had fallen into LeMasters' possession, it would have resulted in a catastrophic effect. Secondly, there are indiscriminative destinies. These destinies are neutral and wouldn't cause any significant change to the future if altered. Then, finally, there are adverse destinies. If these destinies are tampered with even in the slightest way, it would cause a chain reaction of events that would wreak havoc in the delicate equilibrium of human existence. I'm sorry to say that saving Dublin Minnows' life would have been the latter."

"What?" he hissed. "There must be a mistake! Mr. Minnows wouldn't hurt a soul! How could changing his...destiny cause so much trouble?"

"I'm sorry, Xavier, I can't tell you that right now. Yes, Mr. Minnows was a great man, and believe me, if I could have changed his destiny, I would have," Abraham concluded, suddenly sounding very old and tired.

Xavier opened his mouth to argue, but Abraham raised his hand, silencing the boy.

"Xavier, hasn't everything I've told you thus far come to pass?"

Xavier clamped his mouth shut and nodded.

"Have I ever lied to you?"

He shook his head yieldingly.

"Then I'm going to ask that you trust in me and believe what I'm telling you now is the truth. Let me take the burden and guilt from you; there wasn't anything you could do. This is simply how it was meant to be."

Slowly, Xavier nodded, tears renewing their paths down his cheeks, as the old man patted him comfortingly.

Then after a moment, he stood. "Well, I hate to leave with everything how it is, but I'm afraid I'm needed elsewhere. So, I think I'll leave you two to it. Goodbye, Xavier. I'll see you soon."

"Abraham, I need to talk to you. Wait for me outside," Jeremiah ordered with such superiority that Abe looked at him with an angled, reproving brow, but in the end, he nodded and left the tent.

"Son?" Jeremiah questioned. "Are you all right?"

Xavier nodded, wiping the tears from his face. "Yeah. I'm sorry I yelled at you and embarrassed you in front of all those people," he muttered.

"I'm sorry too," Jeremiah replied softly, rubbing the boy's arms and kissing his forehead. "You look exhausted. Why don't you take a nap? I'll wake you when dinner's ready."

He nodded and without another word, settled back into the sleeping bags. But the moment his father exited the tent to join the prophet outside, he scrambled forward and listened through the tent flaps.

"What is it, King Wells?" the older man questioned, but by his tone, he already knew what the king wanted.

"You're a time bender, aren't you? That's why your appearance has changed. Something Xavier did changed the future."

Abraham grinned broadly. "Nothing gets by you, does it, sire?"

The king didn't respond, but continued to study the older man vehemently.

Abe sighed. "Yes. When Xavier prevented you from sacrificing your life for his during the retrieval of the key, everyone's future was altered, for the better. If Dublin had survived in your place, he would have been a gentle father figure for Xavier, but he would have been ill-prepared to handle Xavier's turbulent, influx year, the year when the majority of his powers will emerge. This will be a dangerous time for the boy and everyone around him. Without you, he would have severely injured himself and others," he finished thickly.

"Who are you? Do I know you?" Jeremiah asked, his eyes narrowing on the man in front of him.

The prophet smiled. "Oh, yes. You know me. When you settle in at King's Mountain, we'll discuss assigning you as Xavier's keeper. You'll need to have the ability to control his raging powers. The boy needs your wisdom and guidance now more than ever."

Jeremiah opened his mouth to interrupt, but Abraham stopped him. "Please, sire, don't ask questions that I cannot answer. All the answers you seek will be discovered in time. I really must go now. I'll see you both soon," he reassured him, and then simply disappeared.

Xavier's mouth dropped open. A time bender? What was a time bender? He wondered as he slid back into the tent. Obviously, there was a lot more to Abraham Vincent than the task of being a prophet. His mind wouldn't stop toiling over the possibilities and the puzzle that was Abraham Vincent. No longer tired, he gave up on the nap and began rummaging through his father's backpack, looking for paper and a pen to write a memorial letter to Dublin.

Chapter 27

Revenge

Nearly an hour later, Xavier emerged from the tent. The sun had slipped behind the mountains leaving the land bathed in a soft orange light. An enormous bonfire towered at the north end of the lake, a safe distance from the campsites peppering the lake's shore. Loren and Ephraim, their families, and Tamarah and Brittany Minnows sat quietly around the campfire eating canned beef and fire-roasted potatoes. Sliding his letter to Dublin in his sweatshirt pocket, Xavier joined the group.

"Hey, X," Loren called boisterously. "Hungry?"

"Yeah, a little," he mumbled, sinking onto the log between Loren and Ephraim.

Ephraim fetched a plate of beef and a couple roasted potatoes. As he handed the food to him, Xavier asked, "Where's my dad?"

"He's having a little chat with Robbie," Ephraim answered.

"Oh," he muttered, stuffing an entire potato in his mouth and struggling to chew it down.

"Xavier Wells!" Mrs. Hardcastle chastised. "Where are your manners? Cut your food into smaller bites, young man."

The Hardcastle boys snickered.

Xavier spit the half chewed potato back onto his plate and smiled sweetly at the woman. "Yes, ma'am."

Drew, Court, and Caleb burst into laughter which was squelched by a stern look from their mother. Then, she turned and swatted the prince stifling a smile.

"You little heathen! You act more and more like your father each day!"

The group snickered.

"Don't I know it," the king commented dryly.

Xavier spun and looked up his father with a small, sheepish grin.

His hand was clamped firmly on Robbie's shoulder as she stood staring at the toe of her shoe. Her watery, red eyes wandered briefly to Xavier before glancing quickly away.

"Xavier, Robbie has something she'd like to say to you. Robbie?" Jeremiah prompted gently.

She glanced back at him and muttered, "I'm sorry for kneeing you like I did. It was horrible thing to do. Can you accept my apology?"

"Yeah, sure," he replied quietly.

She nodded and began to move away.

"Robbie?" he called after her.

She stopped and turned toward him, not meeting his eyes.

"I'm sorry, too. I really wish...I...I'm sorry."

She nodded vaguely and wandered toward her mother and sister.

Jeremiah gave him a small, encouraging smile. "Give it a little time, son."

Following dinner, what was left of the Premier Royal Guard began trickling into the royal campsite to do their part in Mr. Clarke's penance for treason. Timmins wrapped his royal cloak protectively around his body and looked up at the king apprehensively.

"Sire," he greeted and bowed humbly.

"Let's take this into the woods," Jeremiah announced. "There's no need for this to be witnessed by anyone else."

Xavier watched the men follow his father into the woods. Courtney, who sat next to him by the fire, seemed to be holding his breath, but once the Royal Guard disappeared into the woods, he released it in a quiet whistle.

"Crikey! I'm sure glad I'm not Mr. Clarke, right now. Hey, Xavier! Where are you going?"

"Where do you think? Come on," he called as he jogged into the woods.

When the boys finally found the men, Timmins Clarke had been stripped of his cloak and stood bracing himself against a tree trunk. The rest of the Guard stood several yards behind him, and Jeremiah stood to the side, stripping the leaves from a long switch. Finally, with the leaves removed, Jeremiah turned toward Timmins, switch in hand. Xavier shuddered at the fury he saw in his father's face and prayed that he would never have to see that expression directed toward him.

Then, Jeremiah turned to the motionless Premier Royal Guard. "Your role here is to bear witness to this punishment. This man has been charged with treason. Due to his humble admission to the crime, leniency has been considered and therefore, his punishment will be thus: a twenty-lash caning, a demotion to the rank of private in the regular Royal Guard, and weekly inquisitions for the next two years. For the record, Private Timmins Clarke, how do you plea?"

"Guilty, sire," he choked and began weeping uncontrollably.

Xavier had never seen a grown man cry so hysterically,

and he wasn't sure he could blame Timmins. If his father looked at him like that, knowing he had twenty lashes coming to him, he would certainly bawl, too.

Jeremiah shrugged off his jacket and flung it angrily to the side. Aside from a sigh, the king gave no indication that he dreaded what he was about to do. He turned toward Timmins and swung, hard. The whip lashed against Timmins's bare skin with a loud crack, and he screamed like a baby. Xavier felt a strange sense of satisfaction but immediately felt guilty for it. Soon, he felt only pity for the man as he endured lash after lash. Although it was far from the torment his father had endured, Timmins fell on the ninth swing. Jeremiah waited patiently as Timmins struggled to his feet. Once Timmins stood and hugged himself against the tree again, the king resumed the whipping. By the fifteenth lash, Timmins could no longer stand, and Jeremiah backed away from him.

"Jer," Ephraim muttered, "you must finish it; you know you must. The men must see you as a man of your word, good or bad. And you know Timmins wouldn't feel he had redemption unless you finish his punishment."

Dread and remorse swept across the king's face, and he closed his eyes. After a long moment, he raised his head with a hard, taunt expression in place. Jeremiah finished the beating quickly, and with a strangled growl, he threw the whip into the surrounding trees and stormed off into the forest with Ephraim on his heels. The remaining Guard silently began to disperse as Loren helped Timmins to his feet.

Xavier nudged Courtney with his elbow and mouthed the words, "Come on."

The boys crept farther into the woods after their fathers. They hadn't traveled far when they heard a loud crash and cussing, and Xavier pulled Courtney behind a clump of shrubs. They found the two men in a small clearing: a very calm Ephraim standing off to the side and a very agitated king stomping in circles.

"Are you done, Your Highness?" Ephraim asked dryly amused.

Jeremiah was pacing and panting madly. "No, damn it! I'm not!" he spat, picking up a large branch from the forest floor and smashing it several times against a tree trunk. Then, he continued to stomp around the clearing huffing and ranting. His tantrum would have appeared funny if the situation hadn't been so serious. Finally, the king's rage seemed to deflate, and he sank onto a fallen log.

Ephraim paused a moment before asking quietly, "Now are you done?"

The king didn't speak but simply nodded. Ephraim sighed and sat next to him. They sat in silence for several minutes before Jeremiah buried his face in his hands and whispered, "Sorry about that."

Ephraim nodded. "It's all right, Jer. I've been expecting it. Bloody Hell, with everything you've had to endure over the last month: the near death of your son, the discovery that the woman you've been dating is *Lucifer's mistress* and attempts to murder your son in a bathtub, the trial, the sentencing of crimes that should have been thrown out, the caning, the invasion of *Lucifer* himself, the death of Dublin, and the discovery that one of your highest, most trusted guards has betrayed you. Crikey, I'm surprised this blow-up didn't happen sooner."

He gave him a small reluctant smile. "Well, when you put it like that, maybe I should have another go at it."

"No, I think that was more than enough, Your Highness," Ephraim chastised playfully. "If you go berserk like that again, I may have to restrain you."

He huffed. "You think you could?"

"I have before," the general challenged with a raised eyebrow.

Jeremiah growled an inaudible response and tackled his friend to the forest floor. The men wrestled a moment and it wasn't any surprise to see Jeremiah come out the victor.

Xavier couldn't resist the temptation to rib Courtney. "My dad can beat up your dad."

"Quiet, you." Courtney laughed, giving Xavier a playful shove.

"My dad can beat up your dad. My dad can beat up your dad," Xavier taunted as Courtney wrestled him to the ground and pinned him there.

"Oh, yeah?" Ephraim growled from above as he snatched Xavier off the ground. "But I bet his dad can still whip your butt, young sire!" And before he knew what was happening, Ephraim held him upside down and swatted him playfully.

When the general lowered him to the ground, Xavier grinned up at him. "That didn't even hurt," he taunted.

Ephraim's severe expression was so blatantly fake that Xavier burst into laughter. The general smiled devilishly down at him as he teased, "One would think that you learned your lesson the last time you said that."

Ephraim's smile widened, and he exploded into laughter as Xavier blushed and threw a fretful glance at his father's puzzled, questioning eyes.

Shortly before midnight, the large crowd gathered quietly around the bonfire. Xavier stood next to his father, staring at the enormous flames waving into the sky. The area was silent and all that could be heard was crackling and an occasional loud pop from the fire. Jeremiah reached down, took Xavier's hand, and led him toward the fire. As the immense heat grazed at their bodies, Jeremiah pulled a letter from the hip pocket of his corduroy slacks.

"Got your letter, son?" he asked quietly, and Xavier answered by pulling it from the pocket of his sweatshirt. "Okay, then." Jeremiah smiled sadly. "Let's pay our respects to Dubby and send him our messages."

Jeremiah stepped forward, tossed his letter into the flames, and quickly crossed himself as he muttered a short prayer.

Xavier watched as his father's letter curled and quickly diminished into ashes, before stepping forward with his letter. Sighing painfully, he tossed it into the fire and watched as it too was transformed into ashes and smoke. Jeremiah's hand grasped his shoulder, and he looked up to see his father's head bowed and tears on his grief-stricken face. He wrapped himself around his father's body and hugged him tightly. Then, his father dropped to his knees and enveloped the boy in his arms.

Finally, father and son stood and made their way through the crowd and toward their tent. They settled in for the night and nearly an hour later, the Minnows joined them. Sleep didn't come easily for Xavier, and he cuddled against his father, resting his head on his solid chest and listening, thankfully, to his heartbeat.

Jeremiah pulled him closer, stroked his hair, and murmured sleepily, "Are you all right?"

"Yeah," Xavier whispered, but he wasn't.

As he lay listening to the thumping from his father's heart, his thoughts went to William. The man's smug, teasing words about murdering Dublin sent a hot wave of anger through him. His father was right; they were definitely down, but they weren't out. In his memorial letter, he had promised Mr. Minnows that he would always look after Robbie and that William LeMasters would pay for all the pain he caused. The intense fear Xavier had once felt toward LeMasters was gone. All that remained was pure, utter hatred. He had murdered Maggie and Mr. Minnows, and he had slaughtered his mother. For that, Xavier would kill him, and when he did, it would be slow and painful. He swore before God, it would be excruciatingly painful!

An Excerpt from Book Three:

The Prince of Warwood and The Sword of the Chosen

Xavier felt his heart jerk painfully as he whipped around and found Danson LeMasters strolling into the room. The man seemed to thoroughly enjoy the swell of terror he created in his wake and gleamed malevolently down at the child soldiers as he approached Daniel, who was fighting to stand straight and still. When Danson's eyes bore into Xavier, he met them with unwavering defiance. The man's glee slipped as he stepped past Daniel and stopped in front of Xavier.

For several seconds, the two simply glared at one another in a silent battle, with Danson trying desperately to collapse the boy's mental defenses and Xavier effortlessly keeping him at bay with a small smile. Danson no longer held any power over him. It was at this moment that Xavier realized that his abilities had surpassed Danson's. He was now the stronger telepathist, and his smile broadened.

"What are you grinning at, boy?" Danson blared testily before drawing back and slapping him across the face.

He stumbled and fell, slamming his head on the concrete floor.

"You dare to mock me, boy?" Danson roared as he withdrew a leather strap coiled at his waist. "No one,

ABSOLUTELY NO ONE mocks me, especially a flea like you!"

A faint whistling noise was the only warning Xavier heard before the strap struck him. He rolled onto his side and tucked his exposed flesh under his cloak. Although the cloak shielded him from the worst of the beating, he knew there would be welts and bruises when Danson was through with him.

"Sir! Sir, please!" Daniel cried. "Please forgive my friend, Adam. He's new. He doesn't understand how it works here. Please, sir, stop. Please!"

"Oh, shut up Daniel!" Danson spat.

Xavier heard another whistling sound, but this time the strap didn't strike him. It struck Daniel, and the small boy cried out. The bullish man drew back to hit Daniel again, but he strap never made contact with its target. Xavier propelled a powerful force at the man and sent him hurling across the room. He smashed against the wall and crumpled heavily to the floor where he lay motionless.

The room erupted into thunderous applause and cheers, and Xavier found himself surrounded by the other children.

"Well done!" one boy exclaimed, thumping Xavier's back.

"Yeah, I've been wanting to do that ever since he did this," another boy announced gleefully, gesturing to the black eye patch he wore on his left eye.

"What happened in here?" a strangely calm voice questioned.

Instantaneously, the room fell silent, and the boys spun toward the doorway. No one answered as they stood protectively in front of Xavier.

"Children? I asked a question. What happened to my brother?"

But, the group stayed mutinously silent.

"Who's responsible for this?" William barked, sending a shudder rippling through the group of boys.

The children still refused to answer, but Xavier knew that as inept as Danson was at telepathy, William LeMasters was not.

"I am," Xavier announced, stepping out from behind the group. "I did it. He was beating up Daniel so I gave him a little zap."

When William LeMasters' eyes met Xavier's, he immediately felt the familiar sensation of infiltration, and he fought to block the advances. LeMasters' eyes narrowed on him, and for a moment, he thought William had recognized him.

Finally, he said, "Come closer, boy."

He shuffled awkwardly toward the man he feared above all others, fighting the urge to run from the room screaming, but when he thought of Mr. Minnows, his fear twisted into an intense hatred. With a deep breath, he straightened his shoulders and met William's black, bottomless eyes.

William smiled. "My you're an insolent one. If looks could kill, I think you'd have me hung, dismembered, and electrocuted to death simultaneously if that were possible." He cackled ominously. Then, as though someone had flipped a light switch, his face went wildly dark. "Well, *Prince* Wells? Do it! If you think you're *man* enough, draw your sword and strike me down."

Driven by fear more than anything, he fumbled in his cloak for his sword, but before he could dislodge it from his belt, William LeMasters' sword was at his neck, and he froze.

"Really, now! You'll need to be quicker than that, Prince Wells." The evil man smiled triumphantly down at him.

At that moment, Danson moaned, and William glanced over at his unconscious brother. In that briefest of moments, Xavier hurled a force at the dark man and sent him staggering backwards. Then, he quickly drew his sword and swung with all his might at William, but the man had quickly regained his balance and parried the attack with a dismissive laugh.

"My, my, my! Well done, sire. Fight dirty! It doesn't matter how you win as long as you do! It's a shame that I'll eventually have to kill you. You would have made a nice addition to my army," he taunted.

Then, he attacked, wielding his sword with great skill and expertise. It quickly became apparent to Xavier that he was in over his head. LeMasters was a master swordsman whereas he had a mere couple of months of training. What made him think he could do this? Fear swarmed through his body as he backpedaled and tried to keep himself from being disemboweled. But, the dark man was relentless and continued to barrel down on him, swinging his sword and slicing into his arm. He winced, but had no time to inspect the wound for LeMasters was attacking again. He lashed out desperately, but William simply batted his sword aside and lunged. If he hadn't jumped to the side, he would have been impaled. Scared out of his mind, Xavier scrambled away from him and took stock of his situation. He was in trouble. No, not just trouble, he was in grave peril. This was going to end badly, very badly.

LeMasters advanced on him again, twirling his sword lazily and grinning sadistically. Suddenly, he charged at the boy. Xavier managed to raise his sword to deflect the attack, but the force behind the sword was too great, and his weapon clattered to the floor. LeMasters grabbed him, threw him down, and with a wicked smile, stepped on the boy's neck, pinning him to the floor. Xavier clawed at foot holding him captive as panic crashed over him like a tidal wave.

"Stop squirming, boy," LeMasters hissed and increased the pressure on the boy's throat, cutting off his air supply. Xavier froze under this pressure, and William smiled. "Good boy."

Then, with brutal patience, William impaled Xavier in the hip, sinking the blade deeper and deeper. Xavier's screams only made his smile widen.

"That's it, boy, scream! Scream for Daddy to come and save you," he goaded, twisting the sword lodged in Xavier's side.

Screaming louder than he thought possible, Xavier began to cry. He was going to die! He was going to die, and his father was thousands of miles away and couldn't do a thing to save him. He was going to die, and the last thing he'd see in this world was the sneering, smug face of William LeMasters.

Coming to Amazon in May 2013!

"Like" the books at
www.facebook.com/princeofwarwood
to receive updates on new releases, promotions, and contests!

www.ingramcontent.com/pod-product-compliance
Lightning Source LLC
Chambersburg PA
CBHW071249170626
46809CB00001B/140
9780977311538